Nineteen Steps

Millie Bobby Brown is an actress and producer best known for playing Eleven in the Netflix hit series *Stranger Things*, which garnered her international attention, critical praise and awards recognition, including two individual Primetime Emmy Award nominations and two individual Screen Actors Guild Award nominations. She also starred in and produced *Enola Holmes* and its sequel.

In 2019, Brown launched her own vegan and cruelty-free make-up and skincare line, florence by mills. The brand received the 'Launch of the Year' honour at Women's Wear Daily's Beauty Inc Awards, and has quickly become one of the most popular and reliable beauty brands according to The Cosmetify Index.

On 20 November, 2018, UNICEF named Brown the organisation's newest Goodwill Ambassador. The appointment – marked on World Children's Day at United Nations Headquarters and the Empire State Building in New York – made her UNICEF's youngest-ever Goodwill Ambassador at the time. Earlier that year, Brown was also named one of TIME magazine's 100 Most Influential People.

Follow her on Instagram @milliebobbybrown.

Nineteen Steps

MILLIE BOBBY BROWN

with Kathleen McGurl

ONE PLACE. MANY STORIES

HQ
An imprint of HarperCollins*Publishers* Ltd
1 London Bridge Street
London SE1 9GF

www.harpercollins.co.uk

HarperCollins*Publishers*
Macken House, 39/40 Mayor Street Upper,
Dublin 1, D01 C9W8, Ireland

This edition 2023

1
First published in Great Britain by
HQ, an imprint of HarperCollins*Publishers* Ltd 2023

With thanks to Kathleen McGurl

Millie Bobby Brown asserts the moral right to be identified as the author of this work. A catalogue record for this book is available from the British Library.

HB ISBN: 978-0-00-853026-6
Special edition HB ISBN: 978-0-00-864864-0
TPB: 978-0-00-853027-3

This book is set in Sabon by Type-it AS, Norway

Printed and Bound in the UK using 100% Renewable Electricity at CPI Group (UK) Ltd, Croydon, CR0 4YY

For those who lost their lives in this tragedy and for the loved ones they left behind, and for Nanny Ruth who told me this story.

Prologue

It was the first time Nellie had been back to Bethnal Green, her childhood home, in almost fifty years. The first time since the end of the war. As she stepped off the tube train onto the platform and gazed around for signs to the exit, she was taken aback by how different it looked from the way she remembered it. The station had not been finished and the track not yet laid when the station was requisitioned as a public air raid shelter for the duration of the war. Now, people bustled past her as she stood clutching her suitcase, trying to imagine the thousands of triple bunk beds that had lined the tunnels when she was last here. How many endless, anxious nights had she and her family spent down here during the Blitz? Too many. And then again, later in the war, there'd been so many more nights they'd had to take shelter from the frequent bombing raids above.

The train she'd been on pulled away, its wheels clattering against the track as it picked up speed, leaving Nellie on the platform surrounded by her memories.

They'd replaced the escalators, she noticed, as she stepped onto shiny steel instead of the wooden slatted treads of the old ones, dragging her wheeled suitcase onto the step behind her. A busker had set himself up at the bottom of the escalator, and was singing 'Bridge Over Troubled Water', the music echoing up to her. As she rode the escalator, she sang along quietly, remembering how during the war she sometimes sang down here for her friends and family. She reached the ticket hall and thought of dear Billy, how his cheeks would dimple when he smiled at her. This was where she'd so often stopped for a quick word with him, promising her family she'd catch them up as they made their way to the bunks.

Once through the gates of the ticket barrier, she turned automatically to her left. Back then, there'd only been the one entrance and exit to the unfinished station. Now there was another to her right, but if she used that one, she worried she'd be disorientated when she reached street level. It was familiar yet different, advertising posters lined the walls and there was a vending machine instead of the shelter canteen. Her heart began to pound as she climbed the first seven steps to the half landing, then turned left and began making her way up the nineteen steps. Nineteen. They were much better lit these days, of course, with a central handrail that hadn't been there before, but still they were the same nineteen steps. Memories of all those other hundreds of times she'd used these steps came flooding back as she climbed, making her eyes blur with tears and her stomach knot.

She needed to get herself out of the station, find the way to Barbara's house, greet her old friend and have a cup of tea. Babs had written to her a few months earlier, urging her to consider coming back for the fiftieth anniversary memorial service. It had seemed like a good idea, but now here she was, after all these years, with everything in front of her.

A crowd of young people, university students, she guessed, suddenly came charging down the steps towards her. She moved to her right, flattening herself against the wall. Her breath was coming in short, urgent gasps, her heart racing furiously, and she knew it wasn't due to the exertion of climbing the stairs. It was because of what had happened here, fifty years ago. The night that changed her life forever. Clutching her suitcase with one hand and her chest with the other, she cowered against the wall, fighting to regain control, struggling to catch her breath. 'Don't fall, don't fall,' she whispered.

PART ONE

Autumn–Winter 1942

Chapter 1

It was a bright Saturday in September that felt as though it was still summer. Nellie had had a busy week at work at the town hall, where she was assistant to the Mayor, and today she longed for a bit of normality, a little taste of how life used to be before the war. Before the air raids and the rationing and the endless sombre news reports on the wireless radio. She was taking her little sister, Flo, for a picnic in the park. It was hot – the kind of heat that makes you long for the weather to cool down and the leaves to fall, but then you berated yourself for wishing away the good weather.

The autumn chill would come soon enough, Nellie told herself. And with it the dark days of winter when she'd be returning home from work after dark, stumbling along in the blackout, every yard treacherous.

'Come on, Flo. Let's get a move on. More time for our picnic,' she said, tugging her sister by the hand.

They walked through the familiar streets of Bethnal Green where she'd always lived, passing a row of shops with their meagre window displays. Second-hand clothes, rabbit and mutton in the butcher's (it had been so long since she'd had beef!), a queue, still, at the greengrocer's for apples from the orchards of Kent. On one corner stood the remains of a side wall of a bombed-out house, a curtain still flapping forlornly in its window. She averted her eyes from the bomb sites, the hollowed-out shells that had once been people's homes, houses just like her own. She didn't want to risk spoiling her happy mood thinking about them now.

'When will they rebuild it? When can the people have their house back?' Flo asked, looking up at it.

'After the war's over, I expect.' Nellie sighed, adjusting the basket hanging from her arm. But the people who'd lived there were unlikely to ever come home, she thought. For all she knew they might have perished inside when their house took a direct hit.

'What if the war goes on for ever and ever?'

Lately the headlines screamed about RAF bombing raids on Munich and Nellie felt her stomach lurch thinking about it. Whenever the British had successfully bombed a German city, you could be sure there'd be a retaliatory strike coming soon after. And that usually meant London would be hit. Which meant the East End of London would be once more in danger.

Her little sister, only seven years old, could barely remember a time before the war began, and it showed no signs of ending any time soon. As much as the war had marred Flo's childhood, it had robbed Nellie of her teenage years when she should have been having fun without a care in the world. Although, it wasn't as bad these days as it was in the beginning, when the docks and warehouses were targeted, and then during the Blitz when Hitler had sent his bombers over built-up areas, trying to break the British spirit. It hadn't worked. They were still here, still fighting, and would never surrender, as the Prime Minister had said near the start of the war. *Never surrender.* Nellie jutted out her chin defiantly as she remembered Mr Churchill's speech.

'It won't go on for ever, I promise. Look, we're almost here!' Nellie smiled, eager to cheer her sister up as she led them across the bridge over the Regent's Canal and into Victoria Park, past the statues of two dogs which guarded the entrance. Flo, as always, gave each dog a pat as she passed.

These days, with Victoria Park mostly taken over by the military – anti-aircraft guns on part of it and a prisoner-of-war camp at the far end – there were fewer places where one could feel truly free. Still, there was the small section of Vicky Park that was open to the public, and numerous smaller parks and gardens tucked between the streets of Victorian terraced houses. Some had been dug up to grow vegetables but others were still free for children to play, and there was always a game of football going on somewhere or other, with boys using their jackets to mark the goals.

A little farther on they crossed the small bridge that led onto a tiny island in the middle of a pond.

'I remember when children weren't allowed on this island,' Nellie told Flo. 'It was for grown-ups only.'

'Didn't you ever go on the island till you was grown-up?' Flo asked, wide-eyed.

Nellie smiled. 'Actually, we did. Babs and Billy and me – one of us would distract the park-keeper and the others would race across the bridge onto the island. By the time the parkie spotted us, we'd have done a full tour of it and all he could do was chase us off, but we were faster runners than him and he had no hope of catching us.'

Flo laughed, and Nellie chuckled too. Those had been good times, before the war, when she'd still been a school-girl and Flo was only a baby. She, her best friend Barbara and Barbara's brother, Billy, had been inseparable back then. The three of them were close in age, with Billy older than Nellie by one year and Babs younger by one year. They'd grown up together. She was eighteen now, an adult more or less, a working woman with an important job at the town hall, but sometimes she wished she was still a child, playing hide-and-seek in the park with Billy and Babs.

As if thinking about him had conjured him up, she spotted a familiar figure walking towards them, grinning broadly. 'Thought it was you, Nellie Morris! Having a picnic?' Billy called out, pointing to the basket hanging from the crook of her elbow.

'Yes, we've decided to make the most of the good weather, and Flo does like a picnic.'

'She likes a tickle too, I bet,' Billy said, as he lunged

for Flo. She ran off squealing and Nellie stood watching them, laughing. Billy was like an older brother to them both, and she was fond of him. At times like these you could almost forget there was a war on and these were the moments that kept her going.

After a lap of the island the two were back, Billy gasping for breath. 'She's too fast for me these days,' he said, wheezing a little.

'Be careful, Billy. Your asthma.'

He nodded and reached for the medicinal cigarettes he always carried. A few puffs of one delivered the medication it contained deep into his lungs, stopping the wheezing. 'I know. I'll be all right.' He lit a cigarette and inhaled deeply. 'There. All good now. What've you got to eat in there?' He nodded at the basket Nellie was carrying, the picnic her mother, Em, had put together for them.

'Sandwiches, shortbread, lemon barley. Enough for three if you want to join us?' There wasn't, not really, but she felt she had to offer.

He shook his head. 'Sounds good but I can't. On shift later. Air raids don't wait for picnics.' He gave her a mock-salute, ruffled Flo's hair and set off.

Nellie watched as he passed a pair of middle-aged women; one of them had a poodle on a lead. They stared after him and shook their heads disapprovingly, and the dog barked. They made no effort to quieten the animal. No doubt the women thought Billy was a conscientious objector, as he was not in uniform today. They didn't know he was an air raid warden. They didn't know how hard he worked, how many extra shifts he took on, how many nights he spent supervising people in the tube station shelter, despite the fact that being cooped up down there in that damp atmosphere was not good for his lungs.

They all did their bit for the war effort. Her father, Charlie, did a few shifts each week as a fire-watcher, as well as his regular job as a warehouse man down at the London docks. Babs worked in a factory making military uniforms.

'Nellieeee! When are we going to eat our sandwiches? I'm going to save the crusts for the ducks. See them, over there? Ducklings too!'

'Are there? Let's go!' Nellie let herself be pulled by Flo over to the shore of the island. Sure enough, nestled in amongst some reeds, was a family of ducks. The ducklings were tiny, fluffy things and it was all Nellie could do to keep Flo on dry land, watching but not trying to grab at the little creatures.

Across the park, in the closed-off area, the huge anti-aircraft, or 'ack-ack' guns as they were known, stood silent, pointing skyward, ready for action whenever the next air raid occurred. Yet here, at their feet, was a small reminder that life went on just as it always had.

*

They were packing up when the shrill wail of the air raid siren sounded.

'In daytime? Really?' Nellie said in surprise as her heart

began to pound. She stuffed things into the picnic basket and grabbed Flo's hand. 'Come on, we got to run!'

'Nellieee! Where should we go? I don't want to be bombed!' Flo screamed in terror. They were nowhere near the underground station where the family usually went to shelter from air raids, and far too close to the ack-ack guns that could easily be a target for the German bombers. She imagined a direct hit on the guns, shrapnel flying across the park hitting them both. Little Flo falling, bleeding and lifeless . . . No, it couldn't happen. She had to save her sister.

There was a public shelter near the entrance to the park, which they'd passed on the way in. It was just one of those corrugated iron ones dug into the ground but it would have to do. Anything was better than being caught in the open. As Nellie ran, gripping Flo's hand tightly, a wave of German bombers passed overhead low enough for her to make out the Luftwaffe emblem on their wings. Their engines screamed and roared, the sound recognisably different to that of the RAF planes that frequently flew over in formation, off to bomb towns in Germany. Flo stopped and stared up at them. It was possibly the first time she'd seen the enemy, Nellie realised. The air raids were normally at night. She feared the planes overhead would open fire with their machine guns at any moment, never mind the bombs they carried.

'We've got to run, Flo!' she urged, praying she could protect her little sister. They reached the shelter and she pushed Flo ahead of her into it, panting loudly. Inside, she held Flo close to her, resting her cheek on Flo's soft curly hair. Thank God they'd made it.

'Whew, close one, miss,' said a young boy in the shelter, clutching his little dog as he tried to catch his breath.

'I know. Don't understand why the warning was so late. We barely had time to get here.'

'Daylight raid, innit. Our lads only watch for them at night, I reckon.'

Nellie didn't think that could be true and pulled Flo onto her lap, hoping her parents and their brother, George, would all have made it to safety. Like everyone else in the East End, they were old hands at dealing with air raids. But no matter how many times it happened, it still terrified her – the thought that this one might be the bomb with her name on it, that these might be her last moments on earth. She tried to take a deep breath to calm herself, determined not to cry and not to let Flo see how frightened she was.

The ack-ack guns started up, their sound so much louder than Nellie was used to as they were so close, but it was reassuring that the city was being defended. This small shelter could hold just a handful of people. It had only a wooden plank to sit on and an earthen floor, and was a far cry from the warren of the underground station they'd become accustomed to. Down there, they had bunk beds, toilets, a kitchen serving warm food and even a little theatre for entertainment.

'Glad we don't have to come here whenever there's a raid, eh Flo?' she said, tightening her arms around her sister. Flo nodded and snuggled closer to her. It was terrifying, being in that little shelter while you could hear the planes flying above, the boom of the ack-ack guns and occasional distant thuds of bombs. Down in the tube, the sounds of war were more muted and it was easier to bear. Plus, they'd be with Em and Charlie and George, and Nellie wouldn't have sole responsibility for Flo. She blinked away a tear as she tried to look calm.

When at last the sounds of the planes and guns tapered off, the all-clear siren went off. Nellie led Flo out of the shelter, and they began their walk home, through the dusty air and newly created rubble. As they rounded the corner into Morpeth Street, its rows of red-brick Victorian terraced houses facing each other, George threw open the front door of their house, with their father close behind him.

'I was out in the street,' George said, breathlessly, 'when them bombers came over. They was so low!'

'We saw them too from our shelter,' Nellie replied with a shudder as she recalled how they'd swooped down, so close to the ground.

'I could see the whites of their eyes!' George went on. 'Lead fellow, he had blond hair, like Flo's. I had to dive under a bush before he could shoot me down!'

Charlie glared at him. 'What was you doing out in the street? Get to a shelter the minute you hear the air raid siren, ain't I always told you that?'

'I did, Dad, but . . .' George began.

'You're not to go too far from the tube, you hear me? So you can go straight there.' Charlie wagged his finger at his son.

'Nellie and Flo were miles from the tube, when they were in the park!'

'Half a mile, idiot,' Nellie said, giving her brother a scornful look.

'At least they got to a shelter.' Charlie ran his hands through his hair. The thought seemed to have struck him that his children had been in danger, in broad daylight on a bright September Saturday. It sent a shiver down Nellie's spine too. If anything had happened to Flo while they were out, she'd never forgive herself.

Nellie hugged her father then kissed her mother, who ushered them into the house. 'It's all right. We're all safe. It's ramping up again though, isn't it? At least not as bad as the Blitz.' Back in 1940 and 1941 there'd been bombing raids almost every night, and they'd practically lived in the tube station shelter. Nellie couldn't bear to think it might get that bad again.

'Yes, it is,' Charlie said. 'This bleeding war, eh? Soon as you get used to it and think you're coping all right, it throws something new at you, like this. On a sunny afternoon, and all. Just ain't right.'

Nellie was about to reply when there was a knock at the door. 'That'll be Ruth and John,' Em said, hurrying to answer it.

But on the doorstep was only John, with a black greyhound on a lead. 'I'm sorry, Em, Charlie,' he said.

'Ruthie's not well enough to come for tea today. That daytime air raid put the jitters in her.'

Her aunt and uncle had been coming for tea every Saturday afternoon for as long as Nellie could remember. It was a family tradition. Cakes, a card game or two and plenty of laughter – war or no war.

Ruth was Charlie's sister, and Nellie had had a close relationship with them all her life. Nellie and Babs used to run away to their house whenever they were in trouble with their parents. Ruth would feed them biscuits and say they could live at her house and never go home. Although by teatime the girls would be homesick and wanting their mums. All along though, Em and Mrs Waters had known exactly where they were because Ruth would have sent a neighbour's boy with a message.

'Send her my love,' Charlie said. Nellie knew he was concerned about his sister's health. And for a man who was used to being able to fix things, to make things better, it was agony for him that there was nothing he could do about the tuberculosis she suffered from, which had been made worse by the many nights she'd spent in the damp of the air raid shelter.

Since the war had started, families had become more tightknit, depending on one another for support, and she couldn't bear the thought of Ruthie not being there.

Nellie glanced down at the dog, who was sniffing her hand. 'New greyhound? Where's Oscar?'

John laughed. 'This *is* Oscar. Don't you recognise him?'

Nellie frowned. Her uncle's dog Oscar was a brindle

greyhound. This dog was black, but he was licking her hand as though he knew her.

'You trying that trick again?' Charlie said with a chuckle.

'Yeah. Worked before, should work again.'

'What trick, Uncle John?' Nellie asked.

He leaned close to her. 'Oscar is known as a winner. Paint him black, enter him in a different race with a different name, as an unknown. Bet on him with long odds. He wins, we cash in, job done.' John winked at Nellie. 'Don't matter if there's a war on, we've got to make the most of any chances to make a bit of cash.'

'Where you racing him, and what name?' Charlie asked. 'I'll have a flutter. Might win a few bob.'

'Walthamstow, eight o'clock this evening. Get down the bookies now, Charlie. His new name is Lord of the Darkness.'

Nellie laughed. 'Very dramatic! Well good luck to Oscar and love to Auntie Ruth. So sorry we're not seeing her.'

Em returned with the shortbread wrapped in paper. 'Here. For Ruth's tea, and keep that dog away from them.'

'Thanks, Em. She'll appreciate those biscuits. Oh, she said to give you these. We don't need them, we got enough.' He handed over a few ration coupons to Nellie.

'Thank you, Uncle John,' she said with a smile.

'We got to share what we have, eh? Come on, boy.' John led the dog away as Charlie and Nellie waved goodbye.

It was always like this – family and friends sharing

what they had, making the best of things, appreciating little kindnesses from each other. One day things would change, and they'd be back to how things were before the war, when they didn't have much, but there was always enough of everything to go around.

Chapter 2

'Can I borrow your umbrella, Mum?' Nellie asked as she was getting ready to leave for work on a cold and rainy Monday morning.

'Sorry, love, I need it. Got to go to the market today, or I won't have anything to make for tea. All very well your dad winning money on that greyhound race but I've still got to go out and queue if I'm to spend any of it on food. Here, stick that on your head.' Em tossed Nellie a floppy rain hat that had seen better days.

'It'll squash my curls,' Nellie moaned, but put it on anyway. It was either that or get soaking wet on the ten-minute walk to work.

'Don't be late. Oh, and do me a favour? Pick up your auntie's laundry this evening, will you, from Mrs Denning, and drop it off with her? It's on your way home, and Ruth will be glad to see you.'

'I will.' Nellie kissed Em goodbye and set off.

As she hurried along Morpeth Street she heard a familiar voice call her from behind. 'Nellie Morris! Don't you look a picture in that hat!' She turned to see Billy grinning.

'It's bleeding awful!' The rain was coming down too heavy to stop to chat, so she hurried on, giving him a wave as she went.

'I'll marry you one day, and you'll have to wear a hat as fetching as that on our wedding day, Nellie Morris!' he called after her.

'Only if I'll have you!' she teased back. He'd been saying it to her for years. Since she was fifteen and he was sixteen, and they'd spent so much time together and had begun flirting a little, so that their parents had said they'd end up marrying. She adored him but she didn't think they actually would marry – it was all just a friendly joke. Sometimes it was fun to imagine them ending up together; he'd make a fine husband for her, she knew. But she wanted more from life than to marry the boy next door, the boy who'd said he'd never leave the East End. She wanted to travel, to see the world. When the war was over, she intended to do just that.

**

Billy watched her hurrying away. Nellie didn't know how he truly felt about her. How could she? He'd never told her. He worried if he got it wrong and she rejected him, he'd lose her friendship as well. He knew he wouldn't be able to cope with that, and so he'd kept his feelings hidden from her but it was getting harder to keep it a secret. He knew she saw him only as 'the boy next door', an older brother, a friend. Someone to banter with, not someone to love. Somehow he needed to change that, he wasn't sure how but he wanted to prove to her that he'd be right for her, that they could have a wonderful life together. There'd been times, just before the war broke out, when they'd sit in the park together – not chasing each other as they'd done as children but sitting on a bench, his arm around her shoulder, her head resting against him as she talked of her dreams for the future, and he'd dreamed of a future with her.

Billy had lived his whole life right here on Morpeth Street, as had Nellie. For him, the street contained everything he'd ever wanted in life, including her. But he knew that she wanted more. If it hadn't been for the war, she'd probably have moved out of Bethnal Green already. Excitement, adventure, travel – she'd so often spoken of such things with a longing that he couldn't understand. He couldn't offer her those things. He could only offer her his undying love, companionship and security, and he hoped that would one day be enough for a girl as special as Nellie Morris. The girl who'd once saved her pocket money for weeks to buy him a cigarette case for his medicinal cigarettes. He had it still and thought of her whenever he took it out. The girl who'd run after him along the street one day when he'd forgotten his sandwiches, and had given them to him with a smile, patting his cheek. 'Where would you be without me, Billy Waters?' she'd said. Where indeed. One day, soon, he'd ask Nellie out on a date. One day, when he'd plucked up the courage.

Nellie loved her job as assistant to the Mayor of Bethnal Green, Mrs Margaret Bolton. It was varied and interesting, and she got on well with the Mayor. Mr Percy Bolton, the Mayor's husband, had been Nellie's schoolteacher, and it was he who'd recommended her to his wife. He was retired from teaching but now served as senior air raid warden and was Billy's boss. The other girls she knew worked in the clothing factories like Babs did, or in munitions. Her friend had started off making luxury underwear that was sold in top West End department stores, but these days the factory made only uniforms and utility clothing.

Working in the town hall made Nellie feel as though she was right at the heart of Bethnal Green. She was often the first to know what was going on in the borough, and she relished that feeling of importance.

'You're too ambitious, that's your problem,' Em sometimes said to her, but with pride in her voice.

'Too clever for Bethnal Green. My girl's going places, you wait and see,' Charlie would reply, beaming.

She hoped they were right. She treasured Bethnal Green but was itching to see more of the world than this little corner of London. She wanted adventure. She wanted to be someone who would make a difference to the world. When the war was over.

'Morning, Gladys,' Nellie called out to one of the girls in the typing pool she often spent her lunch break with as she entered the first-floor office.

'Morning, Nellie. Fine weather for ducks, ain't it?'

'It is that,' Nellie said with a laugh, hurrying past to take off her wet coat and try to dry her feet at the nearest radiator. That was another good thing about working in the town hall – it had an effective central heating system and she could only hope the heating would be on today to warm up.

'Morning, Nellie,' Mrs Bolton said, as Nellie entered the office and hung her coat on the stand. 'I need you to take minutes in a meeting at ten o'clock but if you could finish typing those letters from yesterday before then, I'd be grateful.'

'Of course.' Nellie had learnt typing and shorthand at school. Her speed and efficiency were what had led to her promotion from the typing pool. She fed a piece of paper into her typewriter, opened her notebook and began working.

By the time ten o'clock came around she'd completed the letters and warmed her feet. She pushed her toes into her still-damp shoes with a grimace, and followed Mrs Bolton into a small meeting room, where a large man in a tweed jacket was sitting waiting for them. He stood up as they entered and held out a hand for Mrs Bolton to shake.

'Mrs Mayor. Pleased to see you again.'

'Mr Smith, good morning. And this is Miss Morris joining us to take notes. Nellie, Mr Smith is an engineer I employed to inspect the Bethnal Green air raid shelter and make any necessary safety recommendations. I've asked Civil Defence before now for funds to improve the entrance but my requests have been turned down. Mr Smith, I'm hoping you'll provide me with the evidence to help make my case more strongly.' She turned to the engineer. 'I understand you've completed your inspection and are ready to report back?'

He nodded. 'Now then, this community is lucky that the station was in the state it was, at the outbreak of war. As you know, it's part of the Central line extension, designed to link the East End with Central London, but it's not yet complete. The tracks weren't laid so it wasn't in use for trains.'

Nellie nodded. They were excited for the tube station opening, when the war was over. The people of Bethnal Green would be able to go up west to the shops or for days out so much more easily by tube than by bus. Nellie wanted badly to feel like a part of the big city, to go shopping with Babs for a new dress and browse the beauty counters in the department stores, or even go to see a show.

'Being deep underground,' Mr Smith continued, 'it makes a perfect large-capacity air raid shelter. Anyone down there in the event of an air raid will be one hundred per cent safe. However . . .'

'However?' prompted Mrs Bolton.

The engineer cleared his throat. 'I have concerns about the entrance, in particular the steps down from pavement level to the ticket hall. They were never finished off properly, and the hoarding at the top was only ever intended as a temporary measure. I've inspected it in detail, both in daylight and at night-time.'

Nellie flipped over to a new page of her notebook and waited for the engineer to continue.

'While the entrance is adequate for normal usage, I think it's very likely unsafe if there are crowds of people all trying to enter at once. There is only one low-wattage light bulb, and even that has been shielded so that the light doesn't shine out onto the pavement – to comply with blackout regulations, you understand. There's no central handrail or indeed any handrails. The gates at the top open inward and therefore could not be closed against a surge of people if the station became too crowded.' He cleared his throat. 'And the steps themselves with those unfinished rough edges can be slippery when wet.'

'I see.' The Mayor's expression was grave. 'But it's been in use since the start of the war. What do you worry might happen if nothing is done?'

'A potential disaster could occur. We've been lucky, I think, that no such calamity has happened yet. But should a large crowd arrive at once, perhaps in a panic and rushing down to the safety of the shelter, there is a danger that the wooden hoarding surrounding the steps at the top might give way, and people would be precipitated down the stairs. Indeed, it would be all too easy for someone to trip, perhaps slipping on wet steps, losing their footing in the poor light, and a fall down those steps could cause serious injury or even prove fatal.' The engineer leaned back in his chair, his arms folded, apparently satisfied he'd done his job and delivered his verdict.

'And what can be done to prevent such accidents?' Mrs Bolton looked at Nellie to check she was capturing all this in her notebook, and Nellie nodded reassuringly. But her mind was on that tube station entrance. She'd always thought that was the safest place to be, sheltering from the dangers of the air raids above. She bit her lip worrying how many times they'd all hurried down there when the siren sounded and wondered if it was in fact as dangerous as Mr Smith seemed to suggest.

'Well, if the wooden hoarding were to be replaced with brick,' the engineer was saying, 'properly supported by concrete piers, and a strong gate installed across the entrance that opened outward or better still, slid across, then that would mitigate the danger of a surge of people collapsing the existing structure. The gate could be closed in the event of too many people trying to access the entrance at once. In addition, extending the roofing over the steps would allow installation of better lighting. The steps themselves should have hard-wearing metal edging added to their treads, and a central handrail should be installed. The work need only take three or four days, and the shelter could remain open for use overnight if there was an air raid.'

Nellie scribbled in shorthand as fast as she could to capture all that the engineer had said.

'Thank you, Mr Smith. You've been very helpful and your suggestions to improve the safety of the station will be invaluable.' Mrs Bolton stood up and shook the engineer's hand.

Nellie followed Mrs Bolton back to the mayor's office. 'Type those notes up for me, Nellie. I'll need them to dictate a letter. We need to apply again to London Civil Defence for authorisation and money to improve the entrance, but I should think after they read Mr Smith's findings and recommendations that shouldn't be too much bother. It doesn't sound as though it should be too expensive or a very long job. With any luck we'll have that station entrance sorted out by the end of next month, if not earlier.'

Nellie sat down to type up her notes. This was just like the Mayor – she always had the community's best interests at the forefront of her mind. Nellie was proud to work for her.

*

By the end of the day the report was complete and the letter dictated and typed. 'Pop it into the outgoing post tray on your way out please, Nellie. The sooner that letter is sent the sooner we'll have the funding and the work can begin. I think tomorrow we should start lining up men who can do the work for us, to Mr Smith's specifications.'

'Ahead of getting the funding?'

'On the assumption the money will be forthcoming, yes. This is people's safety we're talking about. This time, with the weight of Mr Smith's report behind us, I'm sure they won't turn us down again.'

Nellie hoped her boss was right. They owed it to the community to ensure the shelter was as safe a place as possible.

Chapter 3

'Good to see you, Nellie, and thanks for doing this,' said John as he took the bag of laundry from her. 'Your sister's here too. Third time she's come this month to cheer up Ruthie, bless her.'

Nellie went through to the cosy sitting room where Ruth had a bed made up on the sofa. Flo was kneeling on the floor next to her, prattling on about the games she played at school with her friends.

'Nellie! Hi, love. You brought my nighties? Thank you, dear—' Ruth broke off with a bout of coughing, covering her mouth with a handkerchief that was always firmly in her grip.

'Good to see you, Auntie Ruth. Are you keeping all right? Hello, Flo.' Nellie kissed her sister's cheek.

'Ah, yes, love, I've been better, but I shouldn't complain. I was sorry not to have felt well enough to come for tea on Saturday.'

John shook his head sadly. 'She should be in a sanatorium somewhere in the country, where the air's fresh. Not here in London, where we have the dust and fumes and whatnot in the air. It's going down the tube that's done for her. All them nights during the Blitz down in them damp tunnels. If I'd known what it would do to her, I'd have said let's stay up here, take our chances in the old Morrison shelter in the kitchen.'

'You could go to Mrs Thompson's, where I was 'vacuated to,' Flo put in. 'I bet she'd let you stay.'

During the Blitz there'd been a raid almost every night, and Bethnal Green like the rest of the East End had suffered tremendous damage. Some streets had lost half a dozen houses or more, flattened into rubble by the bombs. Three houses in Morpeth Street where Nellie lived were no longer there. One morning, they'd emerged from the air raid shelter to find their own windows blown in. Charlie had put tape in a criss-cross pattern over the remaining windows after that, to stop shards of glass flying in and damaging furnishings if it happened again.

Back then there were only the three of them to have to run to the shelter. George and Flo had been evacuated to the country, spending a year living in a village far away in rural Dorset. Her brother and sister had come back when the worst of it was over, and since then the family had stuck together, sheltering in the tube during the sporadic air raids they'd experienced since.

'Bless you, pet, but they only evacuate kids, not the sick.' John smiled at Flo.

Nellie mulled over what she'd heard today at work, trying to decide whether to say anything about it to her aunt and uncle. She looked through to the kitchen where the cage-like Morrison shelter was. They used it as a table during the day and had slept in it at night on occasions when they'd been too slow to get to the shelter. It was designed to protect against falling debris if a bomb fell close by. It wouldn't stand up to a direct hit, but what were the chances of that? It wasn't like the Blitz had started up again. German bombers flew over but often they were heading for other targets, farther afield.

'I think you're right, Uncle John, about using the Morrison shelter,' she said. 'No point Auntie Ruth having to drag herself down the tube when she's so poorly. The Morrison's much easier, and it'll be safe enough.'

Nellie reached out a hand and patted her aunt's arm. They'd be fine, she reassured herself.

She gazed around the room. There were black marks on the lino and a stain on the seat of an armchair that hadn't been there the last time she'd been round, but she dared not mention them. Ruth was too sick to do any cleaning, and John was too old-fashioned to do it himself.

She turned to John. 'Oscar won on Saturday, didn't he?'

Her uncle grinned. 'He certainly did. We're very proud, aren't we, Ruthie?'

Ruth scowled. 'We are, but . . . tell 'er what happened this morning, John.'

'Hmm. Well. It rained, and I hadn't got round to wash-ing the paint off the dog yet. Took him out in the rain, brought him back and he came in here, and . . . well . . .' John indicated the black marks on the lino and chair. 'He jumped straight up in that chair before I could stop him. Bleeding paint was running off him in streaks. Now Ruthie's on at me to get it all cleaned up.'

Nellie stifled a chuckle. 'Oh dear. Is he back to his usual colour now?'

John nodded. 'I had to finish the job the rain started, didn't I? And I'm going to have to do something about all this.'

'I'll come tomorrow morning before work and help you with that,' Nellie said. 'I'd stay today but our tea'll be ready and Mum hates any of us being late for it.'

Flo looked up at Nellie, her eyes bright. 'Nellie, can I stay here tonight, and clean up Oscar's mess? And I could help Uncle John cook Auntie Ruth's tea for her, and put away that laundry and do *all* the jobs! *Please*, Nellie, say I can! You tell Mum. She won't mind!' In the past, before the war, before Ruth was sick, Flo had often stayed the night, allowing Em and Charlie to have a night out.

'Flo, there's no room for you in the Morrison shelter as well.' She debated for a moment whether to say an air raid was likely, as Billy had told her that morning, but again decided there was no need to scare anyone. She put her arm around Flo. 'I think you'll have to come for a sleepover another night, hey?'

John nodded, looking relieved. 'It was kind of you to offer to do all them jobs, young Flo, but we'll manage, Ruthie and I. How about you come after school tomorrow? I'll get something special from the shops and you can help me make Ruthie's tea then.'

Flo gave a tiny pout, then immediately cheered up.

She never sulked when she didn't get her way. 'All right. And I'll bring more of Mum's shortbread, if there's any left.'

'Thanks for coming round, both of you,' Ruthie said from her position on the sofa. 'You'd best be off home.'

'Come on, Flo-bo. Let's see what Mum's cooking.' Flo got to her feet. Nellie blew her aunt a kiss and hugged her uncle. 'We'll see you tomorrow then, to get that floor cleaned. Look after her, Uncle John.'

'I will, I always do. Thanks again, love.' He gave her a squeeze as she went back out to the street, hand in hand with Flo.

*

Back home, Em was busy frying eels. 'John and Ruth all right, are they? Your brother's outside cuddling his damn chickens again. Honestly, the one that doesn't lay ought to have gone in the pot long ago.'

'He does love his birds,' Nellie said, as she went out the kitchen door through to the small backyard. George was out there, sitting on an upturned pail cradling a chicken. It was his favourite – the white one he'd named Rosie, the one that no longer laid any eggs but which he kept as a pet. He'd brought her and two others back from the country when he returned after being evacuated, and had looked after them ever since.

The family ate most of the eggs his chickens produced but there was usually a small surplus each day that George sold to neighbours, to bring in a little pocket money. Most of which, she knew, he spent on feed for his chickens. There weren't many people who kept chickens in the East End as most backyards were too tiny to do much with, although some of Nellie's neighbours had dug theirs up to grow vegetables as urged by the government's Dig for Victory campaign. Any food you could produce yourself was a bonus, what with so much being rationed these days. And although Charlie might grumble about the chickens, Nellie knew he appreciated the fresh eggs as much as the rest of them.

Just then the high-pitched wail of the air raid siren started.

'Right when we were about to eat,' Em grumbled. 'Should I wrap the food and bring it?'

'We don't have time,' Charlie said. 'Grab your bedding rolls. Flo, leave your doll here, you'll only damage her down in the tube.' He went to the back door. 'George! Come on!'

Nellie felt the familiar rise of fear in the pit of her stomach at the prospect of another night in the shelter but they had to go. It wasn't safe to stay home. She picked up their rolls of blankets and pillows that were stored behind the sofa in the sitting room. The bunk beds in the shelter were equipped with mattresses but nothing more. 'George!' Em shouted. 'We need to be off.'

'Can't leave Rosie,' he called back. 'She's frightened.'

'Leave the bloody chicken, boy. If she's dead when we get back at least it's a Sunday dinner for us.' Charlie went out and grabbed George by the arm, making him drop the chicken, which began running round the yard in a panic.

George struggled and lashed his foot out to kick his father. It was going to end badly, Nellie thought, and there was no time to lose. 'Stop it!' she shrieked, dropping her bedding roll and grabbing George's sleeve with one hand, Charlie's with the other. 'We have to go. George, your chicken will be fine, promise.'

'All right! Fine.'

Out in the street there were dozens of people hurriedly making their way to the tube, clutching bags or bundles of whatever they felt they needed for the night. Sometimes the all-clear went after only an hour or two down there so Nellie hoped it wouldn't be for the whole night and they could return home and eat.

As they hurried towards the tube, Flo grabbed Nellie's hand. 'I brought Spotty,' she said. In the gloom Nellie could barely see the tiny china dog that Flo was holding. It had been a present from Nellie last Christmas – she'd seen the little thing in a shop window and knew Flo would love it.

'Keep him safe in your pocket, Flo,' Nellie cautioned. 'If you drop him out here on the street we'll never find him again.'

Flo nodded seriously. 'I don't never want to lose him, Nell. Will bombs fall tonight?'

'Maybe,' Nellie replied. She couldn't lie and say no. Tears started trickling down Flo's cheeks and Nellie felt bad for upsetting her sister.

They reached the end of Morpeth Street, turned left and hurried along Roman Road to the tube entrance. The siren, housed in the clock tower of St John's church, just across the road from the tube station entrance, wailed louder the closer they got. There was no sign yet of any bombers but it wouldn't be long before they were over-head, dropping their deadly cargo.

Nellie couldn't help but think back to what Mr Smith had said earlier that day. As they went through the wooden gates that had been opened wide, she glanced up at the single, shaded light bulb. It was very dim, that was true. It didn't really shed much light at all on the edges of the steps. She counted them as she went down. Nineteen to the half landing, turn right, then seven more to reach the open space of the ticket hall. *A potential disaster could occur*, Mr Smith had said. He was right. Someone was going to break a leg falling down here sooner or later. She hadn't given it a second thought before, but now she couldn't help but worry.

Billy was on duty in the ticket hall as usual. 'Nellie Morris! And young Flo. Glad you're here. Hurry on down to the platforms now.'

'Flo, you go on with Mum and Dad and George. I'll catch you up. Just want a quick word with Billy.' Nellie gave Flo a gentle push towards Em, who had her hand outstretched towards her youngest daughter. Flo hated walking down the stationary escalators to the bunk beds. She was small for her age and the steps were big.

'What is it, Nellie?' Billy asked.

'Just . . . something I heard today. The Mayor's apply-ing for funding to improve the entrance here. It's too dark, tonight especially, when there's a lot of people trying to make their way down. Just wanted to tell you . . .'

Billy put a hand on her arm. 'Shh, don't say nothing more. People will hear and the last thing we want is them to panic. But you're not to worry. I keep a watch on them all as they come down. If anyone trips, I'm there like a shot to pick them up.'

'You do a good job, Billy.' She smiled and watched as his face lit up at the praise.

'Go catch up with your folks. There's a lot coming down tonight. Barbara's already there.' He waved a hand at the continuing hordes moving towards the ticket hall. Billy's boss – Mr Bolton – was having trouble controlling how many set foot on the stationary escalator at a time. The dark, slippery steps at the entrance weren't the only danger here. That steep escalator could cause all sorts of problems if too many people pushed their way on to it at once.

'All right. I'll see you later, once everyone's settled, perhaps?'

He nodded and Nellie headed for the escalator. She took a deep breath as she went into the depths of the station for another night underground, while German bombers did God knows what damage to the streets above.

Chapter 4

Nellie found the rest of her family alongside the Waters family in their usual place, towards one end of the platform lined on both sides with bunks. They were already settled, George lying on a top bunk, reading a Biggles book, and Em and Charlie sitting side by side on the bottom one of that triple, chatting quietly to Billy and Barbara's parents who were on the one opposite. The next triple bunk housed Babs on the top, Flo on the bottom and Flo's bedding roll on the middle. They were tense, as they always were when faced with a night in the shelter. At least down here, the sound of bombs and ack-ack guns were distant and muffled, and Nellie knew they were safe. She shuddered. She was used to it, but she never ceased to be terrified by it all. Around them was the hum of conversation, a feeling of camaraderie, that whatever happened they were all in it together, they'd support each other and get through it as a community. The 'Blitz spirit', newspapers had called it. Sometimes it was hard to maintain, but Nellie always did her best to stay cheerful, especially for Flo who was now sitting with her arms wrapped around herself, looking small and frightened at the muffled noises from above.

Nellie dug through her bundle. 'There. Five sheets of paper, a couple of crayons and two pencils as promised.' She handed them to Flo. The little girl threw herself down onto her tummy on her bunk and began drawing.

Nellie climbed up to the top bunk and hugged Babs, who was soon regaling her with a tale of how at the factory that day one of the girls had mistakenly sewn pockets onto the back of an army jacket, not the front, to lighten the mood. They'd taken turns trying the garment on, joking about what on earth you'd put in pockets on your back.

Back at the start of the war, Nellie had been fifteen, about to start her year training at secretarial college. They'd thought then that the war would happen a long way off, in France and Belgium, like the last one. But then in 1940 war had been fought in the skies overhead, and then came the Blitz and suddenly they'd all been involved, all the people of London and other cities. War was no longer distant; it was here, all around them, affecting everything they did. Rationing, the lack of goods in the shops forcing them to 'make do and mend'. And of course the endless bombing campaigns.

Nellie and her family had been lucky. They hadn't lost anyone close to them. But with every raid it was a possibility. Someone she'd known a little from school had died along with her whole family when their house was bombed and they'd been sheltering in their cellar. Three lads from her street, friends of Billy, had signed up as soon as war was declared. Two were now dead – one killed during the evacuation of Dunkirk and the other who'd trained as a fighter pilot was shot down during the Battle of Britain. All those young lives lost, and for what purpose?

'Penny for your thoughts?' Babs said, and Nellie realised she'd been daydreaming.

'Oh, nothing,' Nellie replied.

'Well, I've got something for you. It's about Amelia Thomas.'

'What about her?' Amelia was a friend from school who now worked as a barmaid in their local pub.

'She's only gone and got herself up the duff!' Barbara widened her eyes as she spoke, waiting for Nellie's reaction to the news.

'No!'

'Yes. Sure as eggs is eggs!'

'She's been stepping out with Walter Hargreaves for ages, at least when he's not away fighting. He'll marry her, I bet.' Nellie hoped so. Amelia was a cheery, fun girl, and she'd hate to see her left in the lurch.

'Yeah, I reckon so. Probably when he's next home on leave. She'll be the size of a house by then. It's due next February.'

'Bless her. A shop in Roman Road looked like it has a few bits for babies in,' Nellie said. 'I'll go there next Saturday and ask them to put something on hold. Can't bring any baby things home yet, until Amelia's news is known, otherwise Dad'll think it's me and I'd be for it!'

Babs sniggered. 'They might think it was Billy's!'

'What a thought! Me and Billy!' Nellie laughed.

But Barbara's smirk faded. 'I shouldn't have laughed. He really does care for you. A lot, you know.' She took hold of Nellie's hand and squeezed it. 'I know you joke about it, and so does he, but underneath, he really cares. Don't go and break his heart, will you? I know you wouldn't mean to, but he's my brother and all, and I'd hate to see him hurt.'

Nellie blinked. She hadn't realised Billy's feelings for her ran so deep. She and Billy – there'd been a time just after they'd left school when they'd been flirtatious. Billy had never asked her on a date though. He was a wonderful man, but they'd been friends for so long, it was hard to imagine him as anything but. She squeezed Barbara's hand back. 'I won't. You know I like him too, a lot. But . . .'

'Not in that way,' Barbara finished.

Nellie nodded. 'Maybe I've just known him too long. He's more like a brother to me now.'

There was a distant boom as somewhere up above a bomb exploded. Nellie flinched, and Flo squealed in alarm.

'Will Auntie Ruth and Uncle John be all right, staying in their Morrisey shelter?' Flo asked. 'I could've stayed and looked after Auntie Ruth. And Oscar.'

'They'll be fine. Don't you worry. Come on, lie down now.'

Flo snuggled down under her blanket. 'Sing to me?'

'All right. Settle down now.' Nellie sat on the floor by Flo's head, tucking her feet under her. Singing to Flo always helped her nod off, despite what was happening above them. She began to sing softly.

'Sleep, my child, and peace attend thee,
All through the night.
Guardian angels God will send thee,
All through the night.'

As so often when she sang, she found herself forgetting where they were, and the reason they were there. The world around them shrank away until there was only her, little Flo and the song. She let her voice soar and Flo watched her with eyes first wide, before they began to droop until she finally succumbed to sleep as Nellie let the final verse trail away into little more than a whisper.

'Though our hearts be wrapped in sorrow,
From the hope of dawn we borrow,
Promise of a glad tomorrow,
All through the night.'

She adjusted the blanket covering her sister, and kissed her gently on the forehead.

Chapter 5

Nellie breathed in the cool air and glanced around as they emerged from the shelter the next morning. It was always a relief to know you'd survived another night but you were always met with the anxiety of not knowing what you'd find and if your own house would still be standing. There was no obvious sign of damage from bombs in the immediate vicinity of the tube. She felt the wave of anxiety in her stomach start to subside. She checked the time. There was just enough time to go home, drop off her bedding and wash and change before work.

Around them, hundreds of people were doing the same – streaming out of the shelter, blinking in the bright sunlight, making their way home, before heading off to work. The lucky ones would all sigh with relief when they entered their streets and saw their houses still standing, untouched. There'd be others for whom life would never again be the same.

As her family rounded the corner into Morpeth Street, Nellie was relieved to see there was no damage. Not to their house, or any of their neighbours', or to the school that stood at the other end.

'Well, looks like we've had a lucky escape again,' Charlie said.

'I heard loads of bombs though,' George added. 'Loads of 'em.'

Em glanced at Nellie. 'On your way to work, pop in on Ruth and John, will you? Just for a minute. I thought we'd see them down the tube last night. They must have gone to the other platform perhaps.'

'Will do, Mum,' Nellie replied, knowing Em needed to get Flo ready for school. Then she remembered the mess left by Oscar's paint job. 'Was going to go this morning anyway. They might have decided to stay in their Morrison shelter last night. Ruth's chest wasn't too good when I saw her yesterday.' Somehow Nellie found she didn't want to tell them she'd suggested they stay home. Not till after she'd ensured that they were safe.

*

A short while later, in clean clothes, her hair brushed, and with a cup of tea and a slice of toast with margarine inside her, Nellie rushed off to Royston Street. She'd need to be quick getting Ruth and John's lino mopped, and the stain on the armchair would have to wait for another time. As she walked up their street she saw a cloud of dust farther along that made her palms sweat and her heart begin to pound. Emergency services were in the street and people were milling about. She felt sick to the stomach with worry and sped up.

'Oh no. Not here,' she pleaded As she drew closer, she could see with mounting horror that a bomb had hit – it must have fallen very close to their house. Nearby, Mrs O'Brien from number 10 was shaking her head sadly, and the Houghs from across the road stood watching her with sympathetic expressions, and that could only mean one thing. She counted down the house numbers. *It couldn't be, it couldn't be . . .* The missing house was *theirs.* The neighbouring houses had their windows blown out, a chimney collapsed, roof tiles missing, but Ruth and John's – there was just a pile of rubble spilling out across the road where it used to stand. Their familiar sitting room wallpaper was still visible on one side wall. A door, hanging from one hinge, squeaked as it swung forlornly back and forth. A bedstead, mangled and bent, was oddly perched on top of piles of bricks. A fire burned somewhere at the back, with fire hoses trained on it.

'Auntie Ruth! Uncle John!' She screamed their names and ran forward towards the rubble. A fireman stepped in front of her and caught her by her upper arms.

'No, miss, you can't go nearer. It's not safe. Know them, did you?'

'My aunt and uncle,' she managed to say, wanting to free herself from his grip, to run into what was left of the house, find them, pull them free of the wreckage. 'Are they . . . ?' But she couldn't bring herself to say the word.

'If they were in the house then I'm afraid there's no

hope, love,' the fireman said, his tone sympathetic now. 'Took a direct hit.'

'But they'd have been in a M-Morrison shelter?' Even as she said it, she knew it would have made no difference. A Morrison shelter wouldn't stand up to a direct hit.

The fireman just shook his head sadly, patted her arm and returned to his duties. Nellie stood staring at the remains of the house, willing it not to be true, praying that somehow they'd survived.

'Oh Nellie, duckie. I'm so sorry.' Auntie Ruth's neighbour, Mrs Perkins, came up to Nellie, folding her into her arms. 'They pulled out two bodies early this morning. They're gone, love.'

Nellie's knees buckled and she fell to the floor, sobbing. Mrs Perkins crouched down beside her in the street and rubbed her back.

Nellie held her head between her hands and rocked back and forth, squeezing her eyes shut as though that could block out the reality of what had happened. Somehow she had to tell her family. But she couldn't, she couldn't bring herself to tell them that it was *her* fault that Ruth and John had stayed home. If only she hadn't told them to use their Morrison shelter! The sense of guilt was overwhelming. And Flo. She'd adored them. As she thought of Flo her blood ran cold. Her little sister could so easily have been killed last night too, if Nellie had given in to her pleading and let her stay with Ruth and John.

Suddenly she remembered about Oscar. 'The dog, their greyhound? Was he . . . was he killed too?'

Mrs Perkins shook her head. 'He's in my kitchen. He's filthy, poor thing, and has a few cuts, but nothing too bad.'

'I'll take him,' Nellie said decisively.

Nellie followed Mrs Perkins into her house, where Oscar was curled up on a blanket. He raised his head and thumped his tail weakly against the floor when he saw her. She felt a new wave of sobs coming. He was all that was left of her aunt and uncle. She knelt beside him and gently stroked his head. She could see a few cuts beneath the fur and filth. One on his head, another on his right foreleg. 'Oh you poor boy. But you'll come home with me, and we'll patch you up.'

She glanced across the street at the flattened house. Less than a day ago she'd sat in the front room there, with Ruth and John, and now there was nothing left. No matter what Mrs Perkins said, she knew this was all her fault. She trembled at the shock of it all, feeling unsteady on her feet.

'Come, dear,' Mrs Perkins said gently. 'Let me help you home. You can't be alone in the state you're in.'

Nellie was shaking and unsteady. She soberly accepted the woman's arm, allowing herself to be guided home. As they headed to Morpeth Street, her hand on Oscar's collar, she felt an ache in the pit of her stomach, like someone had torn out her insides. Her heart was heavy both with loss and guilt. She couldn't imagine how on God's earth she was going to be able to tell her family what had happened.

Chapter 6

Nellie thanked Mrs Perkins and hugged her goodbye at the corner of Morpeth Street. She'd managed to get a hold of herself on the walk home, but she was still trembling, the aching pain of her loss coursing through her body.

As she walked along the street, Charlie was just leaving for work. 'Dad!' she called, and he stopped, turned and saw her with the dog.

'What the—' he began, and then she saw him register her reddened, wet face, puffy eyes and dishevelled hair. It dawned on him what had happened, the colour running from his face as he grabbed the door frame and his knees sagged beneath him. 'Oh no. Not Ruthie. Not my poor Ruthie.'

Em must have heard something for she too came out to join them.

'I'm so sorry, Dad!' Nellie whispered when she reached them. 'They were in the Morrison shelter. They took a direct hit. They had no chance . . .' Her voice tailed away as she spoke and she dashed away tears.

Em let out a sob and put her hand over her mouth.

Charlie was shaking his head in disbelief, looking from Nellie to Oscar and back again, as if at any moment Nellie would say, *Don't worry, it's not true, it's all a joke, they're fine*. He knelt down beside the dog and held Oscar's face, staring into his eyes as though searching for confirmation, and let out a low moan of anguish.

'Let's go inside,' Em said quietly, and Charlie allowed himself to be ushered into the house. Nellie followed and placed the old blanket from Mrs Perkins by the stove in the kitchen, where Oscar immediately lay down. She put a bowl of water on the floor beside him.

Charlie slumped into a kitchen chair, his elbows on the table, head in hands. 'What was they doing in the Morrison? Why weren't they down the tube with the rest of us? They know it's safer. It'd only be the poor dog dead if they'd gone down the tube.' He looked up at Nellie as he spoke.

'I expect it was 'cos Ruthie was so poorly,' Em said. 'It's just bad luck, is all . . .' Her face was streaked with tears.

'Bad luck? *Bad bloody luck*? They're dead. My only sister and her husband! And you call it bad luck?' Charlie thumped the table, and Oscar gave a little whine.

Nellie bit her lip. She wondered if she should tell him it was her fault, so he'd shout at her and not Em, but no good would come of it. She'd have to explain why and then they'd all worry about going to the tube . . . Suddenly the war seemed so much closer. Nellie stared at her parents for reassurance and guidance, wondering how on earth you were supposed to cope with this kind of loss.

But Em seemed to be in disbelief at what had happened while Charlie was angry at the cruel world that had taken his sister and her husband far too soon. All Nellie could do was cry but nothing would bring back Ruth and John.

'At least our Flo wasn't with them,' Em said. 'Could've been so much worse.'

Charlie let out a roar. 'It's bad enough!' Oscar whined once more and then Charlie turned to stare at the dog as though he'd forgotten he was there. 'Sorry, boy. You've lost them too, I know. Is he badly hurt?' he asked Nellie.

'Few cuts – on his head and leg.'

Charlie slid off his chair and knelt beside the dog, checking him over. 'None of this is too bad. You'll stay with us now, boy. I'll take him to a vet.'

Em looked at Nellie and gave her a weak smile that Nellie returned, wiping away her tears. She knew her mum wasn't keen on dogs but if caring for the dog might help ease the loss of his sister, she wouldn't say anything to Charlie. 'You staying home today, Nellie? Given what's happened?' Em said after a few moments.

Nellie shook her head. 'No, Mum. I think I should go in, I can't let Mrs Bolton down.'

'But . . .' Em began, touching her arm.

'Mum! Please. I need to be there,' Nellie shouted, shrugging off her mother's hand. She knew her mother was just trying to help, but she couldn't be alone with her thoughts, not now. She had to keep busy.

Charlie shushed her. 'Let her go if she wants to.

Nothing she can do here, and work'll distract her. I'll take the day off to sort out the funeral.'

*

It was midday before Nellie entered Mrs Bolton's office warily, anxious at what sort of reception she'd get for being so late. She knew she'd missed at least one meeting that morning.

But the Mayor jumped to her feet as soon as Nellie walked in. 'Nellie! Something's happened, hasn't it? The raid last night? Sit down.' She called to Gladys in the typing pool to make tea and then closed the office door and looked at Nellie with sympathy.

'My aunt and uncle's house was hit.'

'Oh no. And are they . . . ?'

'Both gone,' Nellie whispered as tears started to fall down her cheeks. Crying at work was not something she'd ever thought she'd do but she couldn't help herself.

Mrs Bolton came to her side and put an arm around her shoulders. 'I'm so very sorry. I knew there'd be something. You're never late. We lost a few others in Bethnal Green last night. A family in Roman Road didn't get to the shelter in time. And a fireman was killed when a burning house collapsed on him. All these losses. When will it end?' She shook her head with an air of resignation. 'You shouldn't be here now,' she insisted, patting Nellie on the shoulder. 'Take the rest of the week off. We can manage without you. And please, Nellie, promise you'll come to me if you need anything?'

Nellie nodded. 'Th-thank you. You're very kind.'

A minute later Gladys came in with the tea. 'After you finish your tea, you must go home,' Mrs Bolton said softly to Nellie. 'She suffered a terrible loss last night, Gladys. Perhaps you could walk her home.'

'Of course, Mrs Bolton.'

Nellie took a sip and forced herself to smile her thanks at Gladys. There was sympathy in her friend's eyes. She sat beside Nellie and began chatting quietly, gossip from the Council offices, the latest antics of the kittens her cat had recently had, a memory of a trip to Brighton before the war. Anything and everything to take Nellie's mind off her loss, being careful not to upset her further, giving her time to drink her tea and compose herself before going home.

*

In the end Nellie took just two days off work. Her parents had all the funeral arrangements well in hand and at least at the town hall she could escape the subdued sadness at home and the constant callers offering their condolences.

Babs was the only person Nellie really wanted to see, and they spent several evenings sitting out on the bench in the backyard, talking.

'I suppose they thought it'd be easier to use their

Morrison shelter, what with your aunt being so ill,' Babs had said, and Nellie had nodded.

'Yes, that was why they stayed home. I saw them that day. Delivered their washing. Brought Flo home with me.' She sniffed back a tear. 'To think that was the last time I'd see them and I had no idea. Poor Auntie Ruth. Poor Uncle John.'

Babs put a comforting hand on her shoulder and suddenly Nellie wanted nothing more than to confide in her friend. 'It was me – I suggested they stay home and not go to the tube. To make it easier. If I hadn't said that, they'd—'

'They'd still be dead,' Babs said, cutting her off. 'Because they'd have made the decision anyway, no matter what you'd said.' She turned to look straight at Nellie. 'Don't go blaming yourself,' she added sternly.

Nellie smiled weakly at her friend. 'Thanks. Don't tell Mum and Dad I said they should stay home, will you? They might not be as understanding as you.'

'I'm sure they would, but no, I won't. And come talk to me whenever you need a shoulder to cry on, okay?'

'Will do.'

They sat in silence, Nellie feeling comforted by her friend's presence.

*

At the funeral, all of Ruth and John's neighbours and friends came to pay their respects, as well as Babs and her family. There'd been so many funerals in the community since the start of the war, but every one of them was important and the vicar managed to make each one special.

Later that evening, Charlie called the family together at the kitchen table. 'Right. I don't want to lose no more members of my family. So I've made a decision,' and here he eyed each of them in turn. 'It's time the kids were sent away again. The bombing raids are more frequent again. It's not safe here in London and if anything happened to them . . .' He tailed off, shaking his head. 'I want the kids in the country, where I know they'll be safer.'

Nellie watched as her mother struggled to keep her emotions in check. She'd hated it when George and Flo were evacuated the first time. Like so many other Londoners, the family had taken up the chance of moving the two younger children to safety using the Government Evacuation Scheme. They'd gone as soon as the Blitz started and had stayed away for almost a year. Em had been terrified that Flo, who'd been only four at the time, would forget her. She'd saved every penny she could, so that on two occasions she could take a train trip down to Dorchester to see them. 'Well, I . . . don't know. I mean, it'd be safer for them, but are we going to carry on having this many raids? Or are they all going to finish and we'd look fools for sending them away?'

'There's loads of people sending their kids away again now,' Charlie said. 'Three fellows I work with told me the other day they are. Every day there's busloads of kids being sent off. There's no sign of these raids stopping, and they say we're doing more bombing over there, so it stands to reason they'll retaliate. It's for the best, Em. And if or when it all ends, then we just bring 'em home again, like we did before.'

'Well, I'm not going,' George said, folding his arms. 'I've got me chickens to look after. Wouldn't be fair on Mum or Nellie. Got to be me what looks after them.'

'You'll do what you're told, lad,' Charlie growled.

'I'm thirteen. Nearly fourteen. Nellie didn't get evacuated at the start of the war. You said then she was old enough to stay here.'

Charlie opened his mouth to respond to that but Em put a restraining hand on his arm. 'He has a point. He's old enough to make up his own mind, Charlie. Let him stay if he wants to. As long as he promises he'll go straight down the tube the minute the siren goes. No stopping up here with his hens.'

'I promise that, Mum,' George said solemnly.

'Just Flo, then,' Charlie said.

Nellie was surprised he'd given in so easily. Perhaps he was finally beginning to recognise George was growing up. Her dad told them so often how he'd been just fourteen when he'd left school and started working at the docks. 'Thought I was quite the big man!' he'd say. And he'd been only a year older than George was now.

'Don't send me on my own!' Flo wailed, and flung her arms around Nellie who was sitting next to her.

'Ssh, Flo. Think about how you liked it last time – the

cows and the pigs and all the trees! You'll be somewhere lovely like that again.' Nellie held her tightly, pulling her little sister onto her lap.

'Would I stay with Mrs Thompson? At Hilltop Farm?'

'Probably not at the same farm but you'd be somewhere like that, out in the country with someone just as nice as Mrs Thompson, I'll bet.' Nellie hoped and prayed that would be the case.

'What if it's somewhere horrid where they treat kids badly?' Em muttered. 'You hear such things . . .'

Flo looked terrified. 'I don't want to go! It was all right last time with George. But not on my own!'

Nellie stroked her hair. 'Mum's being silly. We'll send you letters every week, and you can write back and tell us all about the farm animals you'll make friends with.'

'She's going, and that's that,' Charlie said. He got up and left the kitchen, trying to get his temper under control.

'Noooo!' Flo wailed. 'Do I have to go?'

'If Dad says so . . .' It'd break Nellie's heart, saying goodbye to Flo. First they'd lost Ruth and John, and now the war was going to separate her from her sister once more. But it was for the best. She steeled herself; she didn't want to cry in front of Flo, it would only make things worse if she saw how upset Nellie was.

Em slowly nodded. 'Yes, Flo, love. You have to go. It's safer, and your dad and I don't need the extra worry with all these raids. Come here, pet.' She reached out and Flo got down from Nellie and climbed onto Em's lap. Em kissed the top of her head. 'Hopefully it won't be for long, love. There's them that say we're going to win this war. It's just while the bombing's going on. Dad lost his sister, didn't he? That was horrid for him. He doesn't want to risk losing his little girl too, now does he?'

The back door opened and Charlie came back in. He was calmer now but Nellie could see his mind was made up.

'Tomorrow, I'm going to put Flo's name down.' Charlie crossed the kitchen and put an arm around his youngest daughter, who was still on Em's lap. 'It's for the best, my pet. We're doing what's best for you, that's all.'

Flo was still sulking, but Nellie could see she was putting a brave face on, doing her best not to cry. She was an easy-going child. The heart of the family, Nellie often thought. The one they all loved best, the one no one ever got cross with. She'd miss Flo, but Dad was right. It was the best thing to do.

Charlie leaned over and kissed Flo's cheek, brushing away her tears with his knuckle. 'Cheer up, pet. Make it easy for us, eh?'

Flo kissed him back and nodded, her little face set firm, both sad and serious.

As though confirming his decision, at just that moment the air raid siren began its all-too-familiar wail. 'For goodness sake. Not tonight,' Charlie said. 'Ain't we had enough this week?'

There was no point complaining. They wearily collected their bedding bundles and trooped along to the shelter. After what had happened to Ruth and John, Nellie was no longer worried about the safety of the tube shelter. Hopefully as long as people were careful going down the steps, there wouldn't be a problem. And better to risk a fall on the steps than a direct hit on their house, with them inside it.

Chapter 7

'Flo goes tomorrow,' Charlie announced when he came home from work the day after the funeral. 'Saturday. It's all settled. I went to the Women's Voluntary Service office today to put her name down, and they said they have space, and she can go in the next batch of evacuees. That's tomorrow. It's a sign, innit, Em? That they had space at such short notice, that must mean it's right, and she's meant to go. There's a bus that'll pick them all up at the railway arches and take them to Waterloo station, and a WVS woman will meet them there and go with them. Flo's to be on the bus at ten o'clock sharp, with her case all packed. And don't forget her gas mask.'

'I hate my gas mask,' Flo said.

'What, after all the effort I went to, to get you a Mickey Mouse one?' Em said. Everyone had been issued with gas masks at the start of the war, as there'd been fear that the Germans would attack with chemical weapons. Mickey Mouse–shaped masks were given to some of the smaller children, to make them seem less frightening. Nellie didn't think they looked much like Mickey Mouse at all. They were awful things to wear, but children were supposed to take them everywhere. So were adults, though Nellie's own mask had been left by her desk at work for months.

Nellie could tell Em was fighting back tears. She'd overheard her parents discussing it in their room last night after Flo was asleep, going over and over the arguments as to whether it was better to send Flo away or keep her here before reluctantly deciding it was for the best.

'You don't have to wear the gas mask. Just bring it,' Nellie said. 'It'll be all right, Flo-bo. Like I said. Be brave and a big girl now.'

Flo regarded her solemnly and nodded.

'Come on then, Flo. Let's go and do your packing now.' Nellie took her sister by the hand and led her upstairs. There was a little cardboard suitcase she'd used when she was evacuated before, and it still had her name tag attached. Nellie retrieved that from under her parents' bed and took it to the room she and Flo shared. She worked hard to make a game of the packing – who could fold a vest fastest, what was the smallest ball a pair of socks could be rolled into. And all along she pretended it was Flo's doll's case being packed, Dollie's clothes, Dollie who was being evacuated but taking Flo with her for company.

It worked. Flo chuckled the whole time, forgetting why they were packing. And Nellie enjoyed these moments with her little sister. Who knew when the next ones would come along? Maybe it would only be a month or two, or perhaps a year or more. The days while she was still so young were precious, and the thought that Nellie was going to miss so many of them once again was hard to bear. Harder, perhaps, having already been through it once. She would miss her terribly. And surely it must be even worse for Em and Charlie.

*

It was raining the next morning. A grey, damp, drizzly day that matched the family's mood.

Flo said goodbye to each chicken by name, and cuddled Oscar until he struggled to be set free. Charlie and George said goodbye to Flo at the house, as only two family members were allowed to see each child off, and they'd decided it would be best for Em and Nellie to walk her to the bus stop. Nellie carried the little case, as Flo's hands were full with Dollie. Her hated gas mask was slung over her shoulder in its case, and she was wearing her best red shoes. They'd allowed plenty of time, but even so the bus was already waiting, with a crowd of other children and their parents all lingering as they said their goodbyes, as though there was a prize for whoever could be last to board the bus. Many were crying though all were trying not to. That didn't help, Nellie thought, as she looked around at the tear-stained faces. Flo had noticed too, and her bottom lip was already trembling. How unfair it was that they lived in a world in which the youngest, most vulnerable – who were also the ones that brought the most joy – had to go away.

'Come on now. Line up here,' the bus driver shouted.

'I need your first and last name and then you get on the bus. I'll be leaving in ten minutes.' He had a list of names on a clipboard and as each child boarded he ticked the sheet.

Nellie hugged Flo, who was crying softly. 'You'll be all right, Flo. And remember we packed paper and crayons. I want to see lots of lovely pictures when you come back. Maybe you'll even be able to post some to us, if you can spare any.'

Em had given up trying to hold back her tears, which were now running freely down her face as she hugged Flo. Nellie put a comforting hand on her mother's shoulder, trying to give her strength. It wasn't good for Flo to see how upset her mother was. Not when she was still doing her best to be brave. Though Nellie too was fighting back tears.

'Come on then,' Nellie said. 'I'll get on with you and help you find a seat and stow your case. You bring Dollie.'

Reluctantly Em let go after one last squeeze, and Nellie led Flo to the door of the bus. The driver ticked off her name and nodded when Nellie asked to board the bus to settle her down. Flo picked a seat at the back of the bus. Nellie stowed the case under the seat and made a big fuss of making sure Dollie could see out of the window. She received a tiny smile from Flo in return.

'All right now! Say your last goodbyes then all family members need to get off the bus,' the driver called. 'I'm about to leave.'

Nellie kissed Flo. 'Have fun, you,' she said, and forced herself to smile as she got off the bus and rejoined Em.

The bus driver started his engine and the bus coughed out a plume of black smoke from its exhaust. With a crunch of gears it began to move.

'Oh, look at her little face!' Em called out, and Nellie raised her eyes to see Flo's nose pressed hard against the window at the back of the bus. She was crying, wailing if her open mouth was anything to go by. 'Oh, I can't bear it!' Em started running after the bus, waving.

'Mum, stop! It's the best thing, we all decided. Dad said . . . Don't let her see how upset you are!' Nellie caught up with Em and held her tightly.

'I can't . . . I can't let her go! Oh, I can't bear it! She's so little, and she's on her own . . . it was all right when she had her big brother with her but not now . . .' Em turned to Nellie. 'I can't run in these shoes. Stop the bus, get her off! Please! We made a mistake, we'll keep her with us, we'll go down the tube every night . . . just fetch her off for me! I'll tell Charlie . . .'

Nellie stared at Em, hardly believing what she was hearing, but her mother's anguish was real. It was as though her heart was being torn out of her body by that bus, the ties binding her to her youngest daughter stretching to breaking point, and if they snapped, it would be Em who broke. And not just Em. Nellie too. Flo was the heart of their family, and she had a sudden, awful feeling that if Flo left them now, they'd never see her again. She made a quick decision, turned and ran as fast as she could after the bus, down the middle of the road, panting as she tried to get alongside the driver, her coat flapping open.

She was almost alongside the bus, which had slowed in the traffic, her lungs burning with the effort, when she realised a delivery van was coming the other way, its driver paying more attention to the clipboard he was holding than to the road. There was nowhere for her to go. She was going to be caught between the bus and the van. She screamed in panic, expecting at any moment to feel the impact of the van hitting her.

And then strong arms were around her, she was being held tight, as the van rushed past so close she felt it drag at her coat, its horn blaring as the driver finally saw her.

'Crazy broad!' the man holding her shouted, but all she could see was the bus, now picking up speed, as it drove away from her with her precious little sister onboard.

'Stop that bus!' she yelled, fighting free of the man's arms and once more taking up the chase. He ran too, faster than her, shouting in an American accent as he drew alongside it, waving frantically at the driver. He was wearing the uniform of the US Air Force, she realised.

At last the driver noticed him and pulled over, and Nellie ran to the bus door and pounded on it. Flo, she could see, was already out of her seat and making her way forward.

The driver opened the door. 'What's the big panic? Forgotten something?'

Nellie couldn't talk as Flo pushed past him, off the bus and into her arms. 'Nelliiiee! I don't want to go!'

'Mum don't . . . want you to go . . . neither,' Nellie gasped out, as she rested her face on the top of Flo's head.

Her heart was pounding and her breath coming in great gasps.

'What's this all about? You taking this child off the bus? Couldn't you decide before you put her on that you didn't want her to go?' The bus driver threw up his hands in exasperation.

'What's going on? You coulda been killed, running in the street like that!' The American airman was leaning over, hands on his knees, trying to recover his breath.

Nellie flashed him a look. He had no idea what this was all about, no idea that if she'd left Flo on the bus she might not see her again for years. No idea what they'd been through. 'Let me get Flo's suitcase,' she said to the driver, 'then you can be on your way. Sorry for . . . changing the plan.'

'You did all that to take a kid off a bus?' the American said. 'What was she on it for?'

'Being evacuated, but not any more,' Nellie said brusquely. She pushed past him onto the bus to fetch Flo's case.

'What's her name? I got to cross her off the list,' the driver grumbled, as Nellie returned with Flo's suitcase. The other children on the bus were staring, open-mouthed, some of them crying that they hadn't been the ones taken off it.

'She's Flora Morris,' Nellie replied.

'I reckon being evacuated to the country is safer,' the American said. 'You shoulda let her go. There's too many bombs falling on London these days.'

'You think I don't know that?' Nellie snapped. 'You should mind your own business.' The arrogance of him, trying to tell her what to do! He knew nothing about it. 'We'll make our own decisions as to what's best for her. Come on, Flo. Let's get back to Mum.' Em was hurrying up the road towards them, relieved to see the bus pulled over.

'Don't I get any thanks? I saved your life back there,' the American called after them, as Nellie took Flo's hand and began walking back the way they'd come.

'Thank you!' Flo called out, giving the man a wave.

'Don't talk to him, he's a stranger,' Nellie said, sounding more cross than she'd meant to. The man *had* helped, she had to admit, but she was sure she'd have caught up with the bus soon. There were traffic lights further along the street. If the bus had stopped at those, she'd have made it, without the help of that man who'd called her a 'crazy broad'. And wasn't it a bit overdramatic of him to say he'd saved her life?

'You got me off, I didn't want to go,' Flo kept saying as they walked back.

'Mum wanted you back,' Nellie said, 'and I'm glad to have you. Go on, give her a hug.' She gave her little sister a gentle push, and the child ran into Em's arms.

Nellie watched as Em and Flo clutched each other, sobbing. Charlie had been so adamant that Flo should be evacuated. But now, looking at her sister, she knew the months would have been long and dark without Flo's sunny presence in the family. It'd be like those dreadful months of the Blitz. They couldn't face that again.

Ray Fleming watched the crazy girl who'd chased down a bus walk away hand in hand with her little sister. She sure was feisty, and quite attractive, but God, how ungrateful and rude! Not even a word of thanks to him, after all his efforts to help her. He'd saved her goddammed life! She was not at all like the girls back home, or those strait-laced girls from the Auxiliary Territorial Service – ATS they called it – who worked at his airbase. He'd only been in the country a couple weeks, sent over from the US as part of the Eighth Air Force to fly bombers over Germany. He'd yet to meet anyone from outside the airbase.

This girl, with her obvious love for her little sister, her spirit, her unconventionality, her disregard for danger – now she was different all right. An enigma. She had that – what did they call it? – British Bulldog spirit. He couldn't help but admire her for it. In a different situation he might have wanted to get to know her more.

Ray stood for a moment watching while the child ran into her mother's arms, and then turned away. He had one precious day off, and a lot that he wanted to do with it, before he met his friend in a pub that evening. He put the girl out of his mind and walked on up the road in the opposite direction to where she'd gone.

Chapter 8

'He's gonna kill me,' Em muttered to Nellie as they went back in the house with Flo.

'What the blazes . . . ?' Charlie said, running his hands through his hair. 'Didn't the bus turn up?'

'It did, but . . .' Em began.

'We put her on it, but then . . .' Nellie added.

'Then Nellie ran after it and so did a man and they stopped the bus and got me off,' Flo finished. She jutted her little chin in the air as though daring her father to be cross with her.

'This true?' he asked, looking from Em to Nellie and back again. He was like an unexploded bomb, Nellie thought. At any moment he'd go *Boom!* and they'd all have to run for cover.

'Erm, yes . . . Oh Charlie, it was heartbreaking, her little face! She looked so terrified being all alone and I couldn't . . . I just couldn't . . . Maybe if George had been with her, but we decided just her on her own and she's so little still . . .'

'Bloody hell, woman. How dare you! We talked about

this! Endlessly! We decided, you and me, it was the best thing to do. And then you . . . you . . .' He waved a hand vaguely and paced back and forth. Flo shrank against the wall, watching him with round, frightened eyes.

'I know we did, but . . .' Em held her hands out in a placatory gesture.

'I'll put the kettle on,' Nellie said. 'Come on, Flo. You can help me.' Tea fixed most things, didn't it? She went through to the kitchen and Flo followed her.

'Is Dad really cross?'

'He is now but give him a few minutes and he'll be all right,' Nellie said. At least, she hoped so. But Nellie could hear raised voices in the next room, her parents going over the same arguments as before.

'Thank you for getting me off that bus. I was frightened, all by myself,' Flo whispered. Nellie held her close, and then Flo was crying, her tears wetting Nellie's shoulder.

A moment later Charlie came stomping through the kitchen, off to the yard, no doubt to try to calm down. He cast them both a glance, and Nellie thought she saw a hint of acceptance in it.

'It'll be all right, Flo-bo,' she said, kissing her sister's head.

*

Nellie spent the rest of the morning helping Em with housework. And in the afternoon, when it began to rain

70

and they had no choice but to stay indoors, she played Beggar My Neighbour and Snap with Flo, old games that Ruth had taught them all, that they always used to play with her. As Nellie laughed with her little sister, it felt impossible how close Flo had come to being taken away. She felt her body glow with happiness brought on by Flo's presence.

'You coming down the Angel and Crown tonight?' Babs asked her, when they met outside in the yard during a brief respite from the rain. 'Billy's not working tonight, and says there's no likelihood of a raid. He's going, so am I. And I bet you could do with a bit of fun, you've had a hard time of it lately.'

Nellie nodded. Babs was right, it had been tough, and she'd barely been anywhere other than work since Auntie Ruth and Uncle John had died. It was about time she went out and had some fun. She smiled at her friend. 'Yes, I'll come. Thanks for asking me.'

'Good. And then you can tell me all about how come little Flo ain't halfway to Dorset by now.' Babs grinned. She'd seen Flo's face at the window. 'Lawks, here comes the rain again. Run!'

The two of them dashed into their respective houses. Nellie's legs ached from running after the bus that morning, and her feet were sore. She was pleased to have something to look forward to that evening.

*

Nellie took her time getting ready to go out. She put on her favourite blue dress, set her hair into fashionable victory rolls, curling the sides up high on the top of her head and pinning it so it would stay in two even rolls, while the back hung loose. She debated drawing a charcoal line down the back of her legs to look like she was wearing stockings but decided against it. It fooled nobody. She borrowed a string of jet beads from Em to hang around her neck and added a slick of lipstick. Not much, because she didn't have much left in the tube and it was very hard to find in the shops these days, but enough to redden her lips. It was exciting getting dressed up, even if it was just to go to the pub. A night out with her friends was just what she needed.

'You look like a princess,' Flo said. She'd been lying in bed cuddling Dollie and watching Nellie get ready.

'I feel like one, too,' Nellie replied, twirling around so that her skirt swung out around her. 'Now you get off to sleep, and I promise I'll be quiet as a mouse when I come back so I don't wake you.' She crossed the room and kissed her sister's head. 'Nice to have you back, Flo-bo.'

'I was never even properly gone.' Flo giggled.

The rain had eased off, though there was still thick cloud cover, which would hopefully keep the German bombers away for the night. Nellie skipped over puddles on her way to the Angel and Crown. She had arranged to meet Babs and Billy at the pub since they had no baby sisters to put to bed. As she neared its entrance she could hear raucous laughter, some rowdy singing, a piano tinkling away. It was an East End night in full swing. She grinned happily.

'Here she is!' Billy's face lit up as she walked in. He was sitting with Babs in a corner near the piano. A young lad in a soldier's uniform was attempting to play a ragtime tune on it but kept fluffing the notes and having to start again. Billy jumped to his feet. 'What will you drink?'

'Gin and tonic, if you're buying, Billy. I'll get the next round. Evening, Amelia! How's things with you?' Amelia was on duty serving behind the bar. It was a good way to hide her growing belly, Nellie thought, though surely soon her condition would be common knowledge.

'All good, thanks, Nellie. Going to be busy tonight I think.' Amelia took the order from Billy, winking at him as she did, which made him blush to his roots.

'You heard from your Walter lately?' Nellie asked Amelia.

'I did, yes,' the other girl said with a grin. 'Got a letter this morning. He's doing fine. Missing me. Some big push coming, but he can't say what, not with letters home having to go through the censors. Trying to arrange some leave for when . . . you know . . . my time comes.'

'Good to hear he's okay. You take care now,' Nellie said, and went to join Babs at her table.

'You all right?' Babs asked.

'Better for being out. Honestly, it's been quite a week.'

Babs put her arm around Nellie's shoulders. 'I know. Let your hair down tonight, eh?'

'I intend to.' Nellie shrugged off her friend's arm. Too

much kindness right now would tip her over the edge and she'd cry – at the loss of her aunt and uncle, the stress of nearly sending Flo away and then getting her back. Better to not talk about it. She wanted to enjoy her night out. She gave Babs a bright smile that she hoped would also serve as a warning not to offer too much sympathy while they were in public.

'Here you are, gorgeous,' Billy said, as he put a drink in front of Nellie. 'You're looking a picture this evening. Cheers!'

'Cheers!' Nellie raised her glass and clinked it against her friends'.

'Your mum happy Flo's staying?' Billy asked.

'She is. She can't stop cuddling her. It was the right thing.'

'So what happened, you put her on the bus and then took her off?'

'Pretty much. Had to chase after it, down the road. An American fellow in uniform joined in the chase.'

'Dramatic!' Babs said, with a grin.

'Yes, s'pose it was a bit!'

A cheer went up from the bar as the soldier stopped playing the piano. 'Let's have a decent tune now!' someone shouted. 'Amelia! You can play!'

There was a chorus of people cheering for Amelia to play the piano, and eventually, blushing, she was persuaded out from behind the bar to sit at the piano.

'Putting a bit of weight on, are you, love?' said one man who was sitting on a bar stool. He gave her a lascivious wink.

'None of your business,' she replied.

'Whose is it, anyway?' he went on, reaching out a hand to try to pat her bump.

'Get off me!' Amelia batted the man's hand away.

'Oi, leave the lady alone,' Billy said, jumping to his feet. He squared up to the man. Billy was skinny, but taller than the other man, and there was a look in his eye that said he'd put up with no nonsense. Nellie watched, feeling strangely proud of him. He might not be able to fight in the war because of his asthma, but he hadn't hesitated to fight to protect a woman.

'She ain't no lady. Look at 'er! Not married and up the duff.'

'If you can't be polite, get out of her pub.' Billy took a step forward.

Babs gasped. 'Billy, don't you get in a fight, now,' she warned.

'He won't. The other fella's backing down, look,' Nellie said, and indeed he had taken a step away.

The landlord, Amelia's boss, had noticed what was going on. He went over and had a quiet word with the man, who then took his drink to a table in a corner. 'Thanks, mate,' he said to Billy. 'She don't need no trouble.'

'Thank you, Billy,' Amelia said. She flashed him a smile, then sat at the piano. 'Right then, lads. What'll I play?'

There was a chorus of requests of all sorts, everything from 'Knees Up Mother Brown' to 'Ave Maria'. Amelia listened to a few then struck up a medley of traditional music hall songs that had everyone singing along.

Nellie, Billy and Barbara joined in with gusto. After a few songs Babs turned to Nellie. 'You should sing us all something. With your beautiful voice, you'd have everyone listening.'

'Ah, rubbish. I can't.' Nellie blushed at the compliment, but felt a surge of excitement. Yes, she would love to sing, to lose herself in music for a few minutes.

Billy gazed at Nellie. 'Babs is right. You have an amazing voice. Sing us something.'

'What shall I sing?'

'Something by Vera Lynn?' Barbara asked. She tapped Amelia's arm. 'Nellie here will sing, if you'll play? Is that all right?'

'Certainly,' Amelia replied, as she rounded off her current piece, then turned to Nellie. 'What'll it be, Nellie?'

Nellie thought for a moment. 'Do you know "The White Cliffs of Dover"?'

Amelia smiled. 'I certainly do. Okay then, here we go.' She launched into the intro. Nellie stood up, and soon was joining in, her voice soaring above the piano. She found herself lost in the music as always happened when she sang. The music, the song filled the space around her until she was barely aware of anything else, only Amelia and the piano and the song existed and everything else faded away.

As she sang, conversations fell silent, people put down their drinks and everyone listened, watching this girl whose voice was entrancing.

'Better than Vera,' a voice muttered and was quickly shushed. More than one person had to extract a handkerchief from a sleeve or pocket and dab at their eyes.

***

Billy could not take his eyes off Nellie. He could feel his sister was watching him closely, but he didn't mind. Let her, let everyone around see how much he cared for this girl, whom he'd known all his life, but who now occupied every waking thought. She was his world. His whole world. And maybe, just maybe, there'd come a time when she cared for him as much as he cared for her, and then his world would be complete. He couldn't help but dream of such a future.

He made himself a promise. Tonight, as they walked home, he'd take Nellie's hand and draw her away from Babs. Then he'd ask her out on a date, a proper date, just the two of them. To the pictures if she liked, or for tea and cake at the Lyons Corner House. Whatever she wanted.

If she said yes, it would be a start, a small step towards fulfilment of his dreams. If she said no . . . well. He wouldn't dwell on that possibility. Not now, not when she was singing, and he could imagine she was singing only for him.

Chapter 9

US airman Ray Fleming was sitting with his friend Clayton. It was his first time in an East End pub, which was so different to what he was used to back home, where it was so rural, he had to drive twenty miles to find a bar. Here, everyone was a local who'd walked into the pub and seemed to know everyone else in the room. Even the British soldiers must be billeted nearby as they seemed to be on familiar terms with the barmaid.

He and Clay had had a couple of pints of warm, flat beer. Bitter, they called it over here. 'You like this stuff?' Clay had asked, pulling a face. Ray had shrugged. 'Guess we'll have to get used to it.' And it wasn't so bad, after the first couple pints.

They'd stopped chatting when the barmaid began playing the piano and leading a singalong, to which everyone seemed to know the words apart from them. But it was fun anyway. 'Ain't no pianos in our bars back home,' Clay said, grinning as they attempted to join in with a chorus.

And then a young woman got up to sing, and everyone stopped to listen. Ray stared, immediately recognising her.

'Say, that's the girl,' he whispered to Clayton.

'What girl?'

'The one I told you about. The one who chased down a bus and took her little sister off it.'

'That's her?'

'That's her.'

She instantly captured Ray's attention, as she did the rest of the people in the pub, with the beauty of her voice as it swooped and soared, singing of better times to come, tomorrow, just you wait and see. He knew this song. Who didn't? It was on the radio so often.

'Tomorrow, when the world is free,' Ray whispered, as she sang that line. Now that he could really look at her he could see she was naturally beautiful – yet she seemed totally unaware of the fact. Her hair was dark, her eyes wide, her mouth generous, a smear of lipstick accentuating her lips. She was slim yet curvy, clothed in a blue dress that suited her very well. There was a warmth about her, the way she was lost in her music but at the same time managing to bring her audience along with her.

And yet she'd been so rude and offhand, ignoring him after he helped stop the bus. *Don't talk to him, he's a stranger,* she'd said to her little sister. But what if he introduced himself, so that he was no longer a complete stranger? He hadn't expected to ever see her again, but here she was, a real English rose, singing like an angel. He was intrigued by her. It was her voice, weaving a magic spell around him. He was powerless against it.

'You still with us?' Clayton said with a laugh, as the

song finished. 'Looked like you were on another planet there. Fancy another pint of this soupy stuff?'

'Sure, why not?' Ray replied, and his friend went to the bar for the drinks.

The girl who'd been singing bent to speak to the barmaid who was playing the piano, and a moment later the music started up again. This time she sang 'We'll Meet Again'. Ray, along with the rest of the patrons of the pub, knew the words to this by heart and soon everyone had joined in. She conducted the pub's customers in their singing, a smile on her face, clearly enjoying this immensely. Now, she wanted to envelop everyone in the music rather than just lose herself.

When the song was over, she sat down beside her friend, and it was then that he caught her eye. He saw her gasp and lean towards her friend to say something. The other girl, the blonde, glanced over at him and turned back to say something that made both girls laugh.

Clayton returned with the drinks.

'I'm going over. See if I can break through her British reserve. Come with me, she has a friend,' Ray said.

Clayton raised his eyebrows but followed him carrying their pints, to where the girls were sitting. A few customers turned to watch them. They obviously didn't get too many Americans in this pub, unlike in those near their airbase.

The skinny man who'd been with the girls was at the bar, waiting to be served. Ray hoped it'd be a long time before that fellow caught the landlord's eye. The barmaid had begun playing something else, something that tinkled up and down the keys and was perfect background music for conversations to resume.

'Good evening. We met earlier today, if you remember?' Ray wasn't sure what kind of reaction he'd get. She certainly hadn't been too friendly out on the street.

'Yes, of course I remember. You called me a *crazy broad*.' She looked at him defiantly as she spoke, as though daring him to say anything like that to her again.

He felt himself blushing. 'I did, yeah. But hey, I'm sorry about that now. It was said in the heat of the moment. That van nearly hit us.'

The other girl, the blonde, was staring at him. He tried to appeal to her. 'I helped her get her little sister off a bus. And not a word of thanks.'

The blonde turned to her friend and wagged a finger playfully. 'Nellie, you really ought to thank the man. Where are your manners?' She tutted jokingly, before leaning in closer to whisper something. Ray thought he caught the word 'handsome'. Whatever it was, the girl, the singer, blushed right to the roots of her hair.

'Is she all right? Your little sister?' Ray asked.

'Um, yes, she's fine. Look, I'm sorry too. Heat of the moment, as you say. I'm not normally as . . . rude to strangers. So . . . thank you. Flo's happy to be home, and we're all so relieved she didn't go.'

'I'm glad about that. Ray Fleming.' He held out a hand and she took it. It was a good sign, a thawing of the ice.

'Nellie Morris.'

'Pleased to meet you, Nellie Morris.'

She blushed as she shook his hand. 'Thank you too, for saving my life.'

'Don't mention it.' He grinned. 'Actually, *do* mention it. Not every day I save a lady's life.'

'How often?' There was a cheeky, flirty look in her eye as she asked.

'How often what?'

'Do you save ladies' lives?'

'Ah now, let's see.' He pretended to think about it, counting on his fingers. 'Ahem. You're the first.'

She laughed, seeming pleased with this answer. At that moment, the skinny guy returned to the table, carrying two drinks for the girls. He glared at Nellie as he sat down, a look that wasn't wasted on Ray. Was this Nellie's fella, then? Or brother? Ray gave Nellie a questioning glance, and she took the hint.

'Oh, this is Billy Waters. My next-door neighbour, and Barbara's brother. Billy, this is Ray Fleming. He's the man who helped me get Flo off the bus this morning.'

'You should have let her go,' Billy said tersely. 'Would have been better for her, in the long run.'

Ray was about to respond but then thought better of it. He turned to Nellie instead.

'I also wanted to say, you have a mighty fine singing voice, Nellie Morris. I've never heard anything like it. You had the whole pub in raptures.'

She smiled, dimples appearing in her cheeks, and gave a little laugh. 'You're exaggerating again. Raptures is a bit strong, Mr Fleming. But I'm glad you liked it.'

'Call me Ray, please.' God but she was pretty. And there was an odd combination of vulnerability underneath that feistiness that he liked. Liked a lot. 'Will you sing again?'

She glanced over to where the barmaid was playing the piano – a ragtime tune now, which showed up the inadequacies of the soldier who'd been trying one earlier. 'I don't think so. I think the moment has passed.'

'Amelia would let you if you wanted,' Barbara said. 'Shall I ask her?'

'No, I'm happy sitting here now.' She smiled, and Ray hoped that it was his presence making her happy. 'Come on, Ray, tell me about yourself. Where are you from?'

'Michigan,' he replied, and she frowned.

'You'll have to tell me where that is.'

'North of the country, tucked between Lake Michigan and Lake Huron. You know the Great Lakes, right?' He hoped he didn't sound condescending. He had no idea how much of American geography and history was taught in British schools.

She nodded. 'Yes. Chicago's on Lake Michigan, isn't it?'

'Yes, but that's in Illinois, at the southern end of the lake. My folks' place, where I was raised, is kind of round the corner from there.'

'East or west?' She was staring into space as though picturing the map in her mind's eye, and he, he couldn't help but stare at her profile.

'East.'

'Do you live in a city?'

He laughed a little and shook his head. 'No. My folks have a farm, and their land extends down to the lakeside. We're in the middle of nowhere. Nearest big city is in fact Chicago, and we have to cross two state boundaries to reach it. Indiana,' he added in response to her questioning look. 'Three-hour drive.'

'I can't imagine being that far from a city,' she said, staring at him. Oh, but he could lose himself in those huge brown eyes!

'Have you always lived in London?'

She nodded. 'Yes. I was born here, in the house I still live in. But I've always wanted to move away, to travel and see the world, visit exciting places. Farthest I've ever been is Southend.'

'Well, you are one up on me, Nellie. Some of the other guys, including Clayton there, have taken a trip to Southend but not me. They say the pier's closed to stop the Germans landing, and the beach is strewn with anti-tank devices.'

'I haven't been there since before the war. That's not how I remember it. Then it was all donkey rides on the sand and ice creams on the prom,' she said, and Ray was struck by the note of sadness in her voice. It must be hard, he thought, seeing your hometown targeted by enemy bombers night after night, seeing your favourite holiday destination closed off, having no idea when it would all end.

'They'll put it all back to how it was, when the war's

over,' he said gently, and was rewarded with a dazzling smile.

'I hope so. I want to take Flo there some day.'

'And you will. I promise.'

'I want to take her to more exotic places too,' she said with a smile.

'Like where?'

'Africa. America. Australia.' She waved her hand expansively as if to encompass the entire globe, and almost knocked his drink out of his hand. 'Whoops! Sorry, Ray.'

He laughed. 'I caught it. Well, I've been all over the States – east, west, north and south. And Hawaii. I was in Mexico once before the war.' Her eyes shone, he noticed, as he talked about the places he'd been and the things he'd seen.

Once they started talking about the wider world, Nellie's eyes sparkled, causing Ray's heart to flutter. Clayton and Barbara, Ray noticed, seemed to be getting along, too, laughing at each other's jokes, flirting gently. The lone male – Barbara's brother whose name Ray had already shamefully forgotten – had wandered off to stand beside the piano, watching the barmaid play.

And as for Ray . . . well, he was besotted already. Nellie wanted to see the world, and suddenly, he realised he wanted to be the one who showed her it. He had to spend more time with this girl. He had to. An idea occurred to him. 'Say, girls, next weekend there's a dance, up at our airbase. Why don't you two come along? There's a bus runs from here up to North Weald, and the last one back runs late enough that you can have a decent length of time at the dance. Whaddya say?'

He held his breath as Nellie looked at Barbara, then at him, and back at Barbara again. There was a slight smile at the corner of her mouth as though she liked the idea, and then joy of joys, Barbara raised her eyebrow and gave a small nod. 'I'll go if you will, Nellie,' she said, and Ray could have thrown himself across the table and kissed her for that.

'Well . . . all right then. Why not?' Nellie said, and she smiled broadly as she lifted her drink for a sip. But her eyes stayed on his. If he was reading her right – and how he hoped he was! – then she liked him too.

'What's all this?' It was that fellow, Barbara's brother, who'd come back over to see what they were discussing.

'A dance, at Clayton and Ray's airbase,' Barbara told him. 'Next Saturday. Will you come too? That would be all right, wouldn't it, Clay?'

'Sure it would be! More the merrier,' Clayton replied, but the brother – Billy! That was his name – shook his head and pulled a face.

'Can't. I'm on duty next weekend, both nights. Babs, are you sure you should—'

'We're both going. Me and Nellie. We'll look after each other.' Barbara spoke firmly and it was clear who was the boss in that sibling relationship.

'We'll take good care of the girls, Billy. We're decent people. You don't need to worry.' Ray hoped his words would reassure the young man. It was nice of him to feel so responsible for his sister and her friend, but they were grown women who could make their own decisions.

'I'd still prefer it if I was there too,' Billy said, a petulant tone creeping into his voice. He was glaring at Ray as though Ray had stolen something from him.

'Oh Billy,' Nellie said. 'It's a shame you have to work that day. But next time, eh? Next time we'll all go. Are there lots of dances at the airbase? Do lots of girls go as well as the airmen?' Nellie had patted Billy's upper arm as she spoke and Ray felt a surge of jealousy at the casual touch. There was clearly a closeness between them. Was it only that they were neighbours or was there more to it than that? He sincerely hoped not.

'Yes, plenty of girls go,' Clayton answered her. 'Local ones and London ones, also lots of girls that work at the base. And there are dances every month.'

'We'll hope to see you at the next one, Billy.' Ray raised his glass to clink against the other man's, but received only a bad-tempered stare instead.

'I better be off home,' Billy said suddenly. 'Got to work tomorrow. See you later, Babs, Nellie.' He got up and walked out of the pub with barely a backward glance.

'Oh, don't mind him,' Barbara said with a giggle. 'He's just jealous. He doesn't like anyone else talking to Nellie.'

'I'm not cutting in and causing a problem, am I?' Ray asked. He had to ask, didn't he? In case . . . there was an understanding between Nellie and Billy . . . He held his breath as he waited for the answer.

'Not at all.' Nellie, thank God, smiled at him as she replied. 'He's like a brother to me too, that's all. He's just a bit protective, like, of both of us.'

'Swell to have someone that's got your back,' Ray commented. He tried not to show it, but he was delighted to be shot of Billy, who'd dragged the mood of the party down. Now they could laugh and joke and get to know each other, with the promise of next weekend's dance to look forward to. As long as he survived the missions he had to fly before then, of course.

Chapter 10

'It would be all right if Billy was going too,' Charlie said, when Nellie asked for permission to go to the dance. It was Sunday evening, Flo was in bed and George in his room. She'd tried to catch her parents in a relaxed mood when they'd be more likely to agree. But Charlie was frowning. 'I'm not happy about our Nellie going off with these men we don't know at all.'

'Dad, I won't be on my own. Babs is coming with me.' Nellie folded her arms defiantly. She didn't like going against Charlie's wishes, but she was a grown woman. She and Babs were able to look after themselves. And besides, she really, really wanted to go to the dance. To have fun, to meet new people and . . . if she was being honest with herself, she very much wanted to see Ray again. Her stomach gave a little flip as she thought about him. There was something about Ray – kindness in his smile, honesty in his eyes – that she'd found beguiling. He was different to the East End lads she knew. Exotic, interesting, well-travelled. He'd been to places she could only dream of: California! New York! Hawaii! She wanted to get to know him better. She was embarrassed now when she remembered her initial impression of him, when she'd thought him arrogant. He'd only been trying to help, and she'd been so rude.

'Let her go, Charlie,' Em put in. 'They deserve some fun. This god-awful war eating away at their youth. Like Nellie says, there's two of them to look out for each other.'

'I don't know, love. I don't know that it's right for you to go. Only thinking of your safety. You hear such things about these Americans.'

'What things, Dad?'

'Over paid, over sexed and over here. You want to watch your step around them, you hear me?'

Nellie gasped, but held her ground. 'If I watch my step, can I go?'

'Hmm.' Charlie stared at the empty fireplace for a moment, considering. 'This bloody war. If it wasn't for that, and the thought we could all be killed tomorrow like my poor Ruthie, I'd say no. But your mum's got a point. Long as you promise me you'll behave and you'll be back before midnight. Otherwise,' he wagged a finger at her sternly, 'it'll be the last time.'

Nellie grinned and flung her arms around him, kissing his cheek. 'Thank you, Dad!'

'Get off me, girl! No need for all that,' Charlie said, his expression a mix of happiness and embarrassment at her show of affection.

*

The following days dragged by for Nellie. Mrs Bolton was fractious all week, worried she hadn't yet heard back from London Civil Defence regarding her request for funding to improve safety at the tube station shelter. Nellie had to tiptoe around her, trying not to add to her boss's stress. But the promise of the weekend dance with Ray kept her going – in fact it was all she could think about – and having Flo home brightened up the evenings. There'd been no further air raids, thankfully, which meant there'd been no need to question whether it had been right to take Flo off the bus or not.

At long last Saturday rolled around. After helping Em with a few chores around the house Nellie could begin getting ready for the dance.

Babs came round with a bag full of clothes, rollers, make-up and accessories. 'Nothing fancy,' she said, 'but I'll share whatever I have.' The girls had Nellie's bedroom all to themselves, as Flo was out skipping in the street with some friends.

'I'll share too,' Nellie replied, grinning. 'We'll make ourselves look drop-dead gorgeous, just you wait. Which dress shall I wear? This red and green one, or the blue?' She held up the two possibilities. She'd already taken them out of the wardrobe and laid them on her bed.

'I love the blue, but you wore it last week. He's seen you in it already! Maybe wear the other.'

'I always think it makes me look like a Christmas tree.' Nellie wished she could have bought something new, but she had no clothing coupons to spare. Anyway, there was nothing new in the shops. She'd have to make do, but oh, how she wanted to look her best for Ray! She imagined him falling head over heels for her and smiled at the thought.

'Rubbish, you look gorgeous in it! What are you grinning about, anyway?' Babs replied.

'Oh, just . . . looking forward to the dance.' Nellie tried, but couldn't stop smiling. She felt giddy with excitement.

'So am I! Hey, open the window. It's warm in here. I don't want to sweat all over my frock.' Babs was fanning her face with her hand.

'Ahem, only horses sweat. Gentlemen perspire, and ladies merely glow.' Nellie put on an upper-class accent and raised her eyebrow as she spoke, causing Babs to dissolve into fits of giggles. She pushed up the sash window a little way, allowing cooler air into the room.

'That's better,' Barbara said.

'Babs,' Nellie said, 'do you think Ray's good-looking?'

'God yes. He's gorrrrrgeous!' Babs drew out the word and gave a dramatic eyeroll, making Nellie laugh.

'What are you girls finding so funny?' Billy's voice came from outside. Nellie pushed the window open wider and stuck her head out. Next door, Billy was leaning out of his window too, puffing on a cigarette.

'Billy! Thought you were at work today?'

'On shift this evening.'

'Poor you.' Nellie pouted. 'Having to work while we're out dancing.' She giggled again. 'Still, someone's got to keep the country safe, eh Air Raid Warden Waters?'

'Yes, well. Have a good evening.' Billy ducked back inside his room and pulled the sash window shut.

'He'll kill me for saying this but he's jealous,' Babs said quietly. 'That you'll be spending an evening with a handsome American.'

'Or maybe more than one!' Nellie squealed. 'The whole airbase is full of Americans. Your Clayton'll be there too!'

'Not *my* Clayton.' Barbara shook her head. 'He's nice enough and makes me laugh but he's not for me.' She gazed at Nellie quizzically. 'You like Ray, don't you? Your whole face lights up when you mention him.'

Nellie turned bright red. 'We got on well enough. And yes, I did like him a lot. But oh Babs, it's early days for both of us, ain't it? Who knows who else we might meet tonight!' But Nellie suspected that no one would measure up to Ray Fleming. She didn't know him at all, but she could not ignore the flutters she felt whenever she replayed in her head their time at the pub.

*

'You'll promise to be on the last bus home? Remember what your dad said about being home by midnight,' Em said, as she helped Nellie into her coat.

'We will, promise.' It was about the fifth time Em had asked her, not that Nellie had been counting. Her mother was concerned, she knew. It was the first time Nellie had gone out of London for a night out, since the war began. In fact, the first time ever. She'd only been fifteen when war broke out.

'And you'll be *sensible*?'

Both girls nodded. Out of the corner of her eye, Nellie could see that Babs was stifling a giggle.

'We will, Mum. We'll look out for each other.'

'Well, you have fun, you hear? Good, clean, sensible fun. God knows you get few enough chances. Your youth disappearing as this damned war goes on and on.' She grabbed each of them in turn and kissed their cheeks. Nellie was astounded to see a glint of a tear in her eye.

'Thanks, Mum.' She hugged her back. 'Come on, Babs, we should get going.' The girls linked arms happily as they left the house and set off to the bus stop. Nellie felt a wave of excitement rise up in her. In a short while she'd see *him* again.

*

A few minutes later they were on the bus that would take them up to the village of North Weald, just north of London. They'd bagged a double seat in the centre of the bus and had been wolf-whistled at by a group of British soldiers who were leaving the bus as they got on. 'Where you going, girls? Wherever it is, you'll have more fun with us, ain't that right, boys?'

They'd grinned at each other but ignored the soldiers. When the bus was on the move Babs turned to Nellie. 'I can't believe we're getting out of the city for an evening out. Away from the risk of an air raid and having to go down the tube.'

'We're not quite safe yet,' Nellie said, though she didn't want to dampen her friend's excitement. 'I mean, we're on our way, but if the siren went off right now . . .'

Babs grimaced and nodded. 'The bus would go to the nearest shelter and drop all the passengers off there. And right now, the nearest shelter is the Bethnal Green tube. God, imagine if that happened and we ended up there, all dolled up in our finery!'

'Come on, bus driver, go faster! Get us out of London,' Nellie muttered. She couldn't bear to think of the possibility that their night out could be scuppered by an air raid, especially now, when they were on a bus, all dressed up. And to make it worse, they would have no way of telling Ray and Clayton why they hadn't come. They would probably never see them again.

She crossed her fingers, silently praying, wishing with all her heart that everything would go smoothly. Beside her, Babs was quiet, staring out of the window as they passed by buildings interspersed with gaps where bombs had hit. Nellie guessed she was thinking the same thing. They'd only relax once they were out of the city and able to enjoy the dance with their dates.

Chapter 11

After nearly an hour, they pulled into a bus stop in North Weald, just around the corner from the dance hall. The hall was festooned with bunting, and there were crowds of people, some in uniform and some not, milling about outside. Nellie gathered her bag and coat and followed Babs off the bus. To her surprise and delight, Ray and Clayton were both there, at the bus stop to meet them, sitting on a wall smoking. As soon as they saw the girls get off the bus they both leapt off, stubbed out their cigarettes and came over.

'Nellie! Barbara! You made it!' Ray exclaimed.

Nellie grinned, her stomach turning somersaults at the sight of him. He was even better looking than she remembered, and seemed genuinely excited to see them. 'We certainly did! Now then, lead the way. There's dancing to be done!'

Ray took her arm and Clayton linked up with Babs, and the four of them made their way back around the corner to the dance hall. 'Mind the kerb there,' Ray said to Nellie, gently pulling her back a little. 'It's a little uneven just here.'

'Thank you.' She clutched his arm tighter, enjoying being looked after by someone so courteous. Enjoying too, the warmth and strength of his arm beneath his jacket.

At the hall, they left their coats in the cloakroom and went inside, where a band was playing the latest Glenn Miller numbers. 'I'll get the drinks,' Ray said. 'G & T, right, Nellie?'

She nodded, and he went off to the bar while Clayton found them a table. The hall was filling up fast with servicemen of every description, girls in Women's Auxiliary Air Force uniforms and a handful of people in civilian clothes.

'You ever think about joining the WAAF?' Nellie asked Babs.

'Nah. Blue's more your colour than mine,' she replied with a wink that set both of them giggling.

'Say, don't you two ladies look beautiful,' Ray said, as he returned with the drinks. Nellie blushed as she noticed his eyes staying on her.

'Did you have a good week?' she asked, as he sat down next to her.

'It was fine. I flew my missions. I survived, and so did all my crew. That's all I ever ask for.' He leaned closer to her.

'I've been wondering, what brought you to Bethnal Green last weekend? It's not the most exciting place. I'd have expected you to go up the West End on your days off.' It was something she'd been thinking about all week.

'Ah, one of my grandfathers was originally from Bethnal Green,' he replied. 'He left for America fifty years ago. I wanted to see for myself where he'd lived. When I wrote my folks and told them I was stationed east of London they suggested I pay Bethnal Green a visit.'

A quarter of him was a Bethnal Green boy, then. The thought made Nellie warm to him even more. 'Do you like it?'

'It's a fine place. Mighty fine. Very different to the big skies and wide-open spaces I'm used to. I told you about my folks' farm, on the shores of Lake Michigan. In the summer we go sailing on the lake. In the winter sometimes it freezes over and we skate on it.'

'Sounds lovely!'

'It is. Maybe you'll see it one day?' He smiled at her as he said it, so that it sounded almost like an invitation.

Suddenly Nellie wanted nothing more than to go with him, sail in the summer and skate in the winter. The nearest to it they had in Bethnal Green was the little pond where Flo had fed the ducks. 'Me go to America? I'd love to.' Nellie sighed. 'By ship? Or by aeroplane? That would be even better. I've never flown anywhere before.'

'I've flown over Paris. Seen the Eiffel Tower, the Seine, Notre Dame. Only from the air, though. Plenty of bomb damage, too, it needs some rebuilding.' Ray's tone was wry.

'So does London.' She pictured the streets in Bethnal Green with their gaping holes where homes had once stood. Ruth and John's house, which had once been a welcoming haven where she had felt nurtured and cherished as a child, now nothing more than a pile of rubble. She shuddered.

Her thoughts must have shown on her face, for he looked at her with sympathy, then reached over and took her hand, sending a surge of warmth coursing through her. 'It will be rebuilt, some day. When we've won this war. Trust me, Nellie.' She gazed deep into his eyes, as though in their depths she might see the future, when the war was over and they were at peace.

And then the band struck up the 'Chattanooga Choo Choo' and he jumped up and pulled her to her feet. 'Time we had a dance, Miss Morris! On your feet, let's go!' Before she knew it she was in his arms being whisked around the dance floor, gasping and laughing.

Ray was an excellent dancer. He was able to guide her with his movements, with pressure here or a pull there, although he held her lightly. All she had to do was relax and let him lead her in a form of Lindy hop, though she didn't know all the steps. She was a little breathless keeping up with his pace, but she loved every second of it.

'Where did you learn to dance like that?' she gasped.

'Lake Shore High. I partnered with a girl with two left feet. She tripped me up at the prom and I near broke my nose.' He grinned. 'You are a vast improvement on her in every way, Nellie Morris.'

When the tune ended, he caught her in his arms and for a moment as he held her and gazed into her eyes it was as though everything around them had melted away.

She loved being in his arms – it felt so good, so right. She'd never felt like this before. It was like those scenes at the pictures, when the leading lady fell in love with the leading man, at first sight. Well, second sight for herself and Ray. She was embarrassed now, thinking back to how she'd treated him the very first time she saw him. But that was all in the past. Right now, in Ray's arms, her face inches from his, gazing into his eyes, now she felt as though she was where she should be. Where she belonged.

It was with huge reluctance that they broke apart. For a moment she'd forgotten they were in a crowded dance hall. Ray took her hand and she allowed him to lead her back towards their table.

'So you learned to dance at school?' she said, as they sat down again.

'Yes, we all had to take lessons. And where did you learn to sing?'

She smiled, pleased that he remembered her singing. 'Same, at school. We had a teacher, Miss Lacey, who taught music and ran the school choir. It was my favourite lesson of the week.'

'I liked math best. You know what I hated most? Geography.' He leaned towards her, speaking in a confidential tone. 'Once, the teacher hauled me up in front of the class for copying from a textbook instead of writing an essay from scratch.' He gave a wry smile. 'I'd copied it word for word, even the part that said "see chapter eighteen". I guess that gave the game away.'

She laughed. 'Ha! Yes, that would be a bit of a give-away. I used to like geography.'

He shook his head. 'I didn't. I wanted to go to all those places around the world, not read about them in dusty textbooks. I wanted to see them for myself.'

'Oh, me too!' She was delighted to hear that, like her, he was keen to travel the world. One day, she promised herself, she would. And as she thought of this she realised she was picturing him with her on her travels, alongside her all the way. It was only their second meeting, but already . . . she was wondering . . . could there be a chance for them? Perhaps Ray would be the one who'd take her out of Bethnal Green and show her the world, just as she'd always longed for.

Chapter 12

'Nellie! We'd best go, or we'll miss the last bus and there'll be hell to pay!' Babs sounded frantic.

'Oh! What time is it?' Nellie glanced around for a clock but there wasn't one on the wall. She'd wanted the evening to last forever, but it had gone so quickly.

'We've got less than five minutes. Come on!'

Nellie had no choice – Charlie would kill her if they missed the bus and she'd never be allowed out like this again. She gave Ray a sorrowful, apologetic look and dashed after Babs. But he and Clayton were on their heels anyway.

A minute later with their coats over their arms, they ran around the corner just in time to see the bus pull away from the bus stop.

'Oh no! We're too late!' Babs cried, but Nellie began running after it. It was worth a try – maybe the driver would see her and stop.

'Always running after buses, you crazy girl!' Ray shouted, as he caught her up and pulled her to a standstill, in his arms. 'This time there's no chance of catching up with it.'

'But, but . . . we can't miss it!' She struggled a moment

to free herself to continue running, but then realised he was right, there was no hope of stopping it and the bus was already out of sight.

Babs ran up to them with Clayton just behind. 'What are we going to do? We're stuck!'

'It's our fault,' Ray said. 'We shoulda kept an eye on the time.'

'No, we should have,' Babs said. 'It's us who had to catch a bus.'

Nellie shook her head. 'What on earth are we going to do?' The four of them stood staring at one another for a minute. Nellie's mind was frantically going over the possibilities. They couldn't walk home, it was miles! Might they try to find somewhere to stay nearby and catch the first bus home in the morning? Would that get them back before her dad got up and realised she hadn't come home? She looked to Babs who had a hand over her mouth. She'd be in as much trouble as Nellie. Clayton was standing, hands in pockets, looking at the ground.

'Say, I have an idea,' Ray said, glancing at Clayton.

'What?' Clayton looked confused for a moment and then his face cleared. 'Ah, I know what you're thinking. Bit dangerous?'

'Dangerous?' Nellie said. What on earth was Ray considering? All she could think about was the fury she'd face from Charlie when she eventually got home, especially if it wasn't until tomorrow morning.

'Not at all. It's Saturday night. He goes to see his

lady-friend on Saturday nights. He'll be nowhere near.' The light of the half moon was enough for Nellie to see a glint of excitement in Ray's eyes. She looked from him to Clayton and back again, wondering what they could possibly be talking about.

'As long as no one sees,' Clayton said, grinning.

'They didn't see us last time,' Ray replied, with a wink.

Babs put her hands on her hips. 'Is anyone going to tell us what you boys are scheming?'

The two airmen laughed. 'It's all right, don't fret, girls. Ray's got a plan for getting you both home. Probably before the bus gets there too. Come on.' Clayton led the way, Ray caught Nellie's hand, and the four of them hurried back past the dance hall, through the village and along a lane that led to the airbase. A few others were making their way back, but the dance was still in full swing so most hadn't yet left the hall.

'Need to be sharpish about it,' Clayton said. 'Before the dance ends and everyone comes back up here.'

'Will do,' Ray said. He led them to the back of the building. 'Wait here with the girls.' He darted around the corner.

'What's his grand plan?' Babs asked.

'You'll know very soon,' Clayton said with a grin, as he casually leaned back against the bonnet of a smart-looking motorcar that was parked there.

'Oh!' Nellie said, clapping a hand to her mouth, as she guessed what the plan was. Clayton's grin broadened and he nodded at her.

'What? Will someone please tell me what's going on?' Babs said, with a small stamp of her foot.

'I think,' Nellie said, with a glance at Clayton, 'that we'll be driven home in this.' She indicated the car.

Babs gasped. 'Whose is it?'

'Belongs to our airbase Group Captain. But he has no need of it right now, and you girls sure do. Successful mission?'

Ray had reappeared around the corner of the building. He nodded and held up a set of keys. 'In you get, ladies. Your carriage awaits.'

No one Nellie knew in Bethnal Green had a motorcar, except for Mr and Mrs Bolton. In the East End, people just didn't have cars. They couldn't afford them and didn't need them. You went everywhere by bus, tube or on foot. Nellie had never even been in one, and as far as she knew, neither had Babs. The nearest they'd experienced was motorbuses and the charabanc that used to take them on Sunday school outings to Southend. But she certainly wasn't going to admit to that. She waited while Ray unlocked the car and opened the rear doors.

'Clay and Babs in the back, Nellie can ride alongside me. Okay?'

'Perfect,' Nellie said, though she had no idea whether it'd be better to be in the back and let Clayton sit alongside Ray. She went round to the passenger side and Ray opened the door for her.

It wasn't like climbing onto a bus. You had to put one foot in and duck your head at the same time. There must be a more ladylike way of getting into a car, Nellie thought, but she was damned if she knew what it was. To Ray's credit he waited patiently for her to get settled, then closed the door once she was inside.

There was a tap on Nellie's shoulder from behind, and she turned to see Babs grinning from ear to ear in the back seat. Her look said it all: *This is so exciting, but don't let on we've never been in a car before!* Nellie suppressed a giggle and waited for Ray to walk round and get into the driver's seat. What an adventure this was turning out to be! Every moment with Ray was exciting.

'All right, ladies?' Ray said. 'This is an Austin 10 Cambridge. It was built in 1938 and it belongs to our boss, so we better be careful with it. But he won't know we've taken it, and we'll have it back soon enough. It has plenty of gas in the tank. I know the way to Bethnal Green so let's get you home safe and sound.'

A thought occurred to Nellie. 'You do know how to drive this thing, right?'

Ray threw back his head and laughed. ''Course I do. I've been driving since I was fifteen. No, earlier than that. Used to drive tractors on my folks' farm when I was twelve. Lots more people have cars in the States than they do here, especially out in the country where we live. You gotta drive. No other way to get to places.' He winked at her. 'And I've driven this car before, but don't tell our Group Captain that! Anyway, we better set off before anyone realises.'

He pressed the starter button and the engine roared

into life. They were soon hurtling along the country lanes. It seemed they were going a lot faster than they would in a bus, but it might have just felt that way because of how low she was sitting. Ray appeared to be a confident driver, navigating the narrow lanes with ease and once they reached the outskirts of London he had no trouble with other traffic. The car's headlights, complying with blackout regulations, were partly covered to deflect their beam downward. Dark buildings flashed by on both sides; here and there they passed people walking with torches partially covered by their hands, on their way home from the pub or friends' houses, Nellie imagined.

Without the stops and starts of a bus the journey passed far more quickly than it had on the way out, and soon Nellie began to recognise the streets. Not far from home there was a sudden loud noise, like two gunshots in quick succession, and Nellie squealed and ducked down in her seat. 'What was that?'

Clayton chuckled, and Ray put a hand on her shoulder. 'It's all right, Nellie. The car backfired, that's all it was.'

'I thought we were being shot at!' Nellie exclaimed, relieved but still feeling a little shaken by the noise.

'There'd be more than two shots if the Germans had landed,' Clayton said. 'It'd be more like rat-a-tat-a-tat!' He performed a good impression of machine gun fire which made them all laugh.

'Left here, then right,' Nellie said, realising they were on Cambridge Heath Road and approaching the turn into Roman Road. A few people were making their way into the tube station for the night.

'Tubes run this late, do they?' Ray asked.

'Oh, our station isn't open for trains yet. It's an air raid shelter. Some people go down every night, just in case,' Nellie answered. Life must be so different for those living outside of London, she thought. Though an air field would be a target in its own right.

'Ah yes, I heard some underground stations were used as shelters. Didn't know your local one was. Do you and your family go there?' He glanced across at her as he asked the question.

'Only if there's a raid. But we used to be down there every night, during the Blitz.'

'Hard to imagine that,' Clayton said, shaking his head.

'This is where we live,' Babs said. They were on Morpeth Street now, approaching Nellie's and Barbara's houses.

'Glad we could see you ladies home safely,' Ray said. He stopped the car, got out and opened Nellie's door. Clayton did the same for Babs and walked her to her front door.

Nellie climbed out of the car with a little more elegance than she had when entering it, and stood in front of him. He reached forward and took both her hands in his. 'Nellie, I have had the most wonderful evening. Thank you.'

She smiled. 'Thank you for inviting us, and for getting us home! I thought we were done for when we missed that bus. We'd have really copped it if we hadn't made it home tonight.' She glanced up at the house. Her parents' room was at the back, so they wouldn't see her now. Flo would be asleep and so there'd only be George who might have heard the car and look out of his window. She gazed back at Ray. Was he going to kiss her? She'd never been kissed before, not properly, only a peck with Billy once, beneath the mistletoe. But now she longed for Ray to kiss her.

Out of the corner of her eye she saw that Babs had gone inside, and Clayton was standing at a discreet distance, apparently fascinated by the night sky. Her eyes dropped to Ray's lips.

'Oh, Nellie,' he breathed, and then his arms were around her and his lips were on hers. The kiss was everything she'd dreamed it might be, warm and long and deep. She reached her arms up and around his neck, pulling him even closer. It felt as though her whole soul was melting into his, as though time had stopped, the world was no longer turning, the war was a distant memory. If ever she had to pick a moment she'd want to last for eternity, she thought, this would be the one she'd choose.

Chapter 13

'You've got a spring in your step, Nellie Morris!' Gladys said to her as they queued in the canteen for morning coffee. 'It's good to see you looking happy.' Back at work on Monday, Nellie felt as though she was dancing on air as she moved around the town hall.

'Thank you,' Nellie said. 'Yes, I am.'

Gladys regarded her carefully, and put her hands on her hips. 'Something's happened, hasn't it? I can tell . . .'

Nellie grinned. 'I met someone.'

'A fella?'

Nellie nodded and looked at her coyly.

'Nice one?'

'Well, I think he is!'

'That's all that matters, then.' Gladys's tone was soft. 'I'm so glad, Nellie. You deserve a bit of fun. Don't let him steal you away from the town hall though, will you? We need you here. Mrs Bolton's always saying how she couldn't manage without you.'

Nellie glowed with pride to hear this. 'Don't be daft. Of course I won't be leaving. I've only just met him, anyway.'

'You're smitten though. I can see that.' Gladys laughed kindly. Nellie beamed at her, trying hard not to bounce up and down in her giddy happiness.

She returned to the mayor's office with her coffee to find Mrs Bolton striding back and forth, waving a letter she'd just opened. 'I can't believe it. They've turned us down.'

Nellie put her coffee cup on her desk. 'What is it, Mrs Bolton?'

'That funding we asked for, to make the tube station shelter safer. They've turned it down.' The Mayor slumped into her chair and flung the letter down on her desk. 'It's too *expensive*, they say. What price for people's safety, I say? What price, Nellie?'

Nellie stared at her boss. What answer was she expected to give? There was no price you could put on people's safety. London's Civil Defence Service must have decided there were better things to spend money on, even though Bethnal Green Council had not asked for very much money for the improvements, if Nellie remembered the letter they'd sent correctly.

'How can they do that, ma'am? Wasn't all that much money you asked for. What are they expecting, that we'll let it drop? We'll fight them, won't we?'

'We will, yes. I shan't let this drop, Nellie. I shall write again and plead our case even more strongly.' Mrs Bolton slammed a hand down onto her desk.

Nellie gasped at the Mayor's strength of feeling, then picked up her notepad and a pencil, ready to take dictation.

Mrs Bolton looked at her and shook her head. 'Oh, not now, dear. I'm too cross about it all. I need to gather my thoughts before sending a letter. That engineer we met with?'

'Mr Smith, ma'am.'

'Smith, yes. He said *a potential disaster could occur.* His words, Nellie, his exact words.' Mrs Bolton stabbed at the air with her finger. 'I quoted them in my letter, and still they turned us down.' Mrs Bolton shook her head and then stood up to pace the room again. 'What are they waiting for – someone to *die* on those steps? Maybe they are. But then we'll have blood on our hands.'

'Mrs Bolton, can't we just go ahead anyway? Aren't there funds in the control of the Council we can use? As it's for safety . . .' Nellie spoke cautiously, scared she might be overstepping the mark, or else saying something stupid that would ruin the Mayor's opinion of her.

'I'm tempted to do just that,' Mrs Bolton replied. 'But I'm afraid we can't just use rate-payers' money without approval. We are legally required to get authorisation to spend money from the relevant government department, and in this case it's the Home Office – Civil Defence comes under the Home Office. If they approved, we'd be reimbursed by the Treasury. But they've said no. Oh, I'm so cross about it all.'

With that, the Mayor walked out of the office, her heels clicking against the tiled floor.

Nellie sipped her coffee then returned to her typing, thinking over what she'd heard. She pictured the tube station entrance – those dark steps with their uneven edging, the inadequate hoarding at the top. The vast numbers of people that so often poured down while the air raid siren sounded. Once you were at the ticket hall level it all felt safer – you were already underground and protected from the worst of the bombing, and Billy and the other air raid wardens were there to ensure everyone progressed down to platform level safely. It was just that bottleneck coming down from the street that was the problem. Why on earth hadn't Civil Defence agreed to the suggested improvements? It was such an easy thing, such a little thing to do and might make all the difference.

She thought about whether to tell her parents but worried if she did, they might think it safer to stay home or use a shelter farther away that they possibly wouldn't reach in time. But if she didn't say anything, and one of them was hurt on their way to the shelter, she'd be beside herself. She decided she had to say something to her family.

*

Later that evening, when they'd finished eating their tea and were chatting about their respective days, Nellie cleared her throat. 'Something happened at work and it's been on my mind. I'm not sure I'm really allowed to tell you but I'm going to anyway.' Em and Charlie looked at her with curiosity, and George and Flo sat in their seats, waiting patiently. Nellie took a breath and went on. 'We had an engineer inspect the entrance to the tube station shelter. Those steps – we've always said you wouldn't want to stumble when you're rushing down them in an air raid.'

'I did, once,' Em said. 'Twisted me ankle.'

'I know. Anyway, the engineer suggested improvements and Mrs Bolton applied for funding to do it, but Civil Defence turned us down.'

'What sort of improvements?' Charlie always wanted to know details.

'Handrails, a crush barrier, better lighting, that sort of thing.'

'Dreadful they've said no to it,' Em said.

'I know, the Mayor's really cross about it. She's appealing the decision. But meanwhile, everyone should be specially careful whenever we have to go down there, right? Flo, you're to always hold someone's hand.'

Flo stared at her with wide, frightened eyes. Nellie put an arm around her shoulders. 'Oh, Flo, don't be scared now. All I'm saying is you're to be extra careful when we go down there. Just in case, eh?'

The little girl nodded solemnly. Nellie smiled. 'There. Said my piece.'

'Thanks, love,' Charlie said, and Nellie knew she'd done the right thing. Warned her family to take care but not frightened them so they wouldn't want to go to the shelter. 'Do let us know whether they decide to do anything to that entrance. Problem is they can't close the entrance while they work on it. They have to keep it open as it's the only way in. I wonder if that's why Civil Defence don't want to make any changes.'

Maybe he was right, Nellie thought. But surely there must be a way the alterations could be safely made during the day, keeping the entrance usable in the event of a night-time air raid. Hadn't Mr Smith said as much?

She shook her head. As long as she lived, Nellie knew she would never forgive herself for what had happened to Ruth and John. At least she'd make sure the same didn't happen to her immediate family. If there was anything she could do to keep them safe she'd do it.

Chapter 14

The year was turning colder as autumn wore on. The days were shorter and the newspapers were full of reports of the war in North Africa, as the Allies pushed back against Rommel's forces. 'That Montgomery's a hero,' Charlie said, as he listened to a news bulletin on the wireless one night. But it was Churchill's words that buoyed Nellie the most, when he pronounced, 'This is not the end. It is not even the beginning of the end. But it is, perhaps, the end of the beginning.' She took some comfort from the Prime Minister's words. The Allies were prevailing. 'We'll win in the end, won't we, Dad?' she said, and when Charlie nodded, she smiled. She could cope, knowing progress was being made.

Ray was making a bleak time exciting though, and Nellie was thrilled by the newness of everything he brought into her life. She felt truly happy, for the first time in a very long time. He'd come to Bethnal Green on every one of his days off since the night of the dance. Together they'd been to the pictures several times, explored parks and walked along canal paths and browsed market stalls.

Nellie had loved showing Ray her home, her community, and even more, she'd loved hearing his stories of life in the US. His parents' farm sounded like an impressive operation, and she could tell how much he'd learnt from helping with the maintenance over the years – he seemed to be an expert on tractors and combine harvesters. It was a different world from what she'd been used to as a city girl. He told her about his younger sister Nora who sounded just like Flo, his older brother who helped run the farm, the mongrel dog named Paddy that he'd found abandoned as a tiny puppy and had brought home and hand-reared and from whom he'd been inseparable until he'd left home to join the US Air Force. 'Poor Paddy. Mom said he didn't know what to do with himself when I went away. But now he's latched on to little Nora. Sleeps on her bed and eats out of her hand, to Mom's disgust.'

'Sounds like Paddy's as much a part of your family as Oscar is ours,' Nellie had said.

'Yes, though Paddy's not as good-looking a dog as your Oscar. Can't run as fast either.'

Her parents knew she was stepping out with Ray though he had not formally met her family yet. Charlie had begun muttering about wanting to make sure he was 'suitable'. And so he was invited for tea one Sunday afternoon.

'I don't know why I feel nervous about meeting him,' Em said, shortly before he was due to arrive. 'Silly, ain't it? Maybe because I never met an American before. To think he was born all the way over the ocean, and now he's here in Bethnal Green!'

'Hmph,' Charlie grunted. 'He's just a fella like any other. Except he'd better be special, as our girl seems to have fallen for him.'

'Well, you'll see for yourself soon enough,' Nellie said, feeling butterflies fluttering in her stomach. 'He'll be here in half an hour.'

'Half an hour!' Em clapped her hands to her face. 'I've lost track of time. I got to brush my hair and finish that cake I baked for him!' She hurried out to the kitchen.

'Bloody Yank gets more attention than I do, in me own home,' Charlie muttered, but Nellie could tell that he was secretly excited to meet Ray too. Her parents' nerves weren't helping. She couldn't stop flitting around, returning to the mirror to check her hair was set properly, and she must have tried on three different outfits before deciding on a red skirt and navy-blue sweater. It's not that she was worried it would go badly, she just wanted everything to be perfect because she was very smitten with Ray.

*

There was a tap at the door. 'That'll be him, now,' Nellie said, jumping to her feet. When she opened the door, she found Ray in his uniform, cap in hand. He looked so smart, so handsome. She couldn't believe how lucky she was to have found him.

'Nellie, you look wonderful today!' he said, greeting her with a kiss on her cheek.

'So do you! Come on. Everyone is dying to meet you.' She led him into the front room and introduced him to Charlie, Em, George and Oscar. 'And Flo, you already met.'

'Ah, I have you to thank, Missy Flo. You're the reason your beautiful sister and I met. Thank you.' He bowed deeply in front of her, which made her giggle.

'Got any gum, chum?' Flo asked, parroting something she'd heard older boys ask of any American soldiers they came across. She giggled again.

'I have something even better,' Ray said. He dug in his pocket and pulled out a little paper bag. 'You like candy?'

'Candy?'

'Sweets, Flo.' Nellie translated for her.

Flo's eyes lit up as she took the little bag and opened it. 'Thank you!' she exclaimed, her eyes as big as saucers.

Ray had gifts of nylons for Nellie and Em and a fat cigar for Charlie. He explained that he'd been advised to bring a stock of such things from the States to use as gifts, since they were hard to get hold of in England. To George, he gave a stack of cigarette cards, which he'd collected himself. Nellie and her family smiled at Ray and thanked him, all touched by his generosity.

'Well, I'll go and make the tea,' Em said, bustling away to the kitchen.

Ray smiled. 'You English and your tea,' he said.

'We do like a nice cuppa,' Charlie said. 'Don't you Yanks drink tea?'

'Not as much as you.' Ray smiled. 'But you sure know how to make a decent cup! Back home, we put lemon in it, instead of milk. Took a bit of getting used to but now I much prefer it your way.'

'Lemon!' Nellie laughed. 'I can't remember when I last saw a fresh lemon. Not since the war began.'

'That's because it's never you who goes and queues up when the greengrocer's got some in,' Em said, returning to the front room with a tray laden with tea things and the sponge cake she'd made. 'Here. A week's sugar ration for the family is in that, so I hope you don't take sugar in your tea!'

'No, ma'am, I like it just with milk. That cake smells great. I'm honoured.'

Em smiled proudly as she cut a slice and Nellie began to relax. Ray was charming them all, as she knew he would. She caught his eye and he smiled, a secret little smile just for her, that made her glow inside. It was the first time she'd brought a boyfriend home. The first time she'd even had a boyfriend! And she really wanted her family to like him as much as she did but she was relieved that Ray was making a great first impression.

The afternoon passed quickly as they ate and chatted. Charlie and Ray fell into a discussion about the war. 'Glad your lot joined in,' Charlie said. 'It'll shorten it, if nothing else.'

'It will, sir,' Ray replied. 'In a way the Japs did Europe

a favour, bombing Pearl Harbor. Otherwise the US's isolationist policies might have gone on longer.'

'Shame it took such a terrible thing to happen to bring you in.'

Ray nodded, and the men fell silent for a moment, contemplating the losses.

After the cake was eaten, George took Ray out to the backyard to meet his chickens, and Nellie found them discussing the best way to deal with egg-bound hens. 'My folks keep chickens,' he told her. 'I grew up with them running around our yard. Your brother here is doing a fine job with this little flock.' Now it was George's turn to smile proudly. 'Although I have to say, I never expected I'd see chickens in the middle of London! Very different from how they're reared back home on the farm, where they've got more acres than they know what to do with, to run around in.' Everyone laughed at that.

Ray looked at his watch. 'I should get going,' he said to Nellie. 'I was hoping to borrow that motorcar today but no luck. I need to catch a bus, got to be back at base in an hour.'

'All right. I'll come with you to the bus stop.' Nellie led him back inside to pick up their coats and say goodbye to the family. Hand in hand they set out for the bus stop. As soon as they had gone around the corner Nellie turned to Ray and heaved a sigh. 'Phew. That went well, but I'm glad it's over!' She was thrilled he'd got on so well with her family. He'd managed to charm everyone and she was so happy everyone seemed to like Ray, getting along well with him.

'Your folks are swell,' Ray said. 'I enjoyed meeting them. I can't wait for you to meet mine.'

'I can't see how that can happen,' Nellie replied quietly.

'Not while the war's on. But it won't go on for ever, Nellie.' Ray stopped walking and pulled her into his arms. 'You gotta believe that. And believe me when I say I hope very much that you and I will last the distance.'

'I hope so too,' she said, and he kissed her for so long that time seemed to stand still.

At last he broke away and they walked quickly to the bus stop, hurrying to make it in time. 'You and me and buses – we don't mix, right?' Ray said with a laugh as he jumped on board.

She waved goodbye to him, still feeling the imprint of his lips on hers and replaying his words in her mind. He hoped they'd last the distance! He wanted her to meet his parents, all the way over in Michigan! The thought sent a jolt of giddy excitement straight through her.

*

The days at work before she would see him again stretched interminably. Only lunch breaks with Gladys, who wanted to hear every last detail of their relationship, provided relief from the monotony. 'When this war ends, you'll be whisked off to . . . where is it? Montana? Missouri?'

'Michigan,' Nellie replied. They were sitting in the canteen at the town hall, finishing the last of their lunch.

'Such exotic place names, ain't they? You're so lucky, Nellie. I'd love an American airman to capture my heart and whisk me away from here.'

Nellie laughed. 'I'm not going anywhere yet though, am I? We've got to win this war first. Ray's over here to help.' She felt a pang of worry. She and Ray never spoke about it, but there was always a constant worry that he might not survive the next mission he flew, or the one after that. Any of them could spell the end.

'He's a good man. They all are. Doing what they can to help us defeat Hitler,' Gladys said.

'Talking of defeating Hitler,' Mrs Bolton said, having appeared behind them unnoticed by Nellie, 'it's time you were back at your desk. I'm going to write one more time to Civil Defence, and need you to type the letter.'

'Sorry, Mrs Bolton,' Nellie said, jumping to her feet. She was only a minute over her allotted lunch break but she knew the Mayor was a stickler for timekeeping.

*

The following Saturday was a grey November day. Nellie and Ray were strolling through the market on Roman Road. There were lots of people about, despite the bad weather. Nellie waved a greeting to Mrs Perkins. They came across a soldier on crutches, his trouser leg pinned up at the knee, and helped him choose a little bar of scented soap as a gift for his mother. Ray had bought Nellie one too, and he also bought a bag of broken toffee pieces for Nellie to take home for Flo. She loved these moments, walking companionably along the street looking at what was for sale. The market was nothing like as busy or vibrant as it had been, but it was still a fun place to go, and Ray seemed to enjoy it too.

'Say, you buy everything here?' Ray said, as they passed a stall selling knitting supplies.

'Pretty much,' she replied, 'though there aren't as many stalls or as much to buy, as before the war.' She'd spotted a knitting pattern for gloves, scarves and hats and was wondering whether she'd be able to manage it. A set of knitted items for the winter would be a wonderful Christmas present for him. She resolved to come back and buy the pattern and some yarn as soon as she could, when Ray was not around so it could be a surprise.

'We don't have markets like this back home. Just regular stores, bigger and less crowded. And newer. I like this, shopping outside.'

'It's good as long as it doesn't rain,' Nellie said, and as if the rain gods had heard her, at that moment the heavens opened.

Ray grabbed Nellie's hand. 'Run!'

She did as he'd said, laughing as they dodged past stall-holders frantically trying to cover their goods with tarpaulins, ran along the street and fell into the doorway of a derelict shopfront. 'We can shelter here until it passes,' he said, pulling her close.

There was very little space, just a square yard between the pavement and the door, covered by a small porch. The shop, which used to be a goldsmith if Nellie remembered correctly, had been closed since the start of the war. No one had any need or money for fancy jewellery since the start of hostilities.

Nellie was pressed against him, her hands on his chest, his face inches from hers. She could feel the warmth and strength of his body through her coat. 'What'll we do while we wait for the rain to stop?' she asked, flirtatiously.

'I've no idea,' he responded in kind. 'No idea at all.' And he bent his head and kissed her. She snaked her hands around his neck, wondering if anyone would see them, anyone who might then tell her parents, and deciding that she didn't care. His lips were warm and soft, and as always when he kissed her, time seemed to stop, the world melted away and there was only them, only that moment, and nothing else mattered.

'Damn. Rain's stopping,' Ray said when they came up for air. 'We had better move from here, before . . .'

He didn't complete his sentence and Nellie thought she'd better not ask what he'd been about to say. She felt a warmth running through her as she took his hand, and they went back out to the street. 'Let's, ahem, cool ourselves down with coffee and cakes,' he said, and she nodded.

They went to a nearby Lyons Corner House, busy with people who'd run inside to shelter from the sudden rain. 'The coffee will be chicory, you know,' she warned him.

'Yes. I kinda like it though. I've gotten used to the nutty aroma and woody flavour. Or look, they have lemonade.'

'Mm, that's what I'll have. And a scone.' She looked at Ray and smiled. What a wonderful day they were having. Who'd have thought an ordinary kind of day, going round the market, getting caught in the rain and then going for lemonade could be so magical. Ray made everyday life feel so fun and special.

Ray ordered and insisted on paying. When the waitress left he reached across the table and took her hand. 'You make me so happy, Nellie. Just being with you is swell.'

'I feel the same,' she said and for a moment they simply sat, holding hands and gazing at each other, breaking apart only when the waitress arrived with their order.

'Christmas is not far away,' Nellie said.

'We should go to the West End somewhere. Have a day out. Then go on to a club. Somewhere swanky, to celebrate Christmas. What do you think?'

'Up west!' Nellie tried to remember the last time she'd travelled to the West End. Had she ever been there for a night out? Possibly not, though before the war she'd been on shopping trips and visits to museums. 'Yes, I'd love that!'

'I'll ask the boys for recommendations then. You deserve to be treated like a princess, Nellie.'

She smiled at that. She certainly felt like a princess when she was with Ray. And how she liked that feeling!

Chapter 15

They were lucky with the weather for their day out, in the West End. It was cold but bright and clear, with a blue sky and weak sunshine. Ray wanted to see all the sights, all the important buildings he'd heard about but never seen. Nellie borrowed a central London street map from Charlie and planned a route for him. They took a bus to Oxford Street, and began the day at Selfridges department store. It had been hit by a bomb earlier in the war and its windows were bricked up, but inside was bustling with people finishing their Christmas shopping.

'I want to buy you something special,' Ray said, but Nellie wouldn't let him.

'We'd have to carry it around all day, and we've miles to walk if you're to see all the sights.'

They contented themselves with browsing, and then headed out to Oxford Circus and down Regent Street. As they passed Hamleys toy shop it was Nellie's turn to long to buy something special for Flo, but she'd already bought her Christmas present.

They walked to Trafalgar Square, where Ray gazed

up at the statue of Admiral Nelson atop his column. 'He helped win a war for Britain, against Napoleon, if I remember my history right.'

'He did. Who's our Nelson these days?'

'Churchill, I guess. Or General Montgomery.'

From there they walked to the riverside and stood at the railings watching barges ferrying goods up and down river, with Westminster Bridge arching across the water to their right. Nellie shivered a little as a gust of cold wind blew, and Ray wrapped an arm around her. She leaned her head against his shoulder.

'We'll come back here, when the war's over, and we'll take a riverboat trip all the way along,' Ray said.

She nodded. 'We'll do it at night, when there's no blackout, and all the buildings will have their lights on, reflections sparkling in the water.'

'That sounds so pretty,' he replied, squeezing her to him.

'Although one of the good things about the blackout,' Nellie said, 'is that normally we can't see the stars as there's too much street lighting.'

'There are thousands of stars to be seen from my folks' place in Michigan,' Ray said. 'Don't you just love that the stars I grew up looking at over Lake Michigan are the same ones that shine over London?'

She looked sideways at him. 'Now you're going to say that if ever we're apart we can look up at the night sky and know that we're seeing the same constellations.' She giggled. 'It's what they'd say in the movies, anyway.'

He laughed. 'It is, and they're right. Spot on, as you Brits would say.'

She held tightly to his arm. 'I don't ever want to be apart from you, Ray,' she whispered.

'Nor I you.'

She leaned against him and tilted her head back, and he dipped down to her and they kissed. Life was perfect right now, she thought, with his lips on hers and a wonderful evening ahead of them.

They continued walking along the Embankment, towards the blackened grandeur of the Houses of Parliament. Big Ben chimed out the hour as they passed it. 'Three o'clock and all's well,' Nellie said, mimicking the call of nightwatchmen of old.

'Where next?' Ray asked.

'We'll take a look at Westminster Abbey, where the King's coronation was held, then through St James' Park to visit him.'

'Visit the King?'

She laughed. 'Oh yes, I know him personally. Seen him so many times.'

'Really?' He wore an expression of disbelief and she laughed again.

'On coins and stamps, yes. I mean, we'll walk up to Buckingham Palace. You can see the King's Guard in their red uniforms standing outside their sentry boxes.'

'We don't have anything like that in the States,' Ray said. 'You have so much tradition here.'

'Yes. And that's why we're fighting to save it, from Hitler.'

They walked for miles, hand in hand, always finding something to talk about, something new to look at. The West End was glitzy and glamorous. Gone were the Victorian terraces with their bombed-out gaps found in Bethnal Green, replaced by larger buildings, shops and businesses. Every now and again there'd be evidence of bombing but not nearly as much as in the East End and it saddened her to realise that her own community were bearing the brunt of Hitler's attacks. The busy streets here seemed to be full of beautiful people in fabulous clothes, even if they were all pre-war fashions. As it began to get dark, Ray stopped outside a restaurant. 'Let's get something to eat, then go on to a jazz club that one of the boys recommended to me.'

'Sounds like fun!' Nellie said happily. What a day this was turning out to be!

*

The bar he'd picked was tucked into a back street somewhere in Soho, and Nellie felt an attack of nerves as they entered it. She'd never been to a jazz club before. She looked down at the pretty pink dress Babs had loaned her and felt herself to be horribly underdressed. Ray's adoring smiled helped lift her confidence as he opened the door for her.

'You look gorgeous,' Ray whispered, squeezing her hand.

He bought them each a gin and tonic and they found a small table not far from the stage, where a female jazz singer was performing. She was wearing a silver dress that caught the light and glittered as she moved. Nellie had never seen anything so glamorous. The woman's voice was husky as though she smoked a dozen a day and the songs weren't any that Nellie knew.

'Sounds like she enjoys her cigarettes,' Ray said with a quirky smile. 'Her voice isn't a patch on yours.'

'Ah, get away with you, you're exaggerating again.' Nellie gave him a playful shove but was quietly delighted with the compliment, especially when Ray held onto her hand and gave it an affectionate squeeze. She applauded loudly when the woman finished singing and Ray fetched them each another drink. While he was at the bar the next act got up to play – a lively five-piece band that was very loud.

As Ray returned, he leaned across and said something, but she couldn't catch his words over the music.

'Sorry, pardon?' she said, and he leaned closer and repeated himself.

'I said, are you a fan of jazz?'

'Not sure. Sounds to me like they're still tuning up.' She giggled, and he nodded and said something in reply. But the band were so loud she couldn't catch his words.

*

When the musicians finally took a break, Ray grimaced. 'You're not much liking this band, are you?'

Nellie tilted her head on one side as though considering his question. He'd brought her here, paid the entrance fee, bought two rounds of expensive drinks and she was loath to let him know that she was hating it, but on the other hand, she didn't want to lie.

'I . . . well . . .' she began, but he laughed.

'It's all right. Your face says it all.'

He put an arm around her shoulder. 'I know it's early still but . . . shall we cut our losses and leave?' He looked at her questioningly then knocked back his drink in one.

She grinned and did the same, then he caught her hand and pulled her after him, out of the club, back into the cool night air and away from that awful music. Outside she fell into his arms laughing. 'Oh I'm so sorry, Ray, but that music . . . just, no. I don't think I could ever grow to like it. I'm all for having adventures and trying new things but I guess I'm not going to like them all.'

'Neither could I. The fellow who recommended this place said he heard a band playing Glenn Miller numbers. He said it was swell and it was what I hoped to hear tonight. So, the night is young, and there's another singer I'd much rather listen to . . .'

She looked at him, frowning. Was he suggesting going on to another club?

'Shall we go to the Angel and Crown?' he said. 'And perhaps you'll sing for everyone? I would do anything to hear you sing again.'

'I would love to,' she said, flattered.

'Let's go find a bus,' he said and they weaved their way through the narrow streets and ended up walking back along the river in the fading early evening light. Ray pulled Nellie to a stop and towards him as he gave her a long, lingering kiss.

'I've really fallen for you, Nellie Morris.' Ray sighed.

'Me too.' Nellie giggled, her cheeks turning crimson. As she kissed Ray again, she thought what a wonderful day out it had been and that this was the perfect way to round it off.

Chapter 16

Billy lit a cigarette and inhaled a lungful of smoke, then opened his bedroom window.

It was a dark night, but clear. No bomber's moon, thank goodness, so there was a respite from the air raids. He gazed up at the stars for a while, leaning on his windowsill, then spotted two people walking up the street, close together, arm in arm. They stopped walking almost under his window, and he realised it was Nellie and that American fella. They were talking, too quietly for him to hear, and then they looked up as though they too were contemplating the stars. He ducked back inside before they saw him, but continued watching from behind the curtain.

They spoke some more, the American pointed out something up above and Billy watched as Nellie followed his outstretched finger. She said something that made them both laugh. And then they looked at each other and the man bent his head and kissed her. Nellie was pressing herself against him, her arms wrapped around his neck, and his arms were around her waist.

That should have been Billy, holding her in his arms, kissing her, loving her. He'd kissed her on the lips once. Last Christmas, beneath the mistletoe if only briefly, and he'd thought then that there was a chance for him. But he'd done nothing to take things forward. It was his own damned fault he'd lost her. He'd been about to ask her out on a date, the night she'd met the American. If only he'd been quicker.

He should have spoken out long ago, told her how he felt about her, talked to her of his hopes and dreams that one day they might be together. What was the worst that could have happened, if he'd been brave enough to tell her? The worst would have been Nellie saying she didn't feel the same way. And that, perhaps, would have been easier to bear than this, than seeing Nellie happy and apparently in love with someone else. It was torture, especially when she didn't even know that he, Billy, could have been hers if she'd wanted him.

There was no hope now for them, he knew that. He'd missed his chance. Nellie wanted more excitement from life than he could offer her. What he wanted was to stay here in Bethnal Green all his life, like his parents and grandparents before him. To live in Morpeth Street or nearby, in a little house with Nellie at his side.

There was a tap at the door, and Babs, returned from her night out at the pub, called to him. 'Billy? Can I borrow your Sellotape? I'm wrapping up a present for Amelia.'

''Course you can. Come in,' he called back. Maybe a chat with his sister would cheer him up a little, stop him descending into the pit of despair that yawned beneath him.

'Cheers,' she said, coming in and dumping an armful of things on his bed. 'Look, I bought her a tin of talcum powder and a little baby's bonnet. Something for her, something for the baby. Do you think this paper's all right to use?' She had a sheet of wrapping paper that he recognised – it was what he'd used to wrap a present to Babs on her last birthday.

'I think it's perfect. Nice of you to get her a present.'

'She's going to be leaving London soon to have the baby, so I thought I should give her something now rather than later. Cor blimey, it's not half cold in here! You've got the window open.' Babs crossed the room and pushed the sash closed.

Nellie and her man must have been still out there, Billy realised, for Babs turned to him, a frown creasing her forehead. 'Were you spying on her?'

'No. I was just smoking out the window, and then she came up the road. With him.' He tried to keep his voice neutral but his sister knew him too well.

Babs came over to him and put an arm around his shoulders. 'Oh Billy. You've got it bad, haven't you?'

He slumped down onto the bed and she sat next to him, still holding him. 'I should have told her. I should have said something to her. Before she met him. I can't, now. I've lost my chance. That American's got her heart.'

'I know. She really cares for him, Billy. I'm so sorry.'

He nodded. 'I know she does. It's bleeding obvious,

when you see her with him. If he ever does a thing to hurt her – I mean in any way at all – he'll have me to answer to. I'd kill him.'

'He's a good man, Billy. He won't hurt her. I'm sure of it. He cares for her very much.' Babs's tone was gentle but firm. She was trying to reassure him, he realised.

Billy turned to his sister. 'All I want is for her to be happy, you know? Nothing else. Just her happiness. I could've made her happy, given half a chance. I'd have worked so hard at it, I'd have done anything for her. But if it's not to be me, then *he* has to make her happy.'

'I think she is happy, Billy my darling brother. I honestly do.' She squeezed him tightly. 'I'd better get on with this wrapping, anyway.'

Billy dug into a drawer for his reel of Sellotape and passed it to Babs. She had managed to reassure him a little, that the American was worthy of Nellie. He would just have to get used to the idea of her being with him. There was nothing he could do, and what he'd said to Babs was the truth. He only wanted Nellie's happiness, whether that was with or without him.

'You'll make someone the best husband one day, dear brother.' She kissed his cheek and left the room with her newly wrapped present.

Billy pushed open the window again. He looked out and caught sight of Nellie as she bounced happily to her front door, waving at the American as he walked back up the street. His heart ached. Would he ever meet a woman who could live up to Nellie Morris? He doubted it.

As he tried to imagine a future with some other, faceless woman, he heard singing. Nellie must have her window open too. Her bedroom was just the other side of the wall from his – how many times had he lain in bed imagining her lying the other side of the wall? He blushed as he considered this.

She was singing that song from *The Wizard of Oz*. They'd gone together to see it, back at the beginning of the war when it had been released. Nellie, Babs and himself. He could remember now how they'd skipped home, arm in arm, singing, 'We're off to see the wizard.'

But now it was 'Over the Rainbow' that she was singing. Perhaps she'd disturbed Flo and was singing her back to sleep. He listened carefully to the lyrics, to the idea that there was somewhere that dreams came true, somewhere over the rainbow, if only you could get there. He mouthed along to the song. It was as though she'd picked it for him, chosen it to put his feelings into music so precisely. As though she was in his head, privy to all his thoughts and desires.

It was an almost perfect moment. Her, so close, singing to him even though she didn't know it. Him, here alone in his room with his dreams and his cigarette, his head filled with nothing but thoughts of her.

His dreams that he knew would never come true, but just for a moment, now, he would let himself believe that somehow, somewhere, they could, and she would be his.

Chapter 17

In December, one year on from the Pearl Harbor attack, the papers reported the full extent of US losses that day, a figure newly released by the American Navy. 'Nearly two and a half thousand dead!' Charlie said, as he read it out to the family. 'It don't bear thinking about.'

Besides that, the papers that month were full of reports of U-boat attacks. It really was a world war, Nellie thought, being fought beneath the ocean as well as on land. Nowhere was safe and despite what everyone was saying, it still seemed to be raging on with no sign of it ending anytime soon. Even so, Christmas was almost upon them, and Nellie's lunch hours were taken up with scouring the shops to try to find presents for her family and friends. And for Ray, of course. She'd bought that knitting pattern she'd seen at the market and made him a scarf and gloves, using wool she'd unravelled from an old jumper. They were dark blue and the scarf was ribbed, and she was pleased how smart it had turned out. For her mother, she'd bought a small bottle of eau de cologne. Probably black market, as she'd bought it from someone at the Angel and Crown, but no matter, Em would love being treated. Books for George and Charlie – second-hand but titles she knew they'd like. Flo's present had given her the most trouble. She'd decided to buy her some watercolour paints, and it had taken weeks of searching to find the colours.

Nellie gave Ray his present a few days before Christmas itself. He was on duty over the festive period, and would not be able to visit Bethnal Green. Nellie also had to work up to Christmas Eve. And so it was the Sunday before when they managed to meet up, walk in the park on a cold, crisp afternoon, and sit on a bench to exchange presents.

Nellie squealed with excitement as she pulled things out of the basket Ray had packed for her. Chocolate, nylons, a pink lipstick, a romantic novel, a silk headscarf, a paper bag of pear drops. 'Those are for Flo, really,' he said, 'but I thought I'd put them in your basket.'

'This is such a thoughtful present. I love everything you picked out, and Flo will love the sweets. Thank you.' Nellie leaned over and kissed him soundly. 'And this is for you.'

Her present to him was wrapped in green paper saved from last Christmas. Actually, she thought, it had probably been used by someone or other in the family every year since before the war. Crumpled and torn, but it did the job and she was nervous as she handed it over. It was the first time she'd had a suitor to buy a present for and she just hoped that Ray liked her gift.

He grinned as he opened it and took out the gloves and scarf. 'Say, these are perfect.'

'The yarn's reused, but I knitted them myself.'

Ray smiled and wound the scarf around his neck. 'I love them. Because I know every inch of yarn in it has passed through your fingers. Thank you. It must have taken you so long to make!'

'About a week,' she replied, blushing. She was not a great knitter but the scarf had come out well and the gloves fit. And it had been relaxing to sit and knit in the evenings, with the coal fire burning and the wireless on. When they hadn't had to go down the tube, that is.

'I've got two days off next week. I'd love to spend it with you, Nellie, see in the new year together.'

'Oh Ray, I'd love that!' she exclaimed, and they kissed once more.

'Brrr!' she shivered, when they broke apart. 'It's turned cold.'

'Here, I can lend you a very fine scarf,' Ray said, draping an end of it round her neck and using it to pull her close for another kiss. 'Let's go to the pictures to warm up.'

'Great idea!' There was a new film showing at the Empire that they hadn't seen, so they headed there. Her life had changed so much since she'd met Ray. She couldn't imagine it without him now. This was the fourth wartime Christmas but the first of many with Ray she hoped. It felt different, exciting in its own way, to have someone special to share it with.

On Christmas Eve, as work at the town hall wrapped up for the holiday, Mrs Bolton gave Nellie a small cardboard hamper of goods. 'Not much, but I hope this'll help make Christmas special for you and your family,' she said, as Nellie looked through the jars of preserves, candied fruit, tinned ham and even a couple of oranges that were in the box.

'This is wonderful, thank you!' All she'd given her boss was a handkerchief with her initials embroidered in one corner. It now seemed an inadequate gift.

'You're worth it, Nellie. Have a good Christmas, and I will see you back here on Monday.' Mrs Bolton smiled as she put on her coat, preparing to leave the office.

'Yes, Mrs Bolton. Thank you again. I hope you and Mr Bolton have a good one too.'

'Ah, he's on duty. He'll be in the shelter, I expect. I'll be down there too, to keep him company on his breaks.' The Mayor gave a little shrug. 'Not the ideal Christmas but we must do what we have to do for the war effort, eh?'

Nellie sent up a silent prayer they wouldn't have to go down the tube that night. For Flo's sake, at least, she hoped that they'd be able to wake up in their own beds at home on Christmas morning.

But it wasn't to be. They'd just eaten a meal but hadn't managed to wash up, when the too-familiar siren went. Flo burst into tears. 'Father Christmas won't find me down there,' she wailed. 'There'll be no presents!'

'Hush, love. Yes, he will. He knows there'll be lots of children down there,' Nellie said, as she bustled Flo into her coat and led the way down to the station entrance that still hadn't been altered to make it safer, down underground with all the others. Percy Bolton was on duty in the ticket hall, not Billy, and Nellie was disappointed not to see him.

It was rowdier than usual in the shelter, with people singing Christmas carols and drinking bottles of beer they'd brought down with them. War or no war, air raid or not, it seemed people were determined to celebrate Christmas.

Babs turned up with her family just after them, letting her know Billy was on duty elsewhere in the shelter. 'And Nellie, I just saw Amelia. She's at the other end of the platform. She looks upset.'

'We'll go and see her, shall we? I have a present for her, for the baby really. But it's at home.'

'Yes, come on, then,' Babs said. 'Let's see if we can't cheer her up. I expect she's missing Walter.'

'There she is,' Nellie said, pointing to a bottom bunk against the wall. Amelia was lying on her side, her swollen belly overhanging the narrow bed. Her eyes were red and her cheeks blotchy, as though she'd been crying a long time.

'Amelia, love, what is it?' Nellie whispered, sitting down beside her, a comforting hand on her hip.

Amelia gulped back a sob, sat up and pulled a crumpled telegram out from a pocket.

'Oh no,' Nellie whispered, horrified. She barely needed to read it to know what it said. 'Walter?'

'K-killed in action.' She gulped between sobs, twisting the engagement ring on her finger. 'N-never got to have a wedding. A-and he never got to meet our b-baby.' She folded an arm protectively across her belly.

'God, I'm so sorry,' Babs said.

'Oh, Amelia, that's . . . that's so . . .' Nellie began. Words were so inadequate at times like this. What did you say? What could you possibly say?

She pulled her friend to her, and wrapped her arms about her, and Babs did the same on the other side.

Maybe words weren't needed. Maybe just being there, holding her, was the best thing they could do for Amelia.

'I remember,' Amelia said between sobs, 'how good Walter was to me when Mum died. He found me the job at the pub, and the flat that comes with it. He looked after me, set me up.'

Nellie stroked Amelia's hair and let her sob, tears running down her own face too at the sadness of it all. Around them, other people shook their heads sadly but gave them space. One woman passed her cushion over, and Nellie and Babs gently arranged it so that Amelia could lie down.

'Here, duckie,' said another woman, passing a blanket. Nellie took it and laid it over her friend.

'Tea,' said a man, pouring some from a flask he'd brought. Amelia took a sip and smiled weakly.

It wasn't much, Nellie thought – tea, a cushion, a blanket

and sympathy. Nothing would bring Walter back, nothing would lessen Amelia's pain, not yet, anyway. But these tiny kindnesses, from people who had so little themselves, touched her. *We're all in it together,* they seemed to say, *and we'll all help each other through it, no matter what comes our way.*

'Try to sleep now,' Nellie whispered to Amelia, who nodded, her eyes already closed.

Babs and Nellie kissed her cheek then stood and gazed down at her for a minute, and the woman who'd donated her blanket spoke. 'I'll keep an eye on her. She's my neighbour. Just sad, what happened, innit?'

'It is. Thank you.'

'You girls get on back to your families now.'

Without speaking they took each other's hands and made their way back. Nellie wiped away a tear and she knew Babs shared her sadness. It was devastating to see such a cruel twist of fate befall Amelia. They were so young that their lives should have been ahead of them but already Amelia's had been marred by tragedy and unimaginable loss.

'Sing for us, Nellie!' The shout went up as they neared their families' bunks.

'You gonna sing?' Babs whispered.

She didn't feel like singing, not after hearing Amelia's news, but it was Christmas Eve and people deserved to be cheered up. 'I suppose so,' she said, blinking away the last of her tears. She stepped forward, smiled at everyone's expectant faces, and launched into a lively rendition of

'Hark! The Herald Angels Sing', which soon had everyone joining in.

But her heart wasn't in it. Here they were, stuck underground on Christmas Eve, not knowing if they'd have a house to go back to in the morning, and poor Amelia having to cope with losing her fiancé. Nellie couldn't imagine how it must feel. If something like this happened to Ray . . . if one day a telegram arrived for her saying Ray was lost . . . well, she'd be . . . she didn't know. She couldn't say, couldn't begin to think how it must feel. It'd be the end of everything. Of all her hopes and dreams, of the joy she felt when she was with him . . .

She stopped herself thinking along these lines. How could she think of herself, of how she'd feel, when the worst had happened to Amelia? Here she was, heavily pregnant, her fiancé lost. And it was *Christmas*. War could be so cruel.

PART TWO

Winter–Spring 1943

Chapter 18

One weekend midway through February, cold but with a gleaming sun to brighten the day, the sky blue and sparkling, Nellie was waiting for Ray to call for her. He had the whole day off and had promised to get himself down to Bethnal Green to take her out for the day. She was excited and already in a good mood after reading the news reports about the surrender of the German Sixth Army, defeated by the Soviets after the end of the Battle of Stalingrad. It was a turning point, the papers were saying, as they gleefully reported that Germany was now fighting a defensive war.

She was wearing a sweater and her favourite tweed skirt, her coat and hat at the ready, when there was a knock at the door and there he was, standing on the doorstep grinning. Behind him, leaning against a lamppost, was a black bicycle.

'Did you cycle here?' she asked, pointing at the bike.

'I sure did. And the crossbar is very sturdy . . . I wondered if you'd be game to ride on it? We could go all over the East End on this. A tour of every park we can find! Your carriage awaits, Miss Morris.'

Nellie laughed. 'I'll give it a try!'

Ray swung his leg over the bike and held it steady while Nellie carefully perched on the crossbar. He reached around her to grip the handlebars and she felt enclosed and safe within his arms.

'Ready?' he asked, and she twisted round and kissed him in response.

'Yes!' She squealed as he pushed away, but after a few wobbles they managed to get going. Nellie held tightly to the handlebars and tried to keep her weight centred on the bike, and soon they were riding along the streets.

They passed the town hall. 'That's where I work!' Nellie said.

'A grand-looking place,' Ray shouted back.

Nellie spotted a familiar figure walking along the road in his air raid warden's uniform. Her joy was so great, she couldn't stop herself from waving and calling out.

'Billy!'

Billy stared at them as they passed by and raised a hand to wave back, but he didn't smile. Nellie felt a pang of guilt. She'd promised Babs she wouldn't break his heart, but what could she do? She couldn't stop seeing Ray just so that Billy wouldn't be hurt. Sometimes you had to think of your own happiness.

There would be someone else for Billy. Some other girl who would see all the good there was in him, who would adore him and be the wife he deserved to have. Someone who would make him feel the way Ray made her feel.

And then they crossed the Regent's Canal where barges

were tied up along its banks, and into Victoria Park, passing Flo's friends, the stone dogs that guarded its entrance.

Ray started singing, and Nellie joined in.

'Daisy, Daisy, give me your answer, do.
I'm half crazy, all for the love of you.
It won't be a stylish marriage, I can't afford
a carriage,
But you'll look sweet, upon the seat of a bicycle
made for two.'

They sang at the tops of their voices and laughed, while Ray steered the bike along the park paths. When Nellie's sides hurt from laughing so much, he stopped pedalling and helped her off the crossbar. She doubled over, gasping, and then squealed as he came up behind her, arms around her middle under her coat, tickling her relentlessly.

'You beast!' She twisted out of his grip and chased after him as he ran away from her, dodging behind a tree. Whichever way she tried to go round it to catch him, he went the opposite, sending her into another fit of uncontrollable laughter.

At last they stopped the chase, breathless, and fell into each other's arms. Their kiss was long and warm, and then Ray pushed her gently away. 'Your face is a bit red,' he said.

'I wonder how that happened? Yours is too.' She reached up and stroked his cheek. She hoped they'd always be like this, having fun, being silly together, but more than anything she wanted to grow old with this man. Life felt so uncertain with the country at war but the one thing she was sure of was that she wanted a future with Ray.

Ray pulled her gently down to a park bench, wrapping his arm around her shoulder as they sat side by side. He turned her face towards his and kissed her again, holding her close. 'I wish today could go on for ever, Nellie. Just us, here in the park, on a beautiful day. No war, no fighting, no worries.'

'I wish for that, too,' she whispered in reply.

He held her a moment longer then took her hand. 'Will we keep a dog, Nellie? You and I, after the war?'

He was assuming they'd be together, living together somewhere, wherever that might be. Nellie opened her mouth, trying to find a way to answer him, when he spoke again.

'I'm sorry, Nellie. I sometimes say what I'm thinking, without thinking what I'm saying.' He took her hand. 'What I mean is, Nellie Morris, I love you. I want to be with you until the end of days. I want us to spend our whole lives together. I don't mind whether we live in England or in the States, or somewhere else entirely once this war's over.'

He sighed heavily and she stared at him. He loved her! He wanted to be with her! Was he . . . *proposing*?

'I mean . . .' He shook his head. 'I've done it again. What I'm trying to say is, Nellie Morris, would you do me the honour of becoming my wife?' He held up a hand. 'Don't answer yet. I mean when the war's over and done with. I couldn't risk it now, not when I could be lost in a raid any time. I can't risk leaving you a war widow. If anything happened to me, I'd want to know you were free to find someone else and have a happy life. But I want you to know that it's what I want, with all my heart, and I hope you feel the same.'

'Oh! I do, Ray. I do feel the same.' She couldn't believe it. Her stomach gave a little flip as a surge of pure joy ran through her. She let the impact of his words take root in her heart.

His eyes shone as he gazed at her. 'I'm so happy, Nellie. I had told myself it was too soon, too early in our relationship and that I should wait to speak to you. But this war – we got to take our chances while we can, that's what everyone says anyway. So . . . that's what I've done, speaking to you now about it. To have an understanding between us is perfect for me. I love you so much, Nellie.'

'I love you too,' she whispered in return. Nellie felt like she was soaring. She was in love, with a man who loved her too, who wanted to marry her. And they would marry, as soon as the war was over. She had never longed for the end of the war so much as she did right at that moment.

Ray's smile was filled with sheer joy. He wrapped her in his arms and kissed her deeply. She could feel their love vibrating between their entwined bodies. She never knew she could feel this way – her whole body was throbbing with passion and happiness.

'Oh Nellie. I'm so happy! But let's keep this our secret until we can make it official.'

'Yes, once the war is over, we'll shout it from the rooftops.' She wanted the world to know. She wanted the world to feel the intense joy she felt right then. It was so marvellous, it was the cure for all problems. If people were in love the way she was, there'd be no war, no killing or bombing. Just love.

He looked at her longingly then kissed her hands. 'Come, let's get out of here,' he said. 'It's getting cold.'

Nellie hopped back on the crossbar, and Ray pedalled them back towards her home. As they approached the tube station entrance, Ray shook his head. 'I still can't believe you spend whole nights down there, on bunks. But I'm glad you do, when there's a raid on. It's the safest place, to be certain.'

'It is. Just those steps down to it . . . they can be slippery when wet and it's very dark down there.'

'You take care going down them, then.' He pulled her close, then stopped the bike. Ray pointed up at the clock tower above the church across the street. 'Say, this is a pretty church. We could marry here, when the time comes.'

She smiled at him. 'I would love that. Everyone local marries here, at St John's. It would be perfect.'

'Come on, let's go over.' He leaned the bike against some railings and Nellie followed him through the wrought-iron gates at the church's entrance and along the side of the building. 'Something I gotta do, now we've decided.' He pulled a penknife from his pocket, chose a clean stone block on the wall of the church, and there he chiselled their initials and the date. Nellie stood guard, terrified the verger would pass by and berate them for defacing the church, but she too wanted their love immortalised in stone.

'There,' he said at last. 'NM and RF, February 1943. It's set in stone now. When we're married, I'll add the date of our wedding.'

She looked closely at the letters. It was subtle, and you'd only spot them if you were looking for them or happened to be standing very close, but he'd gouged deep into the soft sandstone of the block. 'Will it last?'

'It'll last forever. It has to – it has to last as long as our love,' he said, and once more pulled her towards him to kiss.

Nellie thought she had never been so happy. This man, this kind, funny, gentle yet strong man – he was everything she'd ever wanted, and he was hers. The joy inside her bubbled over and she let out a little chuckle.

'Happy?' Ray said as they cycled towards Nellie's house.

'Very.' Soon the war would end and she'd become Mrs Fleming, and they'd travel the world and have adventures together. She wanted to dance and sing and tell everyone her news. It was going to be nearly impossible to keep it to herself, she was so excited and wanted the world to know how they felt about each other. She snuggled into his arms a little, trying not to make the bike wobble. He kissed the back of her head in response, and she felt supremely loved.

Ray didn't want the day to end. This perfect day, the fun they'd had, the new, significant step they'd taken in their relationship. All he wanted was to stay here in this day, on the bicycle, with Nellie in his arms. Her warmth against his chest, her hair blowing in the wind into his face. He had never felt so happy. He loved her so much, more than he'd ever known it was possible to love someone. She meant everything to him.

And with the tide of war turning slowly in the Allies' favour, the war would end and they could marry, and be together for the rest of their lives.

All he had to do was survive the missions he had to fly between now and then. All he had to do was stay alive.

Chapter 19

It was March already; 1943 was flying by. The news was full of the RAF's renewed bombing campaign in Germany, and particularly Berlin. It had been quiet since Christmas, with hardly any air raids, but if the RAF bombed Berlin it would only mean one thing for them in Bethnal Green, Nellie thought, sadly. More air raids in London, as the Luftwaffe launched reprisal attacks. More nights down the tube. She was resigned to it and clung to the hope that each day that passed was one closer to the war ending. What else could they do, but keep themselves safe while they waited for this damned war to finally end? And then she and Ray would be free to marry. The thought sent a little frisson of excitement through her at being Mrs Fleming.

'Here we go,' Em said, as the sirens sounded one evening. It was after eight o'clock and Flo had already been put to bed. 'Knew there was going to be a raid, soon as the wireless went off. It's always a sign. I was going to mend your dad's trousers tonight, where the hem's come down. That'll have to wait now. George, shut Oscar in the kitchen. Nellie, can you fetch Flo?'

Nellie ran upstairs to her room, where Flo was still fast asleep despite the wailing siren outside. She shook her little sister awake. 'Come on. We've got to go down the tube. Put your shoes and coat on quickly. I'll get our bedding bundles.'

Flo stared at her through half-closed eyes, obviously trying to process the instructions through the fog of sleep. Then she rubbed her face and nodded, swinging her legs out of bed.

'Good girl. I'll see you downstairs in a minute, then.' Nellie ran back down and grabbed hers and Flo's bedding bundles from the front room.

George was already there by the door. 'I got all the chickens in their coop quickly this time,' he said with a grin. 'I ain't gonna be the last today.'

'Bloody chickens'll be the death of us all,' Charlie muttered.

'That's not fair, Dad. I've sorted them quickly, this time,' George said. 'Can't bloody win, can I?'

'I can't find Spotty!' came a wail from upstairs. Flo appeared at the top of the stairs, still in her pyjamas but at least she'd put her red shoes on.

'For goodness sake, child,' Charlie pleaded. 'George, help her find the damned thing, as you're so cocky this evening.'

'Find it yourself,' George said, turning his back on them and heading out to the street.

'That boy needs a good hiding. Nellie, go with him. Em and me will sort out Flo.' Charlie charged up the stairs and scooped up the little girl.

'Nellieeee!' Flo cried, and Nellie turned to go to her, but Em pushed her towards the door.

'No, love, you go on ahead with George. Me and your dad will be right behind with Flo. Hurry, now.'

'I'll see you at the tube,' Nellie called to Flo. 'I've some sweeties from Ray for you, as soon as we're in our bunks.'

Nellie ran to catch up with George. 'Dad had no right to have a go at me,' George said as she pulled up alongside him. 'I got the chickens sorted and still he's yelling at me.'

'He's just scared for us all,' Nellie said, trying to placate him. Above them, searchlights were already criss-crossing the sky, trying to pick out enemy bombers.

'Gonna be a big raid tonight,' George said. 'I can feel it in me bones.'

They rounded the corner and arrived at the tube station entrance. As they rushed towards the steps a couple of buses pulled up, and scores of passengers began streaming off them and across to the tube station.

As they made their way down the steps, Nellie counted them like usual. Nineteen, turn right, and seven more. It helped ensure she didn't stumble on the last one, in the darkness.

In the ticket hall, Nellie looked around for Billy as she always did. There were several air raid wardens on duty, but then she spotted him, over by the top of the escalators, his usual place. 'Go on down, George,' she said to her brother. 'I'll be there in a minute, just want to have a word with Billy.'

She crossed over to him, but he ignored her, continuing

to direct people down to platform level. 'Evening, madam. Mind how you go, sir. Canteen's open if you want a cuppa.'

'Billy? Haven't seen you for ages. How've you been keeping?'

'Hello, Nellie. You've been too busy with your American fella, I suppose. Babs is down there already.'

'Oh, good.' Billy hadn't greeted her with his usual smile, and even though he was at work, he'd usually have a chat with her. It was true that she'd seen very little of him since before Christmas. The last two months had passed in a blur but she didn't expect him to be so stiff with her. She'd been busy with work and seeing Ray every spare moment they had but she'd seen Babs often enough – for chats out in the backyard, down the tube if there was an air raid on and at the Angel and Crown once or twice. But Billy's nights off hadn't coincided with their visits to the pub, and she hadn't bumped into him in the street or even seen him in the shelter. Come to think of it, she'd hardly seen him since that day she'd been out on the bike with Ray.

She glanced back towards the entrance where people were still filing down. There was no sign of the rest of her family yet.

'Mum and Dad and Flo are on their way,' she said. 'Got held up because Flo had lost something. That little dog ornament I gave her last year – it's her lucky talisman and she won't come down here without it. Keep an eye out for them, will you? Tell them me and George are getting the usual bunks.'

At last Billy turned to actually look at her. There was hurt in his eyes, and she realised that even though he'd never admit it, he was struggling to deal with her relationship with Ray. And he didn't even know they were promised to each other. She would have to speak to him privately about that. It was only fair, given what he thought of her. She resolved to tell Billy first, before anyone else, and try to get things straightened out between them.

'Yeah, I will, Nellie.' Billy nodded at her and turned away to answer a query from someone.

'Catch you later then, Billy,' she said, as she headed down the escalator. She glanced back once hoping to catch his eye, but he was looking straight ahead.

Chapter 20

God, but she was as beautiful as ever, Billy thought, as Nellie walked over to him on her way down to the platforms. He'd been avoiding her lately. He'd thought that perhaps if he didn't see her, he'd get over her, and stop spending every waking minute thinking about her. She was going to marry that handsome American, who gave her nylons and chocolates, who'd charmed her whole family and stolen her heart. He knew it, and his own heart was broken. Babs kept telling him he'd meet someone else, that there was someone for everyone, but all he could think was that yes there *was* someone for everyone, and the one for him was Nellie. It had always been Nellie. Since they were children playing Knock Down Ginger in the street together. Since she'd kissed him under the mistletoe that Christmas. Since he'd listened to her singing 'All Through the Night' to soothe her little sister one night in the shelter. It had always been her.

He tried not to look at her, but he had to be polite, didn't he? He had to act normal. She was wondering how he'd been. Heartbroken, he wanted to say, but that wouldn't have been fair. She'd never led him on, he just couldn't help the way he felt about it even though it pained him that Nellie didn't love him back.

From somewhere up above there was a loud bang, like a firework, or a car backfiring, and a scream.

He went to the half landing to look up the main flight of stairs for Em, Charlie and Flo, as Nellie had asked.

It was so damned dark in that stairwell, with only that one shaded light bulb hanging overhead. There were dozens of people coming down, and he pressed himself back against the wall out of their way, scanning faces for Nellie's family.

A woman screamed in pain, and he realised she'd fallen, at the bottom of the steps. He stepped forward to help her up, but someone else fell on top of her before he reached her, and then another fell and another and another . . .

It all happened so quickly. They toppled like dominoes in the darkened space, falling forwards, heads down across the bottom few steps, screaming as they went down. And still the people were coming down in their droves, and as they did, they too fell, and their bodies were piling higher. There were shouts and gasps from all around. He pulled on the arm of the nearest person, a woman, but she was stuck fast with the weight of those who'd fallen on top. 'Get me out!' the woman shouted, and all around were the cries of others who were trapped.

But it was so dark, so hard to see what was happening! He fumbled for his torch and switched it on.

'Jesus Christ Almighty!' He couldn't take in the sight that confronted him, it was like nothing he could ever have imagined. This was . . . this was like images of hell, of sinners being cast into the pits . . . piles of bodies, no, not bodies, these were *people*. Men, women, children . . .

'Help me!' a woman's voice screeched from somewhere above him, and nearer, someone made a gasping, choking sound.

'Don't just shine your torch, man! Help us! For the love of God! We're stuck,' a voice shouted, and Billy shone his torch in that direction. A man was caught, his chest and arms free but his legs stuck in the morass of bodies. Billy's heart was pounding as he stepped over to the man and tugged, pulling at his arms, threading his own arms under the other man's and heaving. Surely if one person could be freed the whole lot would come tumbling down, and they would all get up and dust themselves off, laughing at how tightly they'd been stuck for a minute or two, escaping with just a few minor cuts and bruises.

But the man was stuck fast, and no amount of pulling would release him. Further up another man was gasping, 'My back! Ow, my back!' Billy pointed his torch up and saw a fellow facing up the stairs, who must have turned to try to get up to the street. The crush above him was so great he was being pushed over backwards.

'Christ, he'll snap in two,' Billy muttered. He let go of the man he'd been trying to save. There was nothing he could do there. 'I'll get help,' he said, to no one in particular, and he ran back to the ticket hall. Mr Bolton was in charge tonight, and there were at least two other wardens on duty, somewhere in the shelter.

Mr Bolton was in a small room they used as an office. 'Sir! There's a blockage on the stairs!' Billy wheezed, his chest beginning to tighten. He thumped at his chest as though that would help, the last thing he wanted now was to have an asthma attack.

'Blockage? Well, move it, lad!' Mr Bolton said. 'Get some of the men coming down to help—' He broke off and stared at Billy, who was shaking his head.

'Let me see,' he muttered, getting up from his chair and following Billy at a run back to the stairs.

Billy shone a torch again at the struggling mass which had only become worse in the few seconds he'd been away. More people, though perhaps less screaming. The entire width of the stairway was now blocked, and Lord knew how far up the stairs the blockage went. His torch beam picked out red, gasping faces, flailing arms, panicked expressions. Mr Bolton stood still for a moment, his mouth open, and then he shook his head sharply as if testing whether he was seeing things. 'Good God. They're stuck fast. We'll need more manpower. Do what you can, Waters, and I'll get the other wardens and telephone for the police. We'll need to attack this from both sides.'

'Right, sir,' Billy gasped, as Mr Bolton ran back to his office to raise the alarm.

Billy turned to the wall of bodies to try to extricate some of them, anyone he could get to. As he shone his torch around searching for anyone who looked as though they could be pulled free, he was horrified to see faces turning purple, black almost. Were these people . . . he could barely bring himself to think the word let alone say it . . . were they *dying?* From being *crushed?*

He noticed a red shoe, a child's red shoe, like Flo's . . . He reached and pulled, but the shoe came off in his hand. And then he saw a tiny head, wedged between one man's chest and a woman's thigh, part way up. A baby. A tiny young thing, its mouth opening and closing as it gasped for breath. Still alive then. And small enough for him to wrangle free.

He stretched, trying to grab the little child, but couldn't reach. He stepped cautiously onto the pile of bodies below but no cry or shout of pain came. He reached forward again, this time managing to catch the baby by its head and one arm, and pulled, terrified to pull too hard in case he hurt the child further then berating himself for this thought. If he didn't get the baby out, it would die.

And it was working. With a push to the man's chest he managed to make a little room and the baby popped free. It was a little girl, he thought, judging by the dress and tights she was wearing.

Billy stepped back, off the poor soul he'd been standing on. His chest was tight now, and his breath coming in wheezy gasps. It was as though he too was one of these people crushed beneath the weight of so many others. He felt rising panic, but he was holding a tiny child in his arms and if nothing else he would save this little mite.

There were others there now, trying as he had to tug people free. Mr Bolton and another air raid warden were there, grabbing at arms and legs, anything, and pulling as hard as they could.

'Police are on their way,' Mr Bolton shouted. 'Take that baby to the first-aid post.' He stopped what he was doing for a moment and stared at Billy. 'And for God's sake get yourself some medical attention too.'

Billy didn't need telling again. He staggered as fast as he could to the first-aid post that was housed in a room off the ticket hall, gasping and wheezing but clutching onto the baby girl as though she was the one rescuing him. Down at the bottom of the escalators he could see other air raid wardens stopping anyone coming up.

In the first-aid room a nurse was sitting, calmly doing her knitting. She was clearly unaware of the drama unfolding outside. On a normal night she'd deal with nothing more serious than a migraine, or the aftermath of a small punch-up, or a child's grazed knee from tripping over on the platform.

'Take . . . the baby . . .' he gasped, and she reached out and took the child, laying her down on a camp bed.

'You look like you've been in the wars too,' she said to Billy, who slumped into the nearest seat. His body was screaming at him to lie down but he knew that would make it worse. Better to sit up, be upright as he tried to get oxygen to his lungs. As the nurse began checking over the infant he groped for his medicinal cigarettes but they were not in his pocket. Must have fallen out, he thought.

'N-nebuliser,' he managed to gasp out, and the nurse glanced over at him.

'Asthma?'

He nodded, and she quickly opened a cupboard and found the device. She handed it to him and he put the tube in his mouth and used the hand pump to spray a fine mist of medicine into his mouth. He breathed it in as deep as he could and felt it do the trick, opening his airways, reducing the rising panic he'd felt.

'Better?' The nurse was still treating the baby, who was beginning to make little whimpering noises. Billy was glad to hear them, for it meant the child was likely to survive. He'd saved one soul.

He nodded in response, and took a few more lungfuls of medicine, then stood up. He had to get back, to do whatever more he could. No other casualties had been brought to the first-aid post while he'd been in there, he realised. That was not a good sign. Surely by now they should have managed to free some of those caught.

As he made his way back to the entrance he remembered Nellie's plea to keep an eye out for her family. With horror he realised that they might be in the crush – Em, Charlie, little Flo! They could be among those dozens, maybe even hundreds of people trapped on the stairs. That child's little red shoe . . . Thank God Nellie had got through before it all started. Thank God she was safe.

The scene at the foot of the stairs was, if anything, even worse when he got back up there. Several air raid wardens and other men were still trying to disentangle bodies with little success. The air was filled with their shouts and curses, but to his horror Billy realised people in the crush were now for the most part silent, grey and lifeless.

Chapter 21

Ray had been granted permission by his Group Captain to use the motorcar, otherwise he had no hope of getting to Bethnal Green and back by bus at this time. He had to see Nellie, had to tell her his news. It wasn't something he could put in writing and it felt even harder because the last time they'd been together, Nellie had accepted his proposal. It was and would always be one of the happiest days of his life, and he'd been walking on air until this had brought him back down to earth. He just needed to tell her in person.

As he drove along the now familiar bomb-damaged streets of East London with only shells of houses standing he heard the air raid siren starting up. That was all he needed. A damned air raid. He drove a little further, debating what to do. The family would be heading to the air raid shelter so that would be the best place to find her. Babs's brother, he remembered, was an air raid warden stationed in the shelter so he'd be able to help.

As he approached the station entrance he could see crowds of people making their way down the steps. Maybe even now Nellie was among them. He pulled up behind a bus as passengers disembarked. As he did so there was a loud bang and he cursed. Damned car backfiring again. A woman outside squealed, 'It's the Germans! They're here! They're shooting at us!'

Ray jumped out of the car to try to reassure her but she was running, with several others, to the station entrance. Overhead an anti-aircraft rocket went up, making a loud whooshing noise. More people screamed and ran forward.

He followed the crowd, who were moving as swiftly as possible without panic to the entrance and down the stairs.

He was just a few steps down when those in front of him stopped moving. The people behind didn't stop, and he was jostled forward, into the backs of those in front. The pressure increased.

'Stop! Turn around! Go back up and give me some room!' he yelled out.

'We can't! They're pressing on us!' someone else above him on the steps shouted back.

'What's the hold up? Get a move on, there's an air raid on!' other people further back called out, clearly oblivious to the problem below.

It was so dark with just one dimly lit bulb that was shaded so that it didn't shine light onto the street. Ray couldn't see what was holding people up ahead, but dozens of them, hundreds even, were tightly packed and at a standstill.

He waited for the crowd in front to start making their

way down the steps again but still nobody moved. The people behind him were being edged forward by those further back and he felt himself being squeezed. As the crowds grew and he became pushed up against others, his chest was compressed by those around him. There was a feeling of tightness as the pressure grew, and he was unable to expand his lungs to breathe. He felt rising panic at what was happening but when he went to cry for help, he realised he could no longer shout out, his voice was but a faint whisper.

Ray desperately tried to scan the crowds for a sighting of Nellie. He felt his stomach turn at the thought that she could be just further ahead of him and caught up in the crowd too. He prayed that whatever happened to him, Nellie would be okay.

Little lights danced at the corners of his eyes and sound became muffled. He was going to pass out – *oh, Lord no, don't pass out!* He tried to move, to take a step back, but all that happened was that his feet lost contact with the ground. Only the pressure of other bodies around him held him upright. His feeling of panic intensified. In front he saw a woman's head loll back as she lost consciousness. Someone's elbow hit him in the face. There were still shouts, mostly from behind, and still the pressure of other bodies on him increased. A torch flashed over them from somewhere down below, revealing glimpses of dozens, hundreds of people, all as stuck as he was in the crush.

He'd been prepared to die, to give his life to safeguard

freedom for Europe when he signed up to the US Air Force to fight the enemy.

But not like this. He didn't want to die in a crush, struggling to breathe, in a pointless, avoidable tragedy, no, not like this . . .

He tried to call out for Nellie but he couldn't. As his eyesight faded, he pictured her, laughing as they rode their bike around the park and remembered the joy they'd felt that day.

*

Ray tried to open his eyelids, but he was dazed and unsure of what had happened to him. There was pain shooting down his leg. Somehow the pressure on him had released, and he realised he'd fallen and was being pushed against a concrete step. He took a deep breath, remembering his training, to try to bring the oxygen back into his lungs. Another big breath to steady himself and summon the energy to push himself onto his knees. An arm from behind grabbed him, pulling him up, and he crawled up the few steps to reach the top of the entrance.

'You all right, mate?' the stranger checked, and he nodded, still not quite able to focus, still unable to comprehend what was happening.

Ray staggered to his feet and looked around. There was a huge crowd at the entrance to the tube station. Some were still trying to go down, but there was a group of men at the top stopping them. Now and again someone would be dragged up the stairs, as he had been just now, or someone would walk up unsteadily, shaking their head in disbelief.

'What's happening?' he asked the nearest person.

'Dunno, mate,' came the answer. 'I dunno why they're not going down.'

The whoosh of another anti-aircraft rocket caused some of the crowd to flinch, or throw themselves towards the steps. It wasn't the usual, familiar sound of ack-ack guns but more like an enormous firework being set off that left a red trail streaming across the night sky.

He looked back at the crowd hoping with all his heart that Nellie was safe at the bottom of the shelter, or not yet here, still making her way through the streets. Anything rather than being caught up in this and in danger. As he scanned the faces, he saw a familiar figure, her hair awry, her coat hanging off one shoulder, fighting her way back up, out of the entrance.

'Ray! Ray! Oh my God, Ray, are you with Nellie?' Em stumbled towards him, her hair dishevelled and her dress torn from when she'd been caught in the crush.

'Mrs Morris! I was looking for Nellie, I can't find her.'

'I was nearly stuck in there!' Em said, pointing a shaking finger at the tube entrance. 'They're not stuck too, are they? Please say they're not!' She was frantic, clutching at his arm, her eyes wide and terrified.

'I don't think so, I was part way down, didn't see them. Were they not with you?' Ray checked, trying to sound calm so as not to worry Em further.

'They was all ahead of me. I dropped me purse out of me pocket, had to stop to find it, and they went on. I dunno what's happening but I can't get in, I can't get past.'

Ray felt panic rise in him once more, but not for himself. This time it was for Nellie, the love of his life. If she was in that crush, he had to save her.

'I'm gonna see what I can do to help,' he reassured her. 'Why don't you go sit over there?' He pointed across the road, to the low wall that surrounded St John's church. As if she was in a daze, Em did as he'd suggested. The air raid siren wailed on, reminding them all that above ground they were still in danger too.

He fought his way back through the crowds to the top of the steps. The man who'd helped him, who'd pulled him up, was there, doing the same thing for others.

'What can I do to help?' Ray said to him. 'Ray Fleming, US Air Force.'

'Thomas Penn. Policeman. Off duty, but . . .' He nodded towards the entrance. 'I'm gonna try to go over the top of them, see what's causing this. Give us a hand, will you?'

He and Ray ran back over to the steps, where just a few minutes ago Ray himself had been stuck. Now, as far as he could see in the darkness, the space was crammed with bodies and people lying on top of each other. Penn approached and looked across the sea of people, finding the best place to climb on top of them. With Ray's help he launched himself forward and on top of the mass, holding a torch.

'Oi! Stop jumping the queue, mate!' a man behind them shouted.

'Wedged solid down here,' Penn shouted back. As he shone his torch across the human avalanche Ray could see shoulders, heads lolling, purple faces in death grimaces, the occasional arm or even leg poking out. So many of them, and most of them not moving, not screaming, not breathing. It was like nothing he could have imagined. Like the worst depictions of hell. A child's head, wedged beneath a man's stomach. A woman's headscarf slipping back from her grey and lifeless face. An arm, bent at an unnatural angle, emerging between two bodies.

'Help me back up,' the policeman shouted, and as soon as he could reach him, Ray grabbed his arm and pulled him back over the bodies to safety.

Penn's face was ashen. 'Christ alive. There are hundreds. There's no hope for a lot of them. We need manpower, and fast.' He called a teenage lad over to him. 'Run to the police station. Tell them to send every man they can here, now.' The boy nodded and set off at a sprint.

Ray got him to sit down on the kerb, catching his breath. Moments later, a half dozen uniformed police arrived. PC Penn, rubbing at his shoulder where a bruise could be seen forming through a tear in his jacket sleeve, went over to brief them on what he knew, while Ray hurried back to try to be of assistance. They set to work, clearing the area of bystanders, directing them to other shelters in the area. Thankfully the air raid siren that had been wailing from the nearby church tower fell silent at last.

Ray refused to leave, even now the authorities had arrived. Nellie might be down there and he wouldn't go until he'd found her safe. She *had* to be safe. He couldn't bring himself to think of the alternative. She'd brought so much love and happiness into his life. She was his whole world. A few other men stayed near too, as the police officers and other rescuers organised themselves into teams and began disentangling the victims one by one, using force where necessary to bend limbs and pull out bodies, hauling them up from the steps to lay them on the pavement.

And they were bodies, for the most part. Purple-faced, crushed and lifeless. A constable called for water, and a nearby shop was opened to fetch buckets of water. The constable threw that over some of the victims. 'This should revive them. Worked when my missus had a fainting fit.'

But it didn't work now.

Em came over to Ray again. 'They're not . . . dead . . . are they? Just fainted?'

He was about to answer her when the shout went up. 'Got a live one, here!'

A space was cleared on the pavement as several police carried out a woman who was gasping for breath, her face grey and shocked, uncomprehending. A stream of ambulances was arriving now, their sirens taking the place of the air raid warning that had so recently stopped. Medics jumped out to deal with the rescued woman.

Ray looked around. There were so few survivors. His

gaze rested on a young girl whose face was crushed on one side, presumably by someone's boot. There was no hope for her. He caught Em's arm and pulled her away, praying that she hadn't seen it. 'Come on, Mrs Morris. Sit back down again, let me go and look.'

'Charlie . . . Nellie . . . Flo . . . George . . .' Em whispered as she allowed Ray to lead her back to the church wall. His heart gave a lurch. They might all be stuck in there. The next body to be pulled out could be one of them. Could be his Nellie.

And if that happened, and Nellie was brought up not breathing, how could he go on? How could there be life after that? It would be the end of everything, of all his hopes and dreams, of everything he lived for. She was his soulmate. He blinked away a tear as he tried to squash the thought.

He pushed his way through to the entrance, filled with renewed vigour. If there was any way to pull people out alive, then he sure was going to do his utmost to make sure he found Nellie before it was too late.

Chapter 22

'Where are they?' Nellie muttered, half to herself and half to George, who just shrugged in response, his attention firmly on the latest issue of *The Boy's Own Paper* as he spread across his bunk.

'Dunno. Ssh, I'm reading a Biggles story. *Boom! Rat-a-tat-a-tat!*' He made battle noises to accompany his story of the brave fighter pilot in dog fights in the last war.

Nellie climbed off her bunk and set off along the platform. She couldn't say why, but she had a bad feeling. Charlie, Em and Flo should have been just behind them but nobody else was coming into the shelter. Something wasn't right.

'Can't go up, miss.' An air raid warden she didn't recognise was standing guard by the bottom of the escalator.

'I'm just looking for my family. Please let me go and see if they're on their way.'

'No, can't let you up I'm afraid. People are still coming into the shelter, see, and if you try to go up you'll cause a blockage.' But Nellie couldn't see anyone coming down and now she was really starting to worry that something had happened. It wasn't like her family to be so far behind. She felt her heart begin to race.

'Is Billy Waters up there? I need to talk to him.'

The air raid warden shifted slightly so that he stood directly in front of her, closing off her path. 'I'm sure he's busy, miss. You can't go up and that's all there is to it. Now go back to the bunks, there's a good girl.'

Nellie glared at him. She hated being talked to as though she was a child.

But as she turned to go, another woman approached the air raid warden. 'I need to go up,' she told him. 'Feeling unwell down here. I need some air, and I thought I heard the all-clear anyway.'

'You can't go up, madam. The all-clear hasn't sounded, I'll tell you that much.'

Something was wrong because normally once people had stopped coming down, you could go back up.

She began to feel sick to her stomach with worry and swallowed back a wave of nausea as she hurried back to George.

'George, they won't let me back up. Something's not right. Can I take your torch and go and check if Mum, Dad and Flo are somewhere else in the shelter?'

Her concern must have been written on her face for she saw his brow crease with worry. 'I'll come with you,' he said. 'Leave the bedding here to save our bunks. Doesn't seem all that busy tonight anyway.'

No, it wasn't busy, and that was the other thing that didn't feel right at all. There'd been hundreds of people right behind them when they'd arrived at the shelter but they didn't seem to have made it down.

'Mum's friends go up that end, in the tunnel,' Nellie reasoned. 'Maybe they've gone there.'

'We'll go and look, then,' George said. Even for happy-go-lucky George, his usual boyish grin had faded to a look of confusion.

As they made their way along the platform, checking the occupants of every bunk, suddenly Nellie heard the sound of running feet. 'Mind out, miss,' a man called, and she and George flattened themselves against the wall of the tunnel, making way for a dozen policemen who were rushing towards the escalator.

'Come on, let's see where they're going,' George said, but Nellie shook her head.

'They're going up, and we won't be allowed up. Let's see where they came *from*, instead.'

'What do you mean?'

'I mean, they weren't down here when we came down. How did they get in? Wasn't down the escalator.' She grabbed George's arm and pulled him in the direction the police had run from, past their bunks, right to the end of the platform. The bunks here were all empty.

A door she'd never noticed before stood open. Behind was a dark passage. 'Your torch, George,' she said, and he switched it on and shone it along the passage. 'Looks like some steps there. I bet this is another entrance. For emergencies, or maintenance or some such.'

George stared at her. 'Are we going up, then?'

'Yes. Something's wrong and I want to know what. Come on.' Before he could answer she grabbed the torch from him and went through the door, along the passage and onto the bottom step.

'Bloody hell, sis. I don't like this but I ain't letting you go alone. I'm right behind you.' Nellie reached for George's hand not wanting to get separated from any more of her family tonight. The two of them had to stick together – they needed each other.

They took the steps two at a time, going up a flight of a dozen then turned a right angle and went up again, on and on. The steps surely led to the surface, Nellie thought, as she began to breathe heavily with the effort. She didn't like the idea of climbing to the top only to find they couldn't get out and they'd have to go all the way down again with only a torch to light their way. What if someone locked the door at the bottom while they were on the stairs? The thought unnerved her. What would they do if they became trapped and their cries for help were not answered?

Stop thinking like that, she told herself.

And then they turned another corner and could see a glint of light above them at the top of the next flight. A metal ladder stretched above to an open manhole. 'Up we go,' Nellie said, climbing the ladder, with George right behind her.

They emerged into the moonlight, in the middle of a deserted street. Nellie looked around, trying to get her bearings. She could hear distant shouts, and sirens sounded somewhere nearby – not the wail of the air raid siren but those of police cars and fire engines. She shuddered. It felt like the aftermath of an air raid during the Blitz.

'Carlton Square,' she said, recognising where they were. A few hundred yards away and near to the main tube entrance. 'Come on,' she ordered, leading George along.

'Where now?'

'The main entrance.'

George ran, Nellie sprinting to keep up. As they approached the tube entrance, she could see crowds of people there, lots of vehicles, the buses they'd seen disgorging passengers when they arrived, and . . .

'Ambulances! Oh God, George, something really has happened, people are hurt . . .'

'It won't be Mum and Dad. You're getting yourself all worked up, Nellie,' George said, but there was no conviction in his words.

The ambulance crews were carrying stretchers into St John's church, she realised. They must be treating the injured in there.

And then she noticed bundles on the ground. Bundles of clothes, shoes . . . that were still on feet . . . People were lying there in the road. Many of them wet. Something odd about the colour of their faces. 'Give us the torch again, George,' she said.

George handed it to her silently. She shone it at the nearest bundle. A woman, her coat bunched up beneath her. Her mouth open, her skin purple.

'Oh my God. She's dead,' Nellie whispered. Bile was rising in her throat.

'They're all dead,' George replied.

She'd seen a few dead bodies during the Blitz, but this was something else entirely. They didn't have any signs of injuries, they were just lifeless, unmoving. And there were so many.

'Nellie! George! Oh! Oh my darlings!'

Nellie turned around at the sound of their names. It was Em! Nellie ran across the road and into her arms. *Oh thank goodness, thank goodness. Mum was safe, but . . .*

'Mum! Where are Dad and Flo?'

'Aren't they with you?' Em's expression changed.

Nellie could only shake her head. George spoke up. 'You were all together . . . behind us . . .'

'They went ahead . . .'

'What's happened here? Where are they? Flo, Flo, where are you?' Nellie tried to shout, her voice catching in her throat.

She ran over to the entrance desperate to find Charlie and Flo. But she couldn't see them. There were bodies laid everywhere, contorted at awkward angles with bruised limbs sticking out. Tears started to roll down her cheeks at how helpless and scared she felt.

'Nellie! Oh my love . . .' a voice cried out. To her great surprise, it was Ray. He ran over and took her in his arms, kissing her face frantically. For a moment as he held her she felt safe, the frightening confusion that engulfed her retreating. 'Nellie, I thought the worst . . . I thought it'd be you I'd be carrying out . . . oh God, I thought you were down there, one of them . . .'

'Ray! My family . . . I can't find . . . Dad and Flo . . .' Nellie could scarcely get the words out between sobs.

'Nellie, I haven't seen the others . . .'

'George was with me. But Dad and Flo?'

'There are more being brought out. Some are . . . alive . . .' Ray said, but his voice tailed away, and she understood with mounting horror that most of them coming out were not.

More rescue workers were arriving as they spoke, and they were ushered away from the entrance. Ray insisted on staying to help and followed Nellie as she led him over to where Em and George were standing.

'I don't understand,' Em said. 'You was ahead, you two. How did you get out? Ray says it's all blocked down there, with—'

Nellie couldn't bear to hear what was blocking the entrance. She just wished that this was all a bad dream and she'd wake up in her bunk with Flo beneath her. 'Me and George found another way out. There's a maintenance exit.'

'I suppose they're working on getting people out at the bottom end,' Em said. 'They'll find Charlie and Flo, I just know they will, so we've got to hold on to that hope.'

George and Nellie stared at her and both of them nodded solemnly, although no one dared speak. For now all they could do was wait and let the police, the air raid wardens, the ambulance crews and all the other emergency services, helped by Ray and a few other off-duty servicemen, do their job. Nellie put an arm round each of them and pulled them close. 'They'll be found, they'll be all right,' she whispered again, but whether she believed it herself she couldn't honestly tell.

Chapter 23

'Maybe they went home. Maybe they couldn't get through and just went home,' Em said, her voice holding a faint hope for Charlie and Flo's safety.

'We should check,' Nellie mumbled, and George jumped up off the church wall they'd been sitting on, looking relieved to have something to do.

'I'll go. I'll run there and back.' George didn't wait for an answer but took off at a sprint.

Nellie was beside herself with worry and sent up a silent prayer that Charlie and Flo would be at home, Flo in bed, Charlie sitting in the front room with his newspaper and a cup of tea, waiting for them to come back.

She kept a tight hold of Em, both of them hardly daring to breathe while George was gone. Across the street Nellie could see more and more victims being brought out, loaded onto stretchers and then taken away. Some in ambulances, and she prayed they were survivors on their way to hospital, but many had blankets over their faces and were carried into the church behind them. Her mouth was agape in horror at what she was seeing unfolding, it was the stuff of nightmares. Em gave her a squeeze but how was that supposed to make anything better? But every now and again she caught a glimpse of Ray, working tirelessly to free people, and through it all she felt proud that the man she loved was stepping up to help.

Down below, Billy was surely doing the same from the other end. Maybe there were more survivors beneath. Maybe when the steps were finally cleared, they'd all troop out unscathed, Charlie and Flo amongst them?

And then George came running back. He didn't need to say a word. Nellie could see the answer written on his face, the colour drained from it. He shook his head. 'They're . . . not there. I didn't see no sign of 'em anywhere.' He leaned over, hands on knees, to catch his breath.

Nellie's stomach sank at his words, their last real chance dashed to pieces. She stared at George and clutched Em tightly, unable to find any words, any way that they could cling to a final thread of hope. All she could do was sit there in the cold, late night air, fighting back tears that helped no one. With every passing minute it was more and more unlikely that Charlie and Flo would be found alive.

At last Ray walked over wearily to them. 'I've done all I can. The last are being brought up now. I didn't see Mr Morris or Flo, but that does not . . . I mean, I didn't see every face. There are so many . . .'

'What do we do now?' Nellie whispered, her voice breaking. They could not return home and go to bed, as though nothing was wrong. There were others like them, sitting or standing around, faces ashen, wondering where their loved ones were. It didn't seem real, she didn't understand it or know what she should do. It was all so overwhelming.

Ray took her hand and drew her into his arms. 'They've brought a lot of the victims into the church and laid them out. We could go in, try to find the rest of your family . . . I'll do it, to save you the . . .'

'No,' Em said. 'I'll do it. It's my family.' She stood up shakily and George caught her arm to steady her.

'I can come with you, you shouldn't have to do this alone, Mum,' Nellie said, and Em nodded, her lips pressed together in determination.

'I'll stay with George, Mrs Morris,' Ray said and Nellie mouthed her thanks.

Slowly, Nellie and Em made their way over to the church. A policeman stood at the door and let them in when they explained why. 'There's some down in the crypt, and more on the pews,' he said, and Nellie nodded grimly, trying to brace herself for the reality that would confront them.

Arm in arm, holding each other up, Em led her past the rows of bodies. Each had a blanket or a piece of clothing draped over their face. Some they could pass by without looking – any that were obviously not Charlie or Flo, women, children of the wrong size, anyone in clearly the wrong clothing.

But some were covered entirely by a blanket, and in these cases Em had to let go of Nellie, stoop and pull back the cover to expose the person's face. A young boy, who looked as though he were simply sleeping. A woman, with her face dark and drawn, her eyes still open. An old man, his clothes torn and a graze across his face. And worst, a young girl, almost unrecognisable, whose face was half crushed. Nellie closed her eyes to block out the horror, but still she could see each one of those lifeless faces in her mind.

She and Em weren't the only people there looking for loved ones among the rows of pews. Dozens of others were doing the same thing. Occasionally a wail went up when someone found who they were looking for, and each time, Nellie gasped for air, feeling their pain and knowing it was only a matter of time before it would be their turn.

This scene, these horrors would stay with her forever, plaguing her, tormenting her, recurring in her worst dreams for as long as she lived. It would be like that for all of them, she knew, for everyone who'd witnessed it or been caught in it, or like her, narrowly escaped.

*

As they moved across the aisle, Nellie stopped. Brown trousers with a hem that needed stitching, heavy workman's boots. The rest of him covered with a grey blanket. 'Mum?' she said quietly.

'Oh, my Charlie,' Em said as she went over and knelt down. Reverently she pulled back the blanket to confirm.

Nellie sank to the floor, her tears turning to gut-wrenching sobs. Dad looked as if he was just sleeping, his eyes closed. She wanted to go and shake him, wake him up, tell him to get up, lazy bones, and help look for Flo. But his colour was wrong, and the way he was lying slightly twisted was wrong. Then it dawned on Nellie, if Charlie was here that meant they'd find Flo here too. They would have been together. He wouldn't have let go of her for a second.

Em leaned over her husband's body and kissed him, once, on the forehead. She smoothed his hair with a hand. 'Thank you, my love, for our marriage. You were everything to me. I will love you always,' she whispered.

And then Em rose shakily, dabbing her tears with her hankie, the colour drained from her face, and began scanning the church.

'Over there,' she croaked, pointing to the first row of pews, a few yards away. A single, small red shoe poked out from beneath a man's jacket. A pair of white knee socks, the type every child wore, but the one on the left had a small hole near the knee, just like Flo's.

'Noooo! Oh no! My baby, my darling, darling baby!' Em fell to her knees in the aisle in front of Flo and gathered the lifeless little body into her arms. Nellie dropped down beside her, holding her mother and her sister. Someone let out a howl of anguish, a high-pitched piercing sound, and it took a moment to realise it was coming from herself. Both of them, Flo and her dad, gone, just like that. It made no sense. No sense at all! In a few hours, out of nowhere, she'd lost two of her family. How on earth could this be happening?

She clutched Em tightly, wanting desperately to rewind time, back to when she was a little girl and life was carefree, before the war, before air raids, before death touched them with such cruelty.

Nellie didn't want to see Flo, wanting to remember her as she had been, the lively, happy, generous child they'd all loved. Instead, she looked at her mother's distraught face, blurred through the veil of her own tears. She knew then they would never recover from losing Flo and Charlie. The tragedy of it all was crippling. They sat there, both paralysed with grief, sobbing on each other's shoulders.

A medic with a clipboard was standing nearby, waiting to label Flo and Charlie, wanting to place two more ticks on his board. That's all they were to him – bodies to be named. Not people that had been loved and needed. Sobbing, Em told him their names and he wrote their labels silently, his eyes filled with sympathy.

Nellie forced herself to glance down one last time at Flo's little face.

'Oh, Flo. You have no idea how much you were loved and how much I'll miss you. And Dad,' she whispered.

'W-will al-always be loved,' Em said, and Nellie nodded.

'Always and forever.'

Chapter 24

Ray stood with his arm around George's shoulders. He wished it could be him in there with Nellie, supporting her through this hideous ordeal. It was impossibly cruel that her family had been taken away, especially dear young Flo, whom she adored and doted on. She'd never get over this. He knew it without a doubt. None of them would.

'They're dead, aren't they?' the boy asked him in a flat monotone. 'Dad and Flo.'

'We don't know yet,' Ray said, with a squeeze of his shoulders.

'That scream from the church. Sounded like our Nellie.' George rubbed a hand across his face. 'What are we gonna do, without Dad? And Flo? Like, when we thought she was going away, the whole family felt like it was falling apart. If she's gone . . . I dunno how Mum and Nellie'll cope with that.'

'They're strong, George. And so are you.'

Around them, crowds were still milling about, people walking dazed and confused, calling out for friends and relatives. The door to the church opened then as someone was let inside to search for their loved ones. Ray caught a glimpse of Em and Nellie sitting on the floor at the top of the aisle, holding each other and cradling a small body.

He tried to turn so George didn't see but it was too late. The boy let out a heartbreaking sob and Ray could only hold him while he cried. There was nothing he could say that would help.

'I–I argued with Dad. I went ahead . . . with Nellie . . . It's all my fault,' George was saying, between sobs.

'Hush now. It's not your fault.'

As he spoke those words he gazed around at the scene over George's shoulder – the aftermath of the tragedy. Emergency services finishing their work. Exhausted policemen sitting on the ground, helmets beside them, heads in hands. Ambulances were still arriving in a steady stream, taking away bodies for the most part. The buses that had let so many people off all at once, many of them now among the dead, were still parked at the kerbside.

Above them the moon shone down from a cloudless sky. A bomber's moon, but there'd been no sign of German bombers that night. The air raid had been a false alarm. The deaths of so many people were utterly needless.

He glanced over to his Group Captain's motorcar, which had backfired just as he'd arrived. A new wave of dread and horror rose up in him. *Oh God*. Had he caused a panic that had started it all? Was it, after all, *his own fault*? He felt cold and clammy as he considered this. It couldn't be his fault . . . but that woman, shouting about the Germans shooting at them, running to the entrance along with the hordes who'd just got off the bus . . . Maybe he *had* played a part in it.

It had all started with a bus. Chasing down the one that was carrying Flo away. If he hadn't done that and Flo had been evacuated as planned, then she would be alive today, safe in the countryside somewhere. Not lying cold and lifeless in the church with her mother and sister crying over her body.

He realised that Nellie would be feeling the same guilt. She'd started the chase for the bus. Sooner or later she would undoubtedly wish that she'd left Flo on it.

There were difficult times ahead for all of them as they came to terms with this tragedy, if indeed it was something you could come to terms with, ever. All Ray wanted now was the chance to support Nellie through it, as best he could.

But that wasn't going to be possible. He still needed to tell her why he'd come to Bethnal Green that evening. After what had happened, how on earth was he going to tell her? She needed him and yet, he wasn't going to be able to be there for her.

Chapter 25

They walked home in a silent daze, the four of them. Nellie and George were either side of Em, holding her up as she staggered through the streets. Ray walked beside Nellie, his arm around her shoulders. It was late. Past two o'clock when they turned onto Morpeth Street. There was no one else around, and for that Nellie was thankful. She didn't want to explain it to anyone, not yet. She'd seen the Waters family earlier, safely down in the shelter so they wouldn't know what had happened yet. Except for Billy. She realised with horror he must have been involved in the rescue attempt, at the bottom of the steps.

Nellie opened the door to their house and Em half fell inside. 'I'm going straight up,' she said, in a monotone.

'Think I'll go to bed too,' George said. His eyes were red-rimmed.

She nodded and watched them climb the stairs, those stairs that Charlie would never again climb, and Flo would never again bump down on her bottom, giggling. The house felt eerily empty and quiet without them. 'Try and get some rest,' Nellie said softly.

And then there was just the two of them – herself and Ray, and suddenly she realised she didn't even know why he was here, why he'd been in Bethnal Green at all that night. But she was thankful for his presence and grateful he'd done what he had. 'Let's sit in here a while. I can make up a bed for you . . .'

He shook his head. 'No need. I . . . have to talk to you. I don't want to leave you like this but I can't stay.'

She stared at him and nodded, and led him into the front room. It was strange, being in that room. Everything looked so perfectly, awfully normal, the way it had always been but then it wasn't going to be the same ever again.

Ray glanced at the chair by the fireside, the one that had always been Charlie's, then chose a different seat. Nellie perched on a footstool beside him, then turned to Ray, whose expression mirrored her anguish.

He sighed and took her hand. 'Nellie, I don't know how to tell you this, not after tonight. But we're . . . we're being moved. We gotta go . . . tomorrow. Some of the boys have already gone.'

'Go where?' She wasn't taking in his words.

'A different airbase. Up country. Not sure where, but they tell me it won't be possible to come to London, except on a two-day leave or more.' He shook his head sadly. 'It's too far.'

'Too far? You won't be able to come to see me?'

'Nellie, my Nellie, I will come every single time I can arrange a two-day pass. I promise you that.'

'But . . .' *But I need you, now more than ever*, she wanted to say.

'I know, the timing couldn't be worse. But we're . . . committed to each other. We'll survive this, all of it.' He put an arm around her shoulder and squeezed her. 'We will. We will weather this storm.'

'Dad and Flo gone, and now you're leaving me . . .' She felt numb with the pain of it all. If he loved her, how could he do this to her?

'If there was any possibility of me staying, you know that I would,' he said earnestly. 'But my first duty is to fight for freedom. I have no real choice. I came to Bethnal Green tonight to tell you.'

'I wondered why you were here. Were you on one of the buses that dropped so many passengers at once at the shelter?' she asked, dazed as she tried to take in what he was telling her.

'No, I–I drove. My Group Captain lent me his car. I heard the air raid siren and came straight to the shelter to look for you.'

'Were people already . . . dead . . . when you got there?' The details were painful but somehow Nellie felt she had to know, she needed to know everything about how her father and sister had died. Maybe knowing might help her understand.

'No . . .' Ray said, sounding a little hesitant, 'although the crush was forming as I went down to find you. I was pulled out. I got lucky but I didn't realise what was happening. I was so worried you were stuck in the crowd, that you were—' His voice cracked, then he continued softly, 'Going to be taken from me. I love you so much, Nellie.'

'Oh Ray, I love you too. And I can't believe you were caught up in it. I just can't imagine where I'd be if I'd lost you too,' Nellie replied, tears welling up. It was the first time she realised that for her the tragedy could have been even worse than it already was. She might have lost Ray too, without even knowing he was anywhere near.

Ray paused for a moment, looking down at his hands, clasped together in his lap. 'I heard some woman scream that the Nazis were there, firing guns on us. Nellie, I'm worried . . . it was because of the damn car. It backfired as I was parking it, it sounded like – like a gunshot.'

'What? Did it make people panic?'

Ray grimaced. 'Well, it definitely scared a woman. Some kind of rockets were going off too . . . an awful whooshing sound they made. Think that frightened some folks as well.'

Nellie wasn't thinking about the guns. The local people were familiar with the sound of ack-ack guns, and the new rockets surely wouldn't sound much different. She hadn't heard them herself. But if people had thought the Nazis had landed and were firing, she could see how that might easily start a stampede down the stairs, causing falls, a crush . . . and the loss of her sister and father.

'It might have been you that started it,' she said, slowly looking up as the notion dawned on her.

'I don't think—' he began, but she turned then and hit him, square in the chest with the heel of her hand.

'*You* started it. Flo, my dad, all those others that were in the church, all grey and lifeless. All of them . . . all those people, gone, cos *your car* backfired!' Her emotions bubbled over, temper flaring up inside her. The whole thing could have been averted if Ray hadn't been there.

'No, Nellie, listen—'

But she pummelled his chest feebly, sobbing, her heart torn in two for all those souls, for her sweet little sister, her father, for her mother and brother who were heartbroken and trying to come to terms with what had happened.

'You . . . you . . . it was *you*!' she shouted.

He let her hit him, then caught her wrists to stop her and tried to pull her close. 'Nellie, no . . . the car backfired, the woman screamed, but . . .'

'It was you,' she repeated, seething as she pushed him away. He wasn't a hero at all, he was the one who'd started it all off. She got to her feet and stared at him in horror. 'You *knew* that car backfired! You could have . . .' she waved a hand vaguely, 'parked farther away. Not risked f-frightening people. *You* did this . . . my sister, my father . . .'

She stared at him, not recognising the man she saw. He was the man who'd caused all this, the man who'd broken her family and so many other families. The pointless deaths of so many, and all avoidable, if only Ray had not driven that bloody car so near the tube station entrance.

'Nellie, sweetheart,' Ray said, standing up and reaching for her.

But she couldn't, she *couldn't*. A short while ago she'd

needed to be held by him, to gain strength from him to help cope with her loss. Now she needed to get away from him. Far, far away. He'd caused this, and he was leaving her to deal with it on her own. She was shaking with anger.

With her hands out in front to push him if he tried to come towards her, she backed away. 'No, no, no,' she was saying, and the sobs were rising up in her throat once more, choking her, engulfing her. All she could think now was that she wanted him gone, out of the house, out of Bethnal Green, away from the people he'd killed. Away from it all, away from her.

'Go. Get out. Get *out!* I can't . . . I can't . . . I don't want to speak to you . . . ever again!' she screamed, before slumping into the nearest chair, Charlie's, and hid her face with her hands and let the sobs come. In that moment there was only her and her grief, and it filled the world.

***

'Nellie, please, please, honey, just let me . . .' Ray put a hand on her shoulder but she shrugged it off. There was nothing he could do or say now that would make things any better with the woman he loved. It broke his heart to see her sitting there like that, sobbing, her life torn apart. Especially knowing that he'd quite possibly caused it all, it could have been he who'd started the panic that had killed her dad and sister. And all those others. And now he couldn't even be here to support her through the difficult weeks that lay ahead for her, as she struggled to come to terms with it all.

Inwardly he cursed the bad timing of his relocation to a new base. And then remembered, again, that if he hadn't come to Bethnal Green to tell her of it tonight, there might not even have been a crush at the shelter. His car backfiring had scared that woman, but surely there had to be more to it, didn't there? That alone couldn't have caused the tragedy? How would he live with himself, if it really had been all his fault? The feeling of guilt was weighing heavily on him.

He looked down at her as she sobbed. How he wanted to take her in his arms . . . He reached out to her again, and she looked up, her face racked with pain.

'Why are you still here? Go! Get out!' She pushed him in a rage and he took a step away.

She needed time and space. A chance to grieve, and to find a way through all this, if that was at all possible. He'd write to her, he decided, as soon as he could, as soon as he had the address of his new airbase. They'd get over this. They had to. Nellie was everything to him. Everything. He couldn't lose her.

Chapter 26

Nellie cried herself to sleep on the sofa in the end, and woke cold and stiff as the dawn light seeped in through the windows. Her first thought was that no one had drawn the blackout blinds and that Charlie would be furious . . . and then she remembered.

Ray was nowhere to be seen. Her sore throat reminded her how she'd lost her temper and screamed at him to get out. But Ray wasn't her priority. She, George and their mum had to stick together now. Nellie struggled to believe that they were now a family of just three. She stood up, her limbs stiff and aching, her clothes from yesterday rumpled, and went upstairs. She went to her own room, the one she'd shared with Flo, at the front of the house. And there was Em, curled up in Flo's bed, her face resting on Flo's nightgown, her arm around Flo's doll.

Em was awake. 'I slept here. Or tried to, anyway. Probably only managed to drift off for half an hour. Heard you arguing with Ray.'

'We did, yes. He's left.' Nellie was not, under any

circumstances, going to tell Em what the argument had been about.

'George all right?' Em's tone was flat and lifeless.

'I'll check on him,' Nellie said.

George, in his box room next door, was still asleep. Nellie left him to it, washed her face and changed her clothes, then went down to the kitchen to put the kettle on. Em followed her a minute later and took out the bread and margarine. 'Don't seem real, do it?'

'No, it's like we're in a bad dream.'

She sat down heavily at the kitchen table.

'Eat some breakfast, love,' Em said.

'I couldn't.' Nellie just wanted to be left alone.

Em was quiet for a moment, spreading margarine on a slice of bread for herself, then she turned back to Nellie. 'What did you two argue about?'

'None of your business, Mum.'

'Ain't it? I just think he loves you and you're going to need him, not push him away.'

Nellie felt rage rise up in her again, just like last night with Ray. 'You don't understand. You'll never understand.' And she was not going to tell Em what she'd heard from Ray. She had to carry the weight of that knowledge herself.

'You need to talk to me, then, if he's not here,' Em said.

'For God's sake. Stop telling me what to do!' Nellie shouted. George came in the kitchen then, disturbed by the raised voices and stared at them.

'Mum, Nellie, don't fight, I can't . . .'

'Now you're telling me what to do and not do as well. Shut up, both of you, and leave me be!' She couldn't be in that house a moment longer. She grabbed her coat and walked out, slamming the door behind her.

Nellie strode along Morpeth Street and turned the corner, with no real thought as to where she was going or why. She thought back to what Ray had said. In the cold light of morning she regretted the way she'd shouted at him but she couldn't believe he'd abandon her at a time like this. And now the one person she wanted to turn to for comfort had gone but if it was true that it was his fault she wasn't sure if she could ever forgive him.

Everything around her looked normal, just another busy East End morning. A few people she passed wore shocked, dazed expressions but otherwise it was as though nothing out of the ordinary had happened. Not like after an air raid when there was dust in the air and newly ruined buildings to show for it.

But it had all happened, and suddenly she wanted to understand it fully. She wanted to know the cause, what would be done next . . . Her steps had taken her in the direction of the town hall, and she decided she might as well go to work. It was her best chance of finding answers.

Reaching the town hall steps, she took a deep breath to get her emotions under control, and went inside, forcing herself to look normal, to not cry.

Inside, many councillors and other officials were milling about, all with grave faces. Mrs Bolton was passing through the hallway when she saw Nellie. 'Oh thank goodness you're here. I didn't know if you were caught up in . . . the accident at the tube station shelter last night. There is a meeting,' she glanced at her watch, 'beginning in five minutes. It's to be held in secret but I need you there to take the minutes. Upstairs in the conference room. I shall see you there.' She gave Nellie a tight smile and bustled on her way.

Nellie headed up the stairs, hurrying along because if she stopped and reflected on what had happened, she'd break down and she didn't want to do that here and now. Not until she'd heard what would be said at that meeting.

She went into the mayor's office, hung up her coat and picked up her notebook and pen, feeling numb but knowing she had to do this to find out the truth.

The mood was sombre as people filed into the conference room and silently took their seats at the large table. Nellie's place was tucked into a corner behind the Mayor, her notepad on her lap. She glanced around the room at the people gathered – some faces were familiar, others not. Some looked grief-stricken as if they too had lost loved ones. The room seemed blurred and her mind kept replaying her last conversation with Ray, and then drifting to the thought of going home from work tonight but Flo and Charlie not being there. None of this was right, everything felt upside down.

'Thank you, everybody, for coming here early on such short notice,' Mrs Bolton said, opening proceedings. 'You will all be aware that there was a tragedy last night at the Bethnal Green tube station shelter. We need to set in motion a number of things, including an inquiry into what happened and how it can be prevented from recurring. And we must make decisions as to how we handle public communications regarding this. But first, let me introduce everyone as I'm aware you haven't all met before.'

Nellie tried to concentrate, listening carefully to the names as the Mayor introduced them. She already knew some of the Bethnal Green councillors. Then there was Sir Ernest Gowers, the head of London Civil Defence – she'd typed letters addressed to him but had not previously met him. Mr Ian Macdonald Ross, an aide to the Home Secretary Herbert Morrison, was also taking a set of notes for the government.

It was Sir Ernest Gowers who led the meeting from that point on. 'Now then. Firstly I must say that for now, *anything* said in this room must *not* go beyond these walls. Until we have determined how best to . . . ahem . . . play this to the general public, we must keep quiet. A lot of people died last night—' at this Nellie gulped hard, suppressing a sob, fighting to compose herself, 'not due to enemy action, and the last thing we want is for people to become too frightened to use public shelters. We also must avoid demoralising the public or handing the enemy fodder for propaganda.'

He glared at everyone around the table until they all nodded in agreement. 'At first glance, it would appear that a mass panic on the steps leading down to the shelter is the cause. People rushing and pushing each other, causing a pile-up from which they could not extricate themselves.'

Nellie stared at him. Panic, caused by Ray's car backfiring and people thinking it was gunshots and the Germans had landed? If that really was the cause, it was her worst nightmare that the man she loved had made this happen, taking from her the people she held dearest.

'I have the current death toll here,' Sir Ernest went on. He looked down, consulting some notes, and swallowed before continuing. 'I am sorry to say that one hundred and seventy-three lives were lost. A good many of them – sixty-two – were children.'

There were audible gasps as he read out the number. Around the table people bowed their heads in respect, mouthed silent prayers for the lost. Nellie blinked away her tears and wrote the number of victims carefully on her notepad, drawing a box around '173'. Even though she'd seen the bodies, laid out in the church along with those of her father and sister, she could not comprehend that so many had died. Not in that small space, those nineteen steps. And so many had been children, like Flo. Children who'd had their whole lives ahead of them. She tried to pretend that this was just a story, happening to some fictional character in a picture she'd seen at the Empire, not to her. It didn't seem real and even though the Council were gathered trying to make sense of it, she still couldn't understand how this had happened.

'In addition, dozens more were injured and are being treated at several hospitals,' Sir Ernest continued after a few moments. An inquiry was to be opened, commissioned by the Home Office, to get to the bottom of exactly what happened. Survivors and rescuers would be interviewed in detail. Mrs Bolton turned to Nellie and whispered. 'I shall want you to sit in on that, and take notes. It will be harrowing no doubt, but I can trust you to do a good job.'

Nellie stared, her blood running cold at the thought. She had no idea how she would cope listening to the stories of those involved. Hearing how Flo and Charlie had died would be too much to bear.

'I heard it was the Communists that started a panic,' one councillor said.

Another shook his head. 'No, it was the sight of German bombers coming in low. Didn't you hear the bombs falling?'

'No bombs fell on Bethnal Green last night,' the Mayor said firmly. 'That has been established.'

'We will consider all theories during the inquiry,' Sir Ernest said. 'And we must take steps at once to improve the entrance to the shelter.'

Nellie felt sickened and helpless at his words. This was the kind of awful tragedy the engineer Mr Smith had feared might happen. Not a broken leg or two, but a mass crush, hundreds of lives lost in moments. And it could all have been averted by improving the safety of the entrance if they'd been given the funds they needed. She caught Mrs Bolton's eye, and the Mayor cleared her throat to speak. 'Sir, I must remind you that Bethnal Green Council applied on a number of occasions to Civil Defence for authorisation and funds to improve the entrance.'

Nellie gulped back a sob and made herself listen as the Mayor continued speaking. It was true that they'd had fair warning but failed to act on it. And as a result, so many had died needlessly.

'But the monies we applied for were not forthcoming. We foresaw a tragedy might occur—' She was cut off by Sir Ernest raising a hand.

'Now is not the time to point fingers of blame, Madame Mayor. That must wait for the full inquiry.' He looked around the table as though daring anyone else to speak out. 'And now – there are a lot of victims that must each be identified so that their families can be informed and their funerals arranged.'

The meeting drew to a close, and Nellie hurried back to the mayor's office, not wanting to spend a minute longer in the room listening to the men talk.

'You mustn't speak of this to anyone, Nellie. Not even to your family. Not yet,' Mrs Bolton said. 'I know it's hard with so many dead, and I pray there is no one you or I know amongst their number. But as Sir Ernest said, we cannot risk lowering morale at this time.'

Nellie nodded and fed a sheet of paper into her typewriter. And then she stopped and stared unseeingly at the keys. *You mustn't speak of this . . . not even to your family,* Mrs Bolton had said. Mrs Bolton, who could have pushed harder to get that money, who could have diverted funds spent elsewhere in the borough . . . A dam burst inside her and Nellie pulled the paper out of the typewriter, screwing it into a ball that she flung across the room. 'They refused us funding, Mrs Bolton! It's their fault, it's all their fault! We don't need this stupid inquiry. We just need them to see the letter we sent, that I typed, and their reply. It's them, it's all them! They killed them, killed them all!'

She was crying openly now, unable to stop herself. The Mayor looked taken aback by her outburst. Damn her, let her see, Nellie thought, let her know the misery London Civil Defence had caused her and her family.

'Nellie, did you . . . your family . . . are they . . . ?' Realisation dawned on the Mayor's face.

Nellie could only shake her head, picturing Charlie's and Flo's lifeless bodies in the church. She remembered then how she'd shouted at Em and George that morning – her only remaining family. They should be sticking together, not being angry with each other. She sat there, the tears streaming down her face as Mrs Bolton stared at her.

The Mayor reached across her desk and grabbed a sheet of paper, a list of names, the confirmed dead, and ran her finger down it. 'Oh, my love. Your father, your sister . . . Oh Nellie, what are you doing here today? Your place is with your mother, at home.' Mrs Bolton stepped over to Nellie and laid a hand on her shoulder. 'Go on. Go home.'

Nellie stood and put on her coat, numbly. The Mayor was right. She needed to be at home now.

Chapter 27

Nellie left the town hall in a daze, descending the steps at the entrance as she had so many times before, but this time was different. This was the first time she was going home from work to a house with no Dad, no Flo. It didn't feel right. Nothing would ever be the same again.

As she headed towards home, a man approached her. 'Excuse me, do you work for the Council? I saw you leave the town hall just now.' Nellie turned to see a man aged about forty who wore a trilby, his eyes looking tired as though he'd been up all night.

'Um, yes, I do,' she replied.

'May I ask in what capacity?'

'I'm assistant to the Mayor.'

'Then you'll know something of last night's events?' There was an eagerness about him as he asked the question. Nellie shook her head slowly, worried about what to do. She didn't want to lie but the Mayor's repeated warning to not say anything to anyone was still ringing in her ears.

'Not really. I'm sorry, I must go . . .' All she wanted

was to get home to Em and George. She increased her pace, but the man kept up alongside her.

'I apologise. I never introduced myself. Stan Collins, reporter for *The Daily Mail*. I know something happened last night at the shelter, but no one will say what it was.'

'I'm sorry, Mr Collins, I cannot—' she began, but he held up a hand to interrupt.

'I have a personal interest in it, you see. My father always uses that shelter. And he's missing. He's not at home, he's not at work. No one's seen him since yesterday evening. So . . . I just want to know, in case . . .' His eyes pleaded with her to tell him something as his words tailed off.

She looked up at him as he continued, 'If he might be hurt, I need to know. But I've checked at the local hospitals, and with the police. They've said they don't have any record of him, but they're hiding something, I can tell. I don't know what, but they are . . .' He sighed. 'I've been up all night, Miss . . . ?'

'Morris. Nellie Morris.'

'Miss Morris. I'm worried. And I've met others who are looking for friends and relatives too. If there was an accident . . . don't we all need to know?' He reached out to her then, putting a soft hand on her arm.

His father, she realised, might be one of those lying in the church awaiting identification. Surely she could tell him that much, so that he could go there and find out for himself. If he'd lost his father, as she'd lost hers, then he needed to know, and sooner was better than later. She recalled the agony of the previous night, when they hadn't known for certain whether Charlie and Flo were alive or dead. That was what Mr Collins was going through now, and it was unbearable.

She stopped walking and turned to face him. 'Mr Collins, I do know something of what happened. There's to be a full investigation to get to the bottom of what caused it. For now, the Home Office are asking that we don't talk of it until . . . well, until they've decided how it should be communicated to the public.'

'Home Office? Why are they involved? Is it serious?'

She nodded. He'd know the extent of it sooner or later.

'The public have a right to know. *I* have a right to know what happened to my father.'

'Yes, you do. I lost my own father last night. And my sister.' She hadn't intended telling him, but somehow the words just slipped out.

'Oh goodness. I'm so sorry to hear that. Your father *and* your sister? My God. But how? No bombs fell, as far as I'm aware.'

She gazed at him. His eyes were sad, worried, scared. He deserved to know, no matter what Mrs Bolton had said. She took a deep breath. 'There was a crush, at the station entrance, when the air raid siren went off. A lot of people . . . passed away. There are many victims in St John's church, and it's possible . . . your father . . . might be there.'

'A crush?'

'They think perhaps people p-panicked for some

reason, going down the steps.' She was not going to tell him what might have caused the panic. 'There's to be a full inquiry.'

'How many, how many died?'

'I can't say. Listen, Mr Collins, we've been told not to talk of it. Don't put this in your paper, will you? I'll be in trouble . . .' she pleaded, worrying that she'd already said too much and would get in trouble. She desperately needed this job now that she was the only bread-winner to support Em and George.

'St John's church, you say? I must go there . . . and search for him . . .' He looked down at his feet. 'Thank you, Miss Morris. You've been very helpful and kind. I'm sorry for your losses. Good day.'

He raised his hat to her politely and walked off towards the church. Nellie watched him go with sympathy, knowing what he was about to face if his father was indeed among those in St John's. She shuddered as she recalled that horrible moment when she'd seen Flo's lifeless face, the sound of the scream that forced its way out of her, the way Em had collapsed in her arms. She hurried home, feeling exhausted and drained.

*

When she reached home, she found her mother sitting in the front room. Em barely glanced at her as she walked in, and Nellie fell to her knees in front of her, taking her mother's hands. 'Mum? I'm so sorry.'

'What for?' Em's eyes were red as she looked at Nellie.

'This morning. I shouldn't have shouted at you. We got to . . .'

'I don't know what we got to do.' Em's voice was flat, exhausted by the weight of her grief.

'Stick together. Help each other. It's all we can do.'

'The afternoon papers, they're saying it was a bomb.'

'There were no bombs, Mum. I'll make us some tea then tell you what I heard at the town hall.'

Nellie went through to the kitchen and set the kettle on to boil. Through the window she could see George, outside on the bench, with Rosie in his arms. She hoped that somehow the chickens were giving him comfort. Oscar nuzzled against her hand and gave a little whine. He too sensed something was very wrong.

She took their tea to the front room, and despite Mrs Bolton's warnings to say nothing, told Em everything she'd heard at the meeting that morning.

Hearing that the Home Office were involved, that there was to be a full inquiry to get to the cause of the tragedy, seemed to bring Em a little comfort. 'They're to make sure this don't happen again, in other shelters,' she said. 'So my Charlie and Flo ain't died in vain.'

'Yes. And they're going to make some improvements to the shelter entrance here. Think they even started on that today.' Nellie felt her chest tighten at the thought of having to go back there. She didn't know how she could handle it, especially having to walk down those steps wondering where Charlie and Flo were when it happened.

'Even so, I ain't never going down the tube again. Not after that. We'll go to the railway arches shelter, if there's another raid.' Em fell silent, frowning.

Nellie nodded. Her mum was right, they couldn't go back to the station. Not ever.

'What caused the crush, I want to know? What started it all off?' Em said, sounding bewildered.

Nellie took a deep breath. 'They're saying . . . people panicked and pushed forward.'

'But what made 'em panic? When you think of all the other times people have gone down there with no problems. I don't understand it at all,' Em said.

Nellie could only bite her lip and shake her head. She understood it all right, but knowing the truth had only brought her yet more unbearable pain. She made her way to bed, desperate for sleep to come so she could escape for a few hours at least. But as she lay down she felt the weight of Flo's absence, the room feeling so achingly empty without her in the other bed. And every time she tried to close her eyes, she thought about the fight she'd had with Ray, how awfully she'd acted but how hurt she was that he'd left her.

Chapter 28

Two days later a letter arrived for Nellie. She recognised Ray's handwriting immediately and her stomach flipped over in anticipation at what it might hold. She needed to hear from him but at the same time, dreaded what he might say. She ran upstairs with it, ripping it open before she reached her bedroom, slamming the door behind her.

Her hands were shaking as she unfolded the single sheet of paper and began reading. As she'd expected, it began by saying he was sorry they'd parted on such bad terms, but he didn't believe the backfiring could have been the sole cause of the panic. He gave his new address – an airbase somewhere in the Midlands – and asked her to write to him when she was able to. She read the last part through a haze of tears.

I miss you so much already, and I can only once more say how very sorry I am for your losses. We can never fully get over such a thing, but I hope one day the pain will begin to lessen and you will know that life will go on.

'Life go on? Without my little sister and my father, and with my family now having to survive on only my income and George's egg money? You have no idea, Ray Fleming. No idea at all.' She screwed up the letter and threw it into the corner of her room. *Pain will begin to lessen?* It was increasing if anything, eating away at her, filling every part of her. Grieving deeply but also feeling anger at Ray for his part in this, and angrier still at how unfair it all seemed. Would she ever wake up and not feel an overwhelming sense of loss? The hole in her life left by the deaths of Charlie and Flo threatened to swallow her.

She took a long breath and read the letter again, trying to work out if he wanted their relationship to continue or not. All that he'd asked of her was that she write back to him when she felt able. A part of her never wanted to see him again, for every time she looked at him she'd know what he'd done, how he'd inadvertently torn her family apart. But a larger part of her missed him so much, longed to have the weight of his reassuring arms around her, which made her feel so safe, his chest against her cheek. If she hadn't run after the bus that day, she'd never have met Ray. And Flo would still be alive. She'd once thought that a life without Ray would be intolerable. But the life she had ahead of her without Flo's sunny presence was an even crueller fate.

*

'How are you holding up?' Babs asked her. It wasn't the first time she'd asked her that. Nellie was fortunate to have her friend there these past couple of days, lending her shoulder for Nellie's constant tears. They were sitting on the bench in the backyard, while George's chickens pecked at the dirt around their feet. Ray's letter from that morning was still fresh in her mind.

Nellie shrugged. 'It's not getting any easier. Maybe . . . after the funeral . . .'

Babs hugged her. 'To think . . . we were down below with no idea. When you disappeared looking for them and didn't come back, I was worried, but thought perhaps you were all in another part of the shelter. Still can't believe so many died.'

'I know.'

'I'm going to a funeral tomorrow. A woman from my factory. I didn't know her well but I want to . . . you know. Pay my respects. She didn't have a large family.' Babs sighed. 'I can't imagine you'll want to go to any funerals other than . . .' She tailed away and regarded Nellie with sympathy.

Nellie pushed away a tear. She'd thought that after all the tears she'd shed the past few days there couldn't be any more, but there were, much more. Whenever she started to feel like she was coping, something would remind her of Flo or make her think of Ray, and then she would find herself breaking down again. She was lost and there seemed to be no way through this.

'Look, Nellie,' Babs said, 'anything I can do . . . you

know, be here for you and all that . . . you only need ask. Billy too. I know it's hard for you with Ray away as well. But lean on us, yeah? Me and Billy. As much as you need to.'

There were tears in Babs's eyes as she said this, and Nellie squeezed her hand. She considered telling her friend about Ray's car backfiring, but she couldn't bring herself to say it aloud. It was too painful. 'Thanks, Babs. I will. I appreciate it.'

Later, she found a scarf of Charlie's that still smelt of him. She tucked that away beneath her bed. And for a memento of Flo she decided that the little dog ornament she'd once given her would be perfect. She searched everywhere in her room for it to no avail. Em hadn't seen it either. 'Maybe it was in her pocket when she . . .' Em said, and gulped down a sob.

'They gave us all the things from their pockets,' Nellie replied. 'Never mind. I'll look in our— my room again.'

It was such a little thing, but she wanted that ornament. She needed it. Spotty, Flo had called it, and it was the one small thing she'd wanted to keep. It must have been lost in the crush. A picture, one of Flo's brightly coloured paintings of farmyard animals and trees, would have to do instead. Nellie took it down from the wall, folded it neatly and put it under her bed along with Charlie's scarf. It was all she had left of them – a few items, and her memories.

*

The funeral, when it came, was even more heartbreaking than she could have imagined. They held the service in a different church, St John's not seeming right after they'd found their bodies there. Despite the number of recent funerals in the community, there was a good turnout and Nellie appreciated the show of sympathy and support.

'This gentle, innocent child, taken far too soon. This loving family man,' the vicar said of them, and Nellie wanted to shout and scream at the unjustness of God. By the set of Em's pressed-together lips she thought her mother was feeling the same way. George's attention was focused on a spot somewhere above the vicar's head, staring at it as though it was the only way he could get through this ordeal. Nellie reached for his hand and squeezed it.

After the ceremony, they all went to Bow Cemetery for the burials. Em had insisted on two separate graves, with separate headstones. 'She was a person in her own right,' she'd said. 'I don't want her just bunged in with her father. She needs her own place to sleep.'

Behind Nellie, the Waters family stood, and Babs put a hand on her shoulder, lending silent support. Billy did the same to George, Nellie noted out of the corner of her eye. He was trying to say that he'd be there for George, in place of Charlie. George gave a little shrug and Billy removed his hand. An image came to her of Ray supporting George while she and Em had gone in the church to look for Charlie and Flo. They needed Ray, all three of them. But especially her. He should be beside her to help her through her grief. She shook her head sadly. That could never be. Not now.

'Sleep well, little Flo. And Dad, look after her for us,' Nellie whispered, as she threw a handful of soil into the two graves. She stumbled backwards, barely able to see through her tears. Babs caught her and held her upright, and Billy came to her other side.

'All right, Nellie, we've got you,' he whispered, and it helped, somehow, having him there. Billy, whom she'd known all her life. Gentle, steady Billy.

And then came the worst moment of all: when she had to turn her back on her beloved sister's grave, leave her there in the cold, damp earth, unable to do anything more for her ever again. It took Billy and Babs, one on each side, to half carry her away as she cried out in utter anguish.

Chapter 29

Em had insisted that friends and neighbours should come back to their house afterwards, for tea and sandwiches. 'It's what we do,' she'd said when Nellie urged her not to do it, that the strain of it would be too much for them all. 'I got to do right by my Charlie and Flo. It's what Charlie would want.' She'd been adamant so Nellie had backed down, letting her do what she wanted, prepared to help all she could.

There weren't many who came. The Waters family, a few other neighbours, a couple of men Charlie had worked with. There were other funerals on the same day, and more to come, and people were struggling to deal with their grief. The community had been torn apart by the accident.

Nellie was glad it was just a small gathering. Along with Mrs Waters and Babs she'd made little egg or meat paste sandwiches, and plates of jam tarts. It wasn't much but Em had nodded in approval.

Babs and Mrs Waters served cups of tea to everyone, insisting that Nellie, Em and George sit down in the front room and not lift a finger. Nellie would have preferred to be busy, if she couldn't be alone, but it was easier to do as she was told.

Oscar came through from the kitchen and slumped at Nellie's feet. She fondled his soft ears, thinking of how he was a symbol of yet another loss – Ruth and John. At least they'd died because of enemy action, not because of some stupid car backfiring and scaring people into rushing down the tube. The pointlessness of Charlie's and Flo's deaths, the needlessness of it – that was the hardest thing to bear, and Nellie wondered if she'd ever be able to come to terms with that.

'Terrible how things turn out,' Mrs Waters was saying to Em. 'I mean, if Flo had been evacuated like you was going to do, she'd still be with us now. Or if your Charlie had been just that bit quicker, or slower, going down the tube they'd both still be here. Awful. Our Billy says he couldn't pull none of them out, down the bottom. He ended up in the first-aid room himself, what with his asthma.'

'Shut up, Mum,' Billy said.

Nellie stared at him. 'You had an asthma attack?'

He nodded. 'Yeah. I was trying to get people out, and then . . .' It was the first time she'd known for certain he'd been there on the spot, right there at the scene. Billy shrugged. 'You know how it is.'

That shrug, that dismissive gesture, made something snap inside her. Her anger, at Billy this time, bubbled up inside. 'If you'd been there sooner, you'd have stopped it getting so bad,' she said. 'When the first people fell and got stuck. If you'd have been at the bottom of the steps you'd have seen, and you'd have been able to sort it out.'

'I was there . . . I did all I could,' Billy began.

'You were there? What, you saw it happen and did *nothing*?' She jabbed a finger at his chest, struggling to stay in control. 'You could've done more. I know you couldn't have saved them all but . . . you might have . . . saved Flo.'

Billy looked anguished. 'I'd have done anything I could to save her. Thought I'd even seen her red shoe. I was pulling and pulling at it, the shoe came away, and then I couldn't breathe no more and had to . . .'

'You saw her *shoe*? You had a hand on her *foot* and you didn't get her out?' Nellie couldn't believe what she was hearing, remembering how in the church, Flo's body had only had one shoe on. 'You failed her! You . . . *killed* her!' She was shouting, unable to hold her feelings back any longer.

Several heads turned, to see what the argument was about. Babs took a step forward. 'Ah, now, Nellie, don't upset yourself. Loads of kids had those same shoes. Might not have been Flo's foot. Don't blame Billy.'

Nellie pushed her away. 'I *do* blame him! He could have done more, I know he could have!'

Em stared at them both. 'Could he? Our Flo would still be here if you'd left her on the bus that day, Nellie. You ran after it and got her off, and now she's dead. I dunno if I can ever . . .'

'You're the one who wanted her off it! You cried and screamed and made me run after the bus! She'd still be alive if you hadn't, so maybe it's *your* fault!' Nellie knew it was wrong to scream at her mother like this, but she couldn't help it. Em was blaming her. She'd known it would happen sooner or later and God only knew she didn't need Em to make her feel guilty – she'd already done that to herself. She'd replayed that day so many times. If only she'd let the bus go on. They'd have got used to Flo's absence after a few weeks, and now . . . she'd be alive. Maybe even Charlie would be alive too.

Babs took hold of Nellie's arms and tried to steady her. 'Ssh, now. This isn't the time or the place . . .'

'What, on the day of her funeral, in her home? When and where else? *He* could have done more to save people. *She* should have let Flo stay on the bus.' Nellie pointed to Billy and Em. The rage inside her boiled over as she turned to George. 'And you, George. If you hadn't been arguing with Dad when we were on our way out, he wouldn't have been delayed, they'd have been with us, and they'd be alive now.' She threw her hands in the air. 'We're all to bloody well blame, aren't we? All of us. *All of us!*' She screeched out the last words.

George was crying now. 'I know, Nellie, and I keep wishing I'd done things differently that day.'

Babs put an arm around him. 'George, stop. It's not your fault. Nellie, you're wrong. You're not all to blame. None of you is to blame, you hear me? It's a horrible accident, but it ain't no one's fault. No one here, anyway.

You can't go blaming yourselves and each other. We got to stick together, all of us, to get through this.'

'She's right,' Billy said to Nellie. 'Please, let me do whatever I can to . . . comfort you.'

His expression was anguished. Flo had been like a little sister to him, and she guessed that like her, he'd been blaming himself to some extent, bemoaning the fates that had landed him with severe asthma and given him an asthma attack at that crucial moment. Perhaps she'd been wrong to blame him so quickly. But she wasn't ready to apologise. She still couldn't make sense of what was happening let alone know how she was supposed to try to come to terms with it.

Nellie ran out of the kitchen. She needed to be away from other people now, to let her anger simmer down. She leaned against the table and tilted her head back, trying to relieve some of the tension in her neck. It had been wrong of her to explode like that, in front of everybody, but she hadn't been able to help herself. She stayed there, thankful that no one had followed her out, waiting for everyone to go away and leave her alone with her grief.

Chapter 30

It had been a week since the accident had occurred and Nellie was back at work. Every moment of every day she'd been thinking about her dad, and Flo, and also Ray. Despite everything, despite his part in it all, she was missing him immensely.

Most of her day was spent answering correspondence that had been sent to the Mayor asking about the tragedy. Mrs Bolton had prepared a standard response that sympathised with their losses but pleaded with people to await the outcome of the official inquiry, which was due to start very soon. And there was preparation to be done for the inquiry itself.

'I feel dreadful,' Mrs Bolton said, as Nellie sat down to type up a pile of letters relating to the tragedy, 'that everything I'm asking you to do must be serving as a reminder . . . but I'm afraid that's all the work there is at present.'

'It's . . . all right, Mrs Bolton,' Nellie insisted, wanting to carry on as normal. 'In some ways it's better – I feel I am doing something towards finding out the truth of what happened and stopping it happening again. It's all I can do for Dad and Flo.' Her voice cracked on the last words and the Mayor looked at her with sympathy.

'Well, if it ever feels like too much, please tell me. But I am glad you are back here to help. It's not been an easy time.'

Nellie glanced up at the Mayor, and noticed Mrs Bolton seemed to have aged in the last week. There were lines around her mouth and bags beneath her eyes.

'Yes. I should have . . . fought harder for that funding.' Mrs Bolton left the room abruptly, but Nellie had noticed the catch in her voice.

As soon as the Mayor had left the office there was a tap on the door, and Gladys poked her head around. 'Nellie, you're back. I heard what happened. I'm so, so sorry.'

The sympathy in her friend's voice triggered tears in Nellie's eyes once more, and she gulped back a sob.

'Oh God, I've set you off. Listen, I'll fetch us some tea. I'm sure Mrs B won't mind if I sit in here with you for a few moments, eh?' Gladys didn't wait for an answer but ducked out, and came back shortly after with a warm drink, a shoulder to cry on and a sympathetic ear. It was good, Nellie discovered, to talk to someone who hadn't known Charlie and Flo and sharing it somehow just helped her feel a tiny bit better.

*

Nellie got through the day, and despite feeling exhausted from grief and the pretence that she was managing, she was cheered up when she noticed it was still bright outside as she walked home. The days were getting longer, spring was around the corner and soon the trees would be in leaf and the flowers blooming in the parks. New life would be everywhere. It had been Flo's favourite time of year. Nellie let out a pained moan as she thought how unfair it was that Flo would never again experience the joys of spring.

Flo might have been in Dorset again, now, where she'd first fallen in love with the countryside and farm animals. Nellie was beginning to believe she would never be able to live with herself for taking her off that bus. Despite the bright sunshine, her world felt darker than ever.

Chapter 31

Em gave her a weak smile as Nellie entered the house and went through to the kitchen. 'Manage all right at work, did you, lovey?'

'Yes, Mum. It was . . . hard but okay.'

Em nodded, but didn't look at Nellie. She was busy preparing a meal, Nellie noticed. That was good. Since the tragedy they'd relied on food brought to them by Mrs Waters and other neighbours. It was good to see Em had been shopping and was now cooking again, even though every time she set the table for three instead of five, it was a painful reminder of their losses. 'George outside?' she asked.

'No, he's off selling eggs. We . . . don't need so many ourselves now,' Em replied. She rubbed at her eyes with the back of her hand and then patted Nellie's shoulder.

Nellie headed out to the yard to use the lav. Oscar attempted to follow her but she shooed him back inside. George didn't like him to be out there if his chickens were out of their coop.

She did her business and was heading back inside

when Babs came out of her back door. 'Glad I caught you, Nell. Don't know if you heard but Amelia arrived home today. She's moved back into her old digs above the pub. Wondered if you wanted to call round to see her? If you're . . . up to it? She had a little boy, you know.'

Nellie smiled. 'Yes, she wrote to say. Good news that she's back. When are you going round?'

'Me and Billy thought we'd go this evening. Billy's got a little rattle for the baby, and I got a bag of oranges for Amelia.'

'All right, I'll come with you. She'll have heard . . . the news already I suppose.'

'Can't see how she'd be able to avoid it for more than about five minutes now she's back at the pub,' Babs said, grimly. 'Seven o'clock good for you?'

'Yes. I'll meet you out front.'

Nellie went in then, to help Em prepare the rest of the meal: boiled potatoes and a tin of corned beef, followed by tinned peaches. George arrived back in time to eat it but was uncharacteristically quiet after his first day at school since the tragedy.

'Amelia's back,' Nellie announced as she helped clear the dishes after tea. 'Babs, Billy and I are going to see her this evening. If you don't need me here, Mum, of course?'

'No, that's all right, you go and see your friend. Be good for you to get out of the house. Here, let me send her something.' Em got up from the table and went upstairs. She was back a minute later with a set of white knitted bootees. 'These was Flo's. I made them for her just after she was born. They'll be just right for Amelia's baby while the weather's still so cold.'

'You sure you want to give them away?' Nellie asked, and Em nodded, but she couldn't hide the glint of tears in her eyes.

Nellie nodded and took the bootees, knowing that in passing them on she was doing a small, good thing. The feeling was like a tiny speck of light after the darkness of the last few days. Perhaps this was how you coped, how you moved on with life after such tragedy. You just kept going, and looked for little ways to make things better, if not for yourself then for other people. One tiny step at a time.

*

Nellie hadn't set eyes on Billy since she'd shouted at him during the wake. Remembering this, she blushed. She'd need to apologise. Whether or not he'd done his best, it wasn't his fault that people had panicked and now that the red mist of her anger had faded, she regretted what she'd said.

It wasn't the only regret that had been playing on Nellie's mind. She still hadn't written back to Ray. She missed him but she couldn't contact him, not yet. She couldn't imagine what she would say. Not while her pain was still so raw.

Outside, only Babs was waiting for her. 'Let's be off,' she said, taking Nellie's arm.

'What about Billy?'

'Oh, he's . . . not coming. Got things to do, he said.' Babs couldn't meet Nellie's eye. She felt sad that her old, easy-going relationship with Billy had taken such a knock. Yet another loss in her life.

They walked quickly to the Angel and Crown, with Babs chatting nonstop about friends from her factory, people who'd been nowhere near Bethnal Green tube station that awful night, and for whom life was continuing as always. Nellie was grateful for the distraction. They reached the door beside the pub, which led to the flat above it, and rang the bell.

'Think she'll go back to working behind the bar?' Babs asked.

'Maybe, when the baby's a bit older.'

'We can have more sing-songs in the pub then. With her playing piano and you singing.'

But Nellie shook her head. 'I don't feel like I'll ever—'

Amelia answered the door before she finished speaking, and Nellie forced herself to smile brightly. She *was* pleased to see her friend again, and Amelia looked well – her plump cheeks suggested she'd been well looked after in the country.

'Nellie! Barbara! Lovely to see you both! Come on in, 'scuse the mess! God, it's good to be back!' Amelia hugged each of them and led the way up the stairs into the flat. 'We can use the sitting room. Tom, the landlord, is down in the pub.'

She put the kettle on, then went through to her bedroom

while Nellie and Babs took seats on a well-worn sofa. A moment later she returned, carrying a small, squirming bundle. 'Meet William Walter. Isn't he lovely?'

'Oh, he's named after Billy and his father!' Babs squealed, as she took the baby from Amelia and smiled at him.

'Yes, I thought Walter was . . . well, a bit too old-fashioned a name, so I used it as his middle name. I like the name William, and your Billy's always been so good to me. Kind and thoughtful, like. He was passing as I got off the bus today and carried my bags all the way from the bus stop and up the stairs. You're lucky to have him as a brother.'

'He's a good man,' Babs agreed, and Nellie nodded.

'There's some people . . .' Amelia said, 'that've . . . you know . . . sneered at me. For having a baby and not being wed. *No better than she ought to be,* one of 'em said, as I came up the street. But your Billy, he turned and gave her what for, told her it ain't no business of anyone else's, and it weren't my fault Walter was killed, and she was to leave off saying such things. He's nice, your Billy. Used to think he was sweet on you, Nellie. Then you met your Ray.'

Nellie gave her a small smile, and nodded, not wanting to tell her about Ray going away.

'So, what's been happening?' Amelia looked from one to the other of the girls. 'Everyone seems a bit . . . down, like. Tom said some people died? Big air raid, was it? I saw a house on Roman Road had copped it. Hope no one there was hurt. And looks like a few up near Vicky Park gone too, I saw that from the bus. There's a street almost entirely flattened there!' She sighed. 'You start to wonder how it'll ever be rebuilt, don't you? This poor community's had it bad. Hope none of this affected either of you two at all?'

Nellie glanced at Babs, who gave a slight nod, then took a deep breath. 'There was . . . an accident. Not a bomb. At the tube station entrance. Lots of people, all trying to get down at once . . . and yeah, you're right, people died.' God, it was so hard to talk about it to someone who didn't know.

'Fell? Broke their necks?'

'Crushed. Lots of them. And . . .' Nellie looked at Babs to help her out. She couldn't form the words.

'Amelia, Nellie's dad and little sister were killed in it too.'

Amelia clapped a hand to her mouth. 'Oh God. I'm so sorry. And there was me prattling on. Nell, that's just . . . awful. How must you . . . how can you . . .'

'We just got to keep going, ain't we? Nothing else we can do. Here, let me hold the baby now?' Nellie reached out to take him from Babs. Anything to change the subject. Anything to take her mind off it all because whenever she had to talk about it, she felt herself breaking down.

'Here's me feeling sorry for myself losing Walter, and then you . . .' Amelia went on, shaking her head. 'It don't bear thinking about.'

'No. It doesn't.' All Nellie could do was agree. 'After

Walter . . . after you got that telegram, Amelia, how did you manage? How on earth did you keep on going?'

Amelia looked at her silently for a moment as though working out how best to answer. 'It's hard.' She shrugged. 'Go easy on yourself, Nellie. Give in to the tears every now and again. For me, I had my little one to think about, and that helped.' Her tone softened. 'And lean on your friends, as much as you need to. We're all here for you.'

'I keep telling her that,' Babs seconded, patting Nellie's arm.

'Thank you,' Nellie whispered. She dipped her head towards little William to hide her face, to block the tears that threatened to fall yet again, and breathed in his soft milky scent. He was a reminder that throughout all the horror of war, there was still joy in the world, new life, hope for the future. She prayed silently that this child and all others of his generation would know only peace throughout their lives but she'd lived with the country at war for so long, it seemed like it never would end.

*

They were on the point of leaving when that hated noise sounded, the air raid siren winding its way up to full volume.

'Oh God, not today! I can't believe it,' Amelia said, gathering a few things into a bag and hoisting little William over her shoulder. 'You all going down the tube?'

Nellie felt a wave of sickness rise up in her at the

thought of them, of anyone, going down the tube. She shook her head as she quickly pulled on her coat. 'I . . . I . . . can't go . . . not there,' she stuttered, struggling to voice the words. 'Mum, George and I, we're going to shelter in the railway arches instead.'

'Really?' Babs looked dismayed. They hurried down the stairs of Amelia's flat. 'It's not so safe. Jerry targets the railways, and it wouldn't survive a direct hit.'

'We can't go down the tube,' Nellie said, trembling. 'Not after . . .'

'I'm sorry, of course not . . .' Babs put a comforting hand on Nellie's shoulder. 'I got to go there though. Mum, Dad and Billy will wonder where I am otherwise. Amelia?'

Amelia looked torn as to which of them to go with. Eventually she turned to Babs. 'Tube's closest. I'll come with you. Nell, are you going to be okay? You don't look right.'

Nellie gave them a reassuring nod, waved them good-bye and hurried off in the opposite direction to the railway arches, hoping George and Em would already be there. They had to stick together. After the last air raid she was terrified about what could happen tonight, especially being above ground, but she knew she would never again be able to bring herself to walk down those nineteen steps.

Chapter 32

The official inquiry into what had caused the disaster was opened just over a week after the tragedy. Mrs Bolton quietly told Nellie she understood that it would be too much for her to handle being present, taking notes. She would ask Gladys to fill in for her.

'No, I can do it, Mrs Bolton,' Nellie insisted. It had been torture going over it so many nights when she couldn't sleep, not knowing exactly what had happened. She needed answers. Anything to try to help her come to terms with it all. Hearing the truth from this inquiry would be a start.

'If you're absolutely sure . . . I warn you, the testimonies of witnesses might be somewhat harrowing,' the Mayor said, 'but I want us at the town hall to have our own record of what is said, not just the official Home Office report.' She looked haggard, Nellie thought, as though she hadn't slept since the night of the tragedy. She'd lost no one close to her, that Nellie knew of, but her husband as chief air raid warden had been closely involved, and of course as Bethnal Green Mayor she was ultimately responsible for the district.

'I will manage,' Nellie said. If she said it enough times maybe she'd convince herself. But the truth was, she had no idea how she'd be able to get through it. She'd tell herself it was just a story, not real, nothing connected with her. She'd listen to the words spoken but not think about the meaning behind them. And she would do her best to only let the tears fall when she was at home. Not here.

'I don't know how you can bear to do it,' Gladys said, when Nellie told her she was going to sit in on the inquiry.

'Because I have to,' Nellie replied, feeling the weight of responsibility heavy on her shoulders. She couldn't appear weak or incapable in Mrs Bolton's eyes. Surely this wouldn't be the only time the tragedy would be a part of their work. She had to show the Mayor she was strong enough to put her personal loss aside. She was the only bread-winner in the family now, and she couldn't do anything to jeopardise her position. Em was worrying enough as it was about how they'd get by with only her wage to support the three of them.

*

The mood was sombre at the town hall, as the inquiry got underway. Only those specifically involved were allowed in. No press, no members of the public other than those who were to give testimonies, no town hall staff other than Mrs Bolton, Nellie and a couple of other councillors. Mr Ian Macdonald Ross from the Home Office was there once more, as was Sir Ernest Gowers from London Civil

Defence. The civil servant Mr Laurence Dunne was taking notes as copious as Nellie's and had been commissioned to write the official report. Nellie's minutes were for town hall records only.

'We need to establish a record of precisely what happened, of what were the probable causes, as witnessed by those who were actually there,' Mrs Bolton said, setting out what they were trying to achieve. Everyone around the table nodded, but Nellie noticed an odd glance pass between the Home Office aide and Sir Ernest.

In her mind it was crystal clear that London Civil Defence needed to shoulder some of the blame. They'd turned down requests from Bethnal Green Council for funds to improve the entrance. If they hadn't and the work had been done, then whether or not there'd been panic caused by backfiring cars or anything else, perhaps no one would have died.

'I have,' said Macdonald Ross, 'prepared a briefing statement to get us started.' He flourished copies of a type-written paper, stapled together. These were then handed around the room with each official taking a copy. Nellie, sitting in the corner, away from the conference table, did not get one. She longed to read it, to see if it could begin to provide the answers she craved.

There were a few grunts and nods around the table as people read the statement.

Macdonald Ross cleared his throat. 'And now, if we're all ready, we will start with the witness testimonies. We will hear from the police, air raid wardens, doctors and other emergency workers, and from some of the survivors. We will find out how events unfolded, minute by minute, starting from when the air raid siren sounded on that terrible night. We will discover if there is blame to be laid at the door of any organisation, if anyone was negligent of their duties during the course of the accident, or if there was anything that might have been done to prevent it. But I must impress on you all, as at our last meeting, that what is said in this room must, for now, go no further. There are several reasons for this. Firstly, we do not want to alarm people and stop them using the tube station as a shelter in future air raids. Despite what happened, it is still the safest place to be. Secondly, if the enemy found out about this, they might use it as propaganda, saying that the people of London are so scared of raids they stampede to their deaths – that sort of thing. We cannot risk that happening. Morale must be maintained at all costs.'

He took a moment to gaze at everyone in the room, waiting for each to catch his eye and nod. Even Nellie had to nod to say she agreed. There were so many rumours flying around about it already. Survivors had of course spoken about what they'd experienced. No one knew the cause, but it had sent shockwaves through their close-knit community. So many families had lost someone that night. In many cases, like her own, several members of a family had died. And those who'd been lucky had still lost friends and neighbours. The truth of it all needed to be told. It would bring no one back but the people were owed that at least.

With the preliminaries over, it was time to call the first witness. Nellie took a deep breath and steeled herself for what she was about to hear. An image of Ray flashed through her mind. It would all be so much easier to bear if Ray hadn't been involved in all this, if he was still stationed nearby and able to support her through it. But, she told herself sternly, he had been involved, and he was now stationed far away. She needed to know the extent to which his car had caused the panic, and then see if she could ever feel the same for him as she had.

Chapter 33

The first witness to testify was Police Inspector Albert Ferguson, who'd been on duty that night. His account began at the moment when a telephone call had come through, from the chief air raid warden in the tube station, requesting that the police come to the shelter. Shortly after, a boy had come running with a similar message. 'Mr Percy Bolton, who I know well from our dealings throughout the war, told me to send every man available. I put the call out and assembled the men into two teams. One team I sent to the main entrance on the corner, and the other team, at the request of Mr Bolton, I sent to the maintenance entrance. From there they accessed the platform below and then went up to the ticket hall to work on removing people from the bottom of the steps.' He spoke calmly, in a matter-of-fact tone, as if he was reporting an everyday occurrence. Only the tension in his jaw and a vein throbbing in his temple showed the stress he was under.

Nellie noted everything down. The Inspector was asked a few questions confirming the exact time the air raid siren had gone off, the time that he'd received the telephone call, and for how long his men had worked on removing bodies.

'It took about three hours to get everybody out,' he replied, pulling a handkerchief out of his pocket to mop his brow. 'Some of them living, many of them dead. Of course we had to clear them all from the steps and then off the road as soon as possible.' His voice dropped to almost a whisper. 'No one needed to see them all, lying there in the road.'

Nellie swallowed. She and George had seen that. They would never forget it. An image of those lifeless bodies flashed through her mind and she had to fight not to break down sobbing. *Detachment, Nellie, that's what you need,* she told herself. If the Inspector could stay calm as he recounted the events then so could she, as she wrote down what he said.

Dr Joan Martin from a nearby hospital testified next. 'A telephone call came through telling us to expect around thirty "faints",' she said. 'I first thought it was a training exercise, I'll admit. We're a children's hospital, so we had to first of all take down cots and put up beds, and everybody leapt to it to prove we could do it quickly.' She took a deep breath. 'And then they started arriving, and we realised quickly they were all dead. They were blue, and they were wet. I learnt later that the emergency services had poured water on their faces in an attempt to revive them. We had no idea what had caused their deaths. No idea at all. There were far more than we had space for, and the ambulance crews wanted their stretchers and blankets back, so we had to just roll some of the bodies off onto the floor in consulting rooms.'

'Were there any live casualties brought to you at all?' one of the councillors asked in a hopeful tone. Everyone wanted to hear a little bit of good news, learn that someone had been saved, Nellie thought.

'Some, yes. All in terrible shock. A boy of nine years – he was the one who told us what had happened. He had a broken arm and was bruised from his chest down, and he told us how he'd been stuck for a bit then managed to climb up on top of everybody else and was pulled out from there.' Dr Martin looked around at everyone in the room. 'He will make a full recovery. It seemed – either people died, probably very quickly, from asphyxiation, or if they survived they were almost entirely unharmed. That boy's broken arm was one of the worst injuries we had to deal with that night. And those who'd died – many of them weren't injured at all. No blood, no fractures, nothing other than their colour being wrong.'

There was absolute silence in the room as she spoke. Only the scratch of Nellie's pencil, and that of Mr Dunne, could be heard. Nellie was concentrating hard on writing her notes yet at the same time trying to block out the most gruesome details. What she'd seen that night had haunted her dreams ever since and she couldn't bear for them to get any worse.

'The cause of death,' the doctor explained, 'was in almost all cases due to compressive asphyxia. This is when external compression – in this case from other bodies pressing upon the victims – prevents the lungs from expanding. Victims are unable to struggle or shout. Unconsciousness and then death occur very quickly in these cases, unfortunately.'

Nellie looked up at the doctor as she said that last word. *Unfortunately.* If ever there was an understatement . . . She wanted to jump from her chair and slap the doctor, to shout at her and tell her it was far, far worse than merely *unfortunate*. Her job was to record verbatim all that was being said, but she couldn't diminish the agony of Charlie's and Flo's deaths by using that weak term. She replaced it with the word 'tragically'. That was better. She exhaled deeply then looked back up.

Other medical staff were called as witnesses. And several policemen and ambulance crew who'd pulled out victims and taken them to hospitals or into the church. On and on it went, and Nellie took shorthand notes of every single detail they related.

She was exhausted by the end of the day, and they'd barely started on the testimonies. 'I expect it'll take at least a week,' Mrs Bolton said, as they gathered their things after the meeting.

Nellie nodded mutely, doing her best to stay composed but now, away from the meeting room, she couldn't stop the tears from falling.

The Mayor put a hand on her shoulder. 'Go home, get some rest. You've done well today.'

At that moment, Nellie longed to be held by Ray, to be

comforted by him as she cried, releasing the tensions of the day. Realising that was not a possibility made Nellie feel more alone than ever.

*

The next day was no easier, as a policeman named Thomas Penn gave his evidence. 'I was off duty,' he said, 'and was on my way to the shelter with my wife who's pregnant, and our little boy. We got to the entrance and couldn't get in. There were people everywhere, wondering what was going on, wondering why no one was going down, shouting at them to get a move on.'

'Panicking, in other words?' Mr Macdonald Ross put in.

Thomas Penn shook his head emphatically. 'No, sir. Not panicking. They were calm, just confused. They couldn't understand why people weren't going down the steps. Neither could I. There was an American, an airman. I dunno what he was doing in Bethnal Green but I pulled him out of the crush.'

Nellie paused in her note-taking for a moment, realising that Thomas Penn must be talking about Ray. She stared at him, wondering whether Ray himself had been asked to testify. She caught the Mayor's eye, and received a stern glance and a nod at her notebook. She realised the policeman was still talking and quickly returned to scribbling down notes.

'. . . and then with the airman's help I climbed on top

of the pile of . . . people and went over them down below
to see what was what. They were stuck fast. It's . . . hard
to describe but that's how it was. That American fellow
and I, we pulled out some children that were passed up
by some who were caught by their legs but able to move
their arms and breathe. I went down a few times, before
the uniformed police arrived and they took over then.
Me and the American stayed to help however we could,
dispersing crowds, carrying . . . victims into the church
and that. I sent the wife home with our boy. Didn't want
them to see the bodies.'

'But you witnessed no panic at the start?' Mrs Bolton
asked.

'No, not when I got there. There was those new rockets
being fired from Victoria Park. Made a strange whooshing
noise, that startled some. We're used to the ack-ack guns,
and the sound of bombs dropping, but this was different.
A few people thought it was some new weapon of Hitler's,
but they were just saying it to each other, they weren't,
like, running and screaming and whatnot.'

'Hmm.' Macdonald Ross glanced at Sir Ernest Gowers,
and then hastily scribbled further notes. Nellie thought
something seemed off about the whole thing. But then it
dawned on her that if there hadn't been any panic, then
that meant Ray's backfiring car did not contribute to the
accident either. She was confused. He'd been sure it was
all his fault and now she was hearing it couldn't have
been. What was the truth of it?

She became hot and flustered remembering how she'd

shouted at him, blamed him for the tragedy. And they'd parted on such bad terms. She pulled out a handkerchief and dabbed at her face. Not only was it not Ray's fault, he'd worked tirelessly to save whoever he could, despite having been caught in the crush himself for a while. She'd wronged him by blaming him. She felt bitterly ashamed when she recalled her behaviour toward him, it was unforgivable. And now he was far away, and she had no idea when she'd see him again to tell him she was sorry, to make it up to him however she could. She imagined him lying sleepless in his bunk, thinking about her, wondering if he'd ever hear from her, blaming himself for the deaths of so many people. The thought was almost more than she could bear, and she let out a little gasp.

Mrs Bolton looked at Nellie, frowning, then glanced at her watch. 'Perhaps it's time for a quick tea break, everyone. Reconvene in fifteen minutes?'

There were murmurs of assent and then chairs were pushed back and everyone left the room, except for Nellie and Mrs Bolton. 'Are you all right, Nellie?' the Mayor asked.

Nellie nodded. 'Yes, thank you. I'm sorry. I was just . . . picturing the scene.'

Mrs Bolton nodded and patted her arm kindly. 'I know, me too. It's terribly hard. But this is an important job, and the best way we can honour those who died is to get to the truth.'

'And make sure the public knows the truth? They deserve as much.'

'As soon as we are permitted to, yes. Come on, let's get some tea before everyone else comes back in.'

*

Refreshed by the tea, Nellie took her seat again to listen to the rest of Thomas Penn's testimony. He'd ended up with a minor injury to his shoulder that had stopped him being able to pull out any more people.

'We must be particularly gentle with this next witness, one of the survivors,' Mrs Bolton warned the meeting after Penn had left. 'He is just a child. But we do need to hear the story from a variety of angles.' She went to the door to call the boy in, along with his aunt. The aunt sat in the witness's chair while the boy, aged thirteen, stood behind her, a hand on her shoulder.

'Peter, is it?' Macdonald Ross asked, and the boy nodded. 'Please tell us in your own words what happened on the night of third March.'

The boy's eyes darted around the room. He wiped his brow with the back of his hand. Then his aunt patted his arm, and with a nervous voice, he began. 'I was going down when it started. There was a woman who'd fallen, she was holding a child. They went down, an old man went down too, and the people were coming down so fast they all fell over them and on top of them and then no one could move. I was shouting for help but I was stuck.'

'And where were you, exactly?'

''Bout the third step up, on the right-hand side. My

aunt, who I live with since me ma died, was behind me. We was stuck against the wall, and everyone was shouting. There was a warden at the bottom shining a torch at us, and I saw him get a baby out, and then there was more helpers at the bottom all pulling and tugging at everyone. Then I was pulled by my hair. That hurt but I thought it was better'n dying, so I let them do it and I shifted a bit, and then the warden got me under the arms and pulled more and out I popped.'

Nellie stared at the boy. A warden had pulled out a baby and then this boy, Peter. But not Flo. It was so unfair. It was a struggle for her to push the images out of her mind and concentrate again on her note-taking.

'And what happened then?' she heard the Mayor ask.

'Well, I didn't want to leave my aunt,' Peter patted his aunt's shoulder, 'but they said they'd get her out and I needed to go down to the bunks out of the way. And they said I wasn't to say a word to anyone. 'Cos they didn't want people coming up and getting in the way, see. 'Cos no one what was already down there could get out, while it was all going on. So I went down to the bunks, and then later on me aunt came down too, and she was all tattered and bruised. And we didn't say nothing to no one that whole night.'

It should have been Flo, Nellie thought, hauled out and sent down to the platforms. Should have been her darling little sister who was saved.

Macdonald Ross thanked the boy and then turned to his aunt. 'Mrs Hall, perhaps you can give your story now?'

The woman gulped and nodded.

'Well, it was like Peter said, weren't it? We was stuck fast, and then he got out. And then as they pulled out the people they could reach, the others – what were already dead I suppose, even though they was still standing upright, held up by others around them – they just fell and got wedged in even tighter, and I was still stuck for some time. Ripped my coat, sleeve come right off as they pulled me out, and then I went down and like Peter said, we didn't say nothing all night, like we was told.' She folded her arms as though to signify that was all she was going to say on the matter.

'And was there panic?' Macdonald Ross asked, nonetheless.

'Only when we knew we was stuck. Those of us still breathing were panicking then, like, 'cos we could see them all dying around us, their heads falling back and such. But there weren't no panic as we went down the steps. Everyone was just going quickly like they always do, no one was pushing.' She shook her head. 'That poor woman that fell, that's what started it all, and everyone tripped over her. Not that I'm saying it was her fault. Steps were wet, and it's so dark down there.' She jutted out her chin. 'I ain't never going down there no more, that's for certain, and neither's my Peter.'

'We go to the railway arches now,' Peter added, and Nellie looked up, recognising him now from the last air raid.

'Very wise,' Mrs Bolton said. 'You've been most helpful,

Mrs Hall and Peter. Please make sure you get a cup of tea before you leave. I'll ask Gladys to make you one.' She showed them out of the room.

The room was silent as everyone processed the harrowing testimonies they'd heard. Nellie added a few lines to her notes, trying to tell herself it was just a story, it wasn't real. But Flo's little face flashed before her. Why couldn't she have been pulled out, like that boy Peter was? Why not Flo? Billy had said something about a red shoe . . . why had he not managed to save her? Her vision blurred as tears pooled once again.

The Mayor returned to the room looking grey and drawn, and announced that they'd done enough for the day. 'We'll resume after the weekend. Thank you, everyone.'

There was a collective sigh of relief as people gathered up their papers and left the room, still without a word to one another. Nellie was glad to be leaving the stuffy room and longed to get home to be by herself, to think about what she'd heard. There'd been no panic. Ray wasn't to blame for the accident. It wasn't his fault, and yet she'd screamed at him that he'd killed Charlie and Flo.

Chapter 34

On Saturday morning, Nellie sat at the kitchen table with her paper and pen, trying to find the right words to say to Ray.

Dearest Ray,

Thank you for your letter. I am glad you have safely arrived at your new airbase but I wish so much that you were still nearby and we could meet. It seems such a long time since we were together. There is so much I need to say to you that is hard to put in a letter but I suppose I have no choice at present.

At work I am involved in taking notes at the inquiry into the incident. It is not an easy job but I am glad to have the chance to hear the truth of it all.

Ray, it's becoming clear that panic was not to blame for the tragedy at the tube station shelter. Therefore your motorcar backfiring was not the cause of it. None of what happened is your fault and you must not blame yourself for it. I am more sorry than I can say that I shouted at you and blamed you for Dad's and Flo's deaths. It was so soon after the accident, and I was distraught, lashing out at everyone around me. I'm ashamed for how I behaved, accusing you and pushing you away when I needed you more than ever. We have all been blaming each other here – wishing we'd left Flo on that bus, for then she at least would still be alive (but I would never have met you then and I would never want to live in a world in which we hadn't), wishing we'd all been a little bit quicker or a little bit slower going to the shelter that evening. But no matter what we wish, there is no going back to undo it all. You, along with so many others who worked tirelessly to rescue people, are a hero.

I love you, Ray, and I miss you so much. Please, please, accept my apologies and stop blaming yourself if you still are. <u>Please forgive me.</u> I behaved horribly towards you but I can't bear to think of losing you. Please write back and let me know when your next leave is. I long to see you again, to be held by you, to kiss you. Stay well, stay safe.

With all my love, Nellie

Her hands were shaking as she put the letter in an envelope, addressed it and attached a stamp. Her whole future rested on this letter and how Ray received it. She could only pray that despite behaving so badly towards him, Ray would find it in his heart to forgive her and give her the second chance she desperately wanted. She ran downstairs and grabbed her coat from the peg by the door. 'Just off to the postbox,' she called to Em, as she hurried out. She needed to post the letter immediately.

The sooner it reached him the sooner Ray would know the truth and stop blaming himself.

'Gosh, you're in a rush!' Babs was on her way out too.

'Posting a letter,' Nellie told her. 'To Ray. I just really need to hear from him. I miss him.'

'He'll write back as soon as he gets your letter, you'll see. And he'll get leave and be back here as soon as he can.' Babs looked thoughtful for a moment. 'You're not the only one who's been down in the dumps. Our Billy has been depressed lately, because of the accident but also the argument you two had at the funeral.'

Nellie didn't answer. Billy had pulled at Flo's shoe. He might have been able to save her, if it hadn't been for his asthma.

'I–I . . .' Nellie began, but Babs interrupted her.

'You should find a way to make up with Billy. You've been friends all your lives and you adore each other. It's no good to be falling out at a time like this.'

Nellie didn't know how to answer her friend, but Babs was right. Life wasn't the same without Billy. She missed their jokes – he always knew how to put a smile on her face.

'Anyway, he's giving his evidence at the hearing next week. You'll hear everything then, and I hope it helps you forgive him. Come on, post that letter and you'll feel better. Then let's go and see Amelia and her baby, shall we? I quite fancy pushing a pram around the park this fine day.'

Nellie nodded, dropped the letter into the post box

and continued on to Amelia's with Babs. Yes, an hour or so with friends and a newborn baby would help put things into perspective. Anything to take her mind off everything.

Chapter 35

Mrs Bolton spoke clearly and precisely, stating the facts, listing the dates she'd sent letters to Civil Defence, and reading sections of the engineer Mr Smith's report. There was silence in the room as she spoke, and nods and grunts around the table.

But Nellie had the impression that Macdonald Ross was just going through the motions of including her testimony, waiting politely for her to finish.

Mrs Bolton was followed by Sir Ernest Gowers. He acknowledged receipt of the Mayor's requests.

'Was funding withheld?' Macdonald Ross asked, fixing him with a stare.

Sir Ernest held his gaze. 'In our judgement, the proposed amendments to the entrance would have made no difference whatsoever. It would have been money wasted, that could better be spent elsewhere. No amount of gates and hoardings and whatever else they asked for would have made the blind bit of difference to a panicking, surging crowd. The bottleneck at Bethnal Green has always been the escalators, and in stationing several air raid wardens at the top of the escalators Civil Defence has been doing all it could throughout the war.'

'Quite so,' Macdonald Ross said, with a nod, though others in the room – the Mayor and other councillors – let out audible gasps.

Nellie noted those words with gritted teeth. She stared at Mrs Bolton, expecting her to say something, to defend the Council, to force Civil Defence to shoulder at least part of the responsibility. But the Mayor sat tight-lipped, and when Nellie caught her eye she gave a small shake of her head as if to say, *Not here, not now.*

It was becoming clear that Civil Defence would not take any of the blame. They were, of course, part of the Home Office. If it became public knowledge that their refusal to fund improvements had led to 173 deaths then Herbert Morrison's job as Home Secretary was surely at risk. He'd have to resign. It'd be a national scandal.

They were trying to cover it up. They were trying to blame the people for panicking, the Council for not maintaining the shelter – anything rather than blame the government. Nellie could see it all clearly now, and still there were dozens more witness testimonies to hear. She clenched her jaw, furious at the apparent dishonesty of the inquiry. But it was for the Mayor, not Nellie, to speak up, to object to it, if the official report turned out not to be accurate. All Nellie could do was take an honest set of minutes for the Council to use.

***

That afternoon, Billy entered the conference room hesitantly, holding his air raid warden's helmet in his hands, twisting it nervously. He'd never liked speaking in front of lots of people. And what he had to talk about today was not going to be easy. Reliving that awful evening, talking about those events aloud, was likely to be almost as hard as going through it all the first time. He'd barely slept since that evening. He'd had flashbacks, he'd woken from nightmares drenched in sweat, he'd broken out into fits of shaking at all times of the day. He'd been trying to forget, to put it out of his mind, to tell himself that no matter what Nellie had said after the funeral, he knew that he could not have saved Flo, that he could not have done any more than he did. It wasn't his fault he had asthma. It wasn't his fault those people had died in the crush.

But Nellie's words still rang in his ears. *You could have done more. You might have saved Flo.* And the memory of that small red shoe, which he'd had in his grasp, tormented him endlessly. They hadn't spoken since the funeral. He missed her so much.

He took the seat that was pointed out to him and looked around the room. He recognised a few local people – councillors, the Mayor. And there, in the corner at the far end of the room, seated with a notepad and pencil was Nellie. He stared at her and gasped as a surge of nervous energy ran through him. He had not realised she would be there. Of course – as the Mayor's assistant she'd be there to take notes of all that was said, by every witness. Including himself. She caught his eye and gave him a tiny nod, of encouragement, he thought.

Here was his chance, Billy realised, to try to make her understand that he'd done everything he could. It was even more important now that he told his full story as clearly as possible. There was no more he could have done. He needed Nellie to understand. She'd shouted at him, blamed him for not saving Flo. He'd forgiven her for that outburst. And now he needed her to forgive him as well. His life would be meaningless without her friendship.

'Please state your name and occupation,' said a man who seemed to be in charge of proceedings. He sounded tired, mechanical, as though he'd sat through dozens of testimonies and was growing weary of them.

'Billy . . . that is, William Waters. Air raid warden.'

'And where were you, on the evening of third March when the air raid siren went off?'

'In the ticket hall at the tube station shelter. My usual spot. Even if there's no air raid, there's some that sleep there every night, have done since the Blitz. I keep order there on a night shift.'

'Please recount your actions from the moment the siren sounded that night.'

Billy did so, keeping his eyes fixed on Nellie. It helped, watching her. She grounded him, with her quiet, beautiful presence. She barely raised her eyes from her notepad while he spoke. She was scribbling shorthand furiously, recording everything he said. Good.

'So you were first on the scene, witnessing the first person fall?'

He swallowed. 'Yes. I tried to help the woman up but it all happened so fast, the way they all fell one on top of the other.' He shook his head. 'I honestly did all I could, pulled at them, climbed on them, grabbed at anything I could to get them out. It was awful, horrible.'

'Did you get anyone out alive?' a councillor asked.

'Yes, sir. A baby first, then a boy. Three or four other people. Then when the police came up from the maintenance exit, I reckon we saved another ten or so, and sent them down below. But they was mostly dead. We hoped there was more live ones going out the top way.' He looked down at his hands, resting on the table. 'We had no place to put anyone that was dead, see. We didn't want the people down in the shelter to see any of 'em when they came out in the morning. So when we could get through, the police took 'em all out the top, and into the church.'

He lifted his head and caught Nellie's eye. She'd stopped writing and was gazing at him. Her mouth hung a little open and in her eyes he could see horror mixed with sympathy. She'd understood, he thought, that he'd done everything he could. He could not have done more. As he watched her, she mouthed a word – *sorry*.

He'd seen the regret in her eyes, and that was all that mattered to him. He knew he'd lost her, to that American, but even so, he wanted her respect, her friendship, to last their lifetime. They'd been friends nearly their whole lives. In the past they'd spent all their free time together.

These last couple of months when they'd barely spoken, and especially the days since Nellie's outburst at the funeral, had made him miserable. He needed her back in his life so badly.

***

Nellie listened carefully to every word Billy said. She captured it all in her neat shorthand. One thing that had become abundantly clear as he spoke was that there was nothing more he could have done, asthma or no asthma. He'd been a hero down below that night, just as Ray had been up above. Flo and Charlie must have been somewhere in the middle of it all, where there was no chance anyone could reach them either from above or below. She'd been wrong to shout at him at the funeral, wrong to blame him for not doing enough. She would need to apologise to him, to find a way to make it up to him. How could she have doubted him? He was Billy, her lifelong friend, one of the very best of men, and of course he'd have done everything in his power to save people.

She mouthed the word 'sorry' to him, and watched his face light up, his expression clear as he saw that she understood. And she was glad, for it surely wasn't just the survivors who would never get over the tragedy. It would affect rescuers such as Billy for the rest of their lives too. The horrors of that night were going to be etched into the hearts of the community forever.

Chapter 36

It was the last day of the inquiry, a fortnight after the accident occurred, and somehow Nellie had got herself through it. She'd heard all eighty-one witnesses tell their stories. She was exhausted and felt emotionally drained as each recounted their harrowing tales, but she was proud to have played a part in getting to the truth of what happened that night, and eager to finish the work of writing up the inquiry. It would be a significant moment, and one that would allow her to put it all behind her and begin to move on.

That was for another day, Nellie thought, as she hurried home that evening. The clouds were dark and ominous – any moment they'd burst and Nellie would be drenched.

As she hurried along the road she heard her name being called out. 'Nellie Morris! Wait!' It was Billy, running full pelt towards her. Her stomach gave a lurch, seeing him. Now was her chance to properly apologise to him. 'You on your way home?' he said. 'That hearing finished, is it?'

'Yes, last day was today. Then we need to wait for the report. I am glad it's over.'

'Must have been hard, hearing everyone's stories. I'm . . . proud of you, Nellie. For what you've done, all you've been through.' Billy spoke quietly but she could hear the sincerity in his voice.

'I'm proud of you too, Billy. You did well, saving all those people. And Billy, I'm sorry. So sorry for the things I said to you at Dad and Flo's wake. I never should have blamed you. I was overwhelmed by everything that was happening and I think I was looking for a reason to try to make sense of it all. But I shouldn't have taken it out on you and I should have known you'd have done everything possible to help those poor people.'

Billy fidgeted. 'It's all right. I understand. We were all in a right state that day.'

'Even so, I'm sorry. Forgive me?'

''Course I do, Nellie. Did my job, that's all. Hard, though. Can't talk to anyone about it.'

He sounded troubled, as though he was struggling with the memories. 'You can talk to me,' she said, though she wasn't sure she wanted to hear. She'd heard far too much about it these last few days.

He was silent for a moment, then spoke quietly. 'I still see them. Hear them. Those people that were stuck. When I'm in bed, trying to sleep. When I close my eyes.'

'Oh, Billy.' She reached for him and squeezed his arm.

'I still have to go down there, on my shifts. Down those steps, where it happened. And I wasn't even caught in it. Must be worse still for people who were, who survived.'

There was nothing she could say to that. No words

to comfort him. Would it ever fade from their memories or was it too terrible, too horrible an event for that to happen?

'It's the same for me. I can't stop picturing Dad and Flo in the church. And I can't imagine having to go back down the tube. At least we have a choice.'

'I know, but it's me job. Though I miss seeing you come down.' He smiled and she smiled back, pleased that they'd taken the first steps towards reconciliation. They understood each other. They always had.

A few spots of rain fell, and she held out her hand and grimaced. 'Ah no. It's gonna rain and I've no hat or brolly.'

'Here, have mine,' Billy said with a grin, as he pulled his air raid warden's helmet off his head and plonked it on hers. 'Better than nothing, though I can't say it suits you.' The sudden switch to their old light-hearted banter came as a relief.

'Oi! I thought you once said I looked lovely in everything I wore!'

'You do, 'cept for that helmet,' he said with a laugh. 'Here, fancy getting a bag of chips to eat on the way home? My treat.'

'Why not? I'll pay my share, though.'

'Not if I get to the chippy first,' Billy said. 'Come on, race you!' He set off at a sprint.

She chased after him, determined to win, with one hand holding the too-big helmet on her head. They reached the chip shop at the same time and as they piled in through its door she was breathless and laughing – laughing for the first time since before . . . and it felt good.

'Good to see a smile on your face,' Billy said. 'I'm still gonna pay for the chips though.'

She grinned and let him.

With a bag of chips to share they walked the rest of the way home slowly, relieved the rain hadn't started, enjoying each other's company. It was good to be joking with Billy, like the old days, before the accident. Like when they were kids, coming home after school together, and she'd be wondering if he'd ever pluck up the courage to ask her on a date. Would she have said yes, back then, before the war began and everything changed? It was hard to know. She looked over at him, happy to see he was the same old Billy and they could still be friends. A little bit of normality in this crazy, broken world.

As they turned the corner into Morpeth Street Nellie's heart stood still for a moment. There, near her front door, was a man in the unmistakable uniform of the US Air Force. Ray must have got her letter and waited for his leave until he could come to see her so they could smooth things over. Hearing Ray tell her that he still loved her was what she needed most right now. But then the figure turned, and she saw the familiar face of Clayton.

Seeing her, he took off his cap and held it respectfully in front of him. He stayed where he was. Nellie's heart sank, knowing there would be a reason he'd come all the way from his new airbase to Bethnal Green.

'Oh God. No,' she whispered, instinctively clutching

Billy's arm for support. The fun they'd been having evaporated in an instant.

'What? What's wrong?' Billy said. 'Who's that? Oh, that friend of your . . . friend. What's he here for?'

Nellie broke away and began running up the street towards Clayton.

As she reached him and saw the agony on his face she knew that he'd come with the kind of news she'd never wanted to hear.

Billy, panting, came alongside her. 'What? What's happened?'

'Nellie, I'm real sorry,' Clayton said. 'I–I don't know how to say it.'

'Please don't say it,' she whispered, shaking her head.

Clayton gulped. 'I'm sorry, Nellie, I got to . . . tell you. Ray was shot down, over France. No one saw a parachute. He's listed as killed in action.'

'Nooo!' She let out a wail and collapsed, screaming, on the pavement in front of Clayton. This was it, this was her world ending. She was only dimly aware of the strong arms that hauled her upright and held her, but they weren't Ray's arms. They were Clayton's, and he was patting her back and murmuring words that were supposed to be comforting but which did nothing, nothing at all to lessen the pain.

'Nellie, let's get you inside,' Billy said. But she didn't want to go inside, didn't want to face Em and George, didn't want to tell them that someone else had died, someone else they cared for, after all their losses. This was *her* loss. Hers to bear.

'Nellie, come on. I'll make you a cup of tea.' Billy tugged at her arm but she pulled away, stepping back from both men, staring at them as the horror and disbelief turned to anger. How could this be happening to her? Hadn't she already lost enough? How many more people would this war take from her?

'I don't want *tea*,' she said, spitting out the final word. 'I just want, I want . . .' She tailed off. Things back to how they used to be, she'd been going to say. Ray, Flo and Charlie back with them. A few short weeks ago she'd had everything, and now . . . it had all been taken from her. Her mind was a swirl of thoughts and feelings and memories. Ray had proposed, they'd been going to marry, and now . . . now . . . he was gone.

She turned and ran back up the street, just as the threatened rain began to fall. Billy's stupid helmet was still on her head, rattling around, and she pulled it off, flinging it onto the road as she fled, up to Roman Road and along it, to St John's church. She hadn't set foot in it, or its grounds, since that terrible night. She went around the side of it, splashing through the puddles that were forming quickly, along to the stone. The place where Ray had carved their initials on that wonderful day. So long ago it seemed, now, when the world had been a good place despite the war, when there was everything to live for. And yet, it was barely a month ago, and the carving was fresh and clear.

She traced the letters with her fingers. *NM and RF*. Ray Fleming. Her love, the man she'd promised herself to, the man she'd planned a life with. Taken, by this horrible, terrible war. Gone, along with so many others.

She collapsed once more to her knees, her forehead against the wall of the church, and gave way to the sobs that rose up in her, that racked her body and emptied her mind of everything else but grief.

Chapter 37

Nellie woke up in her bed, with no idea of how she'd got there, or what had happened since she'd knelt by Ray's carved initials. As the memory of Clayton's news came back to her she let out an anguished groan, which brought Em running in to her.

'Oh pet. You're awake. Ray's friend told us the news. Oh darling, it's just terrible. Terrible, terrible. Such a shock.' Em sat down on Nellie's bed and took her hand. 'He was such a nice man, your Ray. I thought perhaps . . . I had hopes . . .' She shook her head sadly. 'So many, all gone, and us still here. Makes you think, don't it?'

Nellie turned her face away. It was too soon to be philosophical about it. She'd lost . . . everything.

'Billy's downstairs,' Em continued. 'Wants to see you, when you're up to it. Him and Ray's friend carried you back, you know. You was . . . out of it, completely. Gave me quite a scare.'

'I-I don't want to s-see him,' Nellie stuttered. She didn't want to see anyone right now.

Em sat quietly for a moment then nodded and with a pat of Nellie's hand, left the room.

Nellie was all alone with her thoughts and her pain. She squeezed her eyes shut and released another groan. Had Ray received her letter, before he . . . was shot down? she wondered.

All she could do was hope that he *had* received the letter. It was a small thing, but believing that he'd read it, that he'd known she loved him and that he wasn't to blame, gave her a tiny crumb of comfort in all this horror.

Life was so cruel! Just as she'd thought there was hope once more for herself and Ray, he'd been taken from her in such a horrible way. She turned her face to the wall, remembering that the last words she'd spoken to him had been to scream at him to get out. She'd hit him and shouted at him and now she'd never see him again. And it was all made worse by not knowing for sure whether he'd received her apology and the reassurance that the tragedy was not his fault. The thought that he might have died not knowing Nellie was sorry and still loved him was an even crueller twist of fate. If only she'd written to him sooner. Her body ached with sadness and her skin crawled with frustration.

Em nursed her and comforted her the rest of the day and throughout the weekend, allowing her to stay in bed while she brought meals upstairs. 'Together, love, we'll come through this god-awful time,' Em said, in an attempt to reassure her.

Nellie was grateful, though inside she felt numb and

empty. The grief she'd felt when she'd lost Charlie and Flo was now tenfold. She couldn't see a way through this; no way in which she could return to anything like her old self. At work and at home she'd be just going through the motions, not really living.

*

The official report, by Home Office aide Laurence Dunne, came out exactly a month after the tragedy and a fortnight after the inquiry completed. A fortnight after Nellie heard the news about Ray. It was not made public, but as assistant to the Mayor Nellie would have the chance to read it in full. Mrs Bolton asked her to check in detail what it contained against her own transcript.

'But first, let's read through it together,' the Mayor said, handing her a copy.

They read in silence. Nellie glanced up a couple of times at her boss, to see Mrs Bolton's frown become deeper and deeper. When she'd finished reading, the Mayor put down her copy and sighed deeply. 'So, what do you think?'

'It . . . doesn't exactly chime with what I heard at the inquiry,' Nellie said, cautiously. 'It exonerates the police and air raid wardens, which is good, and correct, but . . .' She'd been glad to read this part – that no blame was to be attached to Billy or his colleagues in any way. They'd done all they possibly could.

'But?'

'It blames "a lack of self-control",' Nellie went on,

quoting from the report. 'If the government really believes it was down to panic, doesn't that mean the Council's off the hook? But then, it goes on to say that "ultimately responsibility lies with the Borough Council". With us. Even though it recognises that we had applied for funding to improve the entrance and were denied it. It actually says,' and Nellie stabbed a finger at it, 'that the Council had foreseen the danger but not taken adequate measures to prevent it.'

Mrs Bolton nodded grimly. 'Yes, that is my reading of it too. "Local authorities, by their intimate knowledge of their own problems, must be the body responsible for their solution." How were we supposed to put in place a solution when we were refused authorisation, let alone funding?' She covered her face with her hands. 'So they're blaming both the public and us. I don't understand what more we could have done. We recognised the danger, took steps to find a solution, then were denied funding to implement that solution. We couldn't spend rate-payers' money without authorisation, which Civil Defence wouldn't give us. And they're now blaming firstly the public for a lack of self-control, despite the many witnesses saying that wasn't the case, and secondly us. They've decided we, the Council, can be sacrificed.'

'You should have spoken up, at the inquiry,' Nellie said, surprising herself with the strength of feeling in her tone. 'You should have said they wouldn't let us make the improvements.' All the anger and emotion Nellie had been keeping a lid on at work since Ray's death came bubbling to the surface. 'It's *your* fault they're blaming us. You should have fought harder.'

The Mayor looked at her coldly. 'I couldn't. They'd already decided, I believe, what they wanted the outcome to be. And you, Miss Morris, need to keep your temper in check. We're all angry about this but it doesn't help anyone.'

Nellie recalled the glances that had been exchanged between the Home Office official and the head of London Civil Defence, and the numerous times witnesses were pressed on whether there was a panic. It was clear that there'd been a hidden agenda and that, ahead of the inquiry, decisions were taken in government as to who to blame, and it wasn't going to be them. She sighed, her anger subsiding as quickly as it had erupted. 'I'm sorry, Mrs Bolton. What can we do?'

The Mayor shrugged. 'Nothing, as far as I can see. Improvements to the shelter entrance have already been made, and this report will ensure other similar shelters review their entrances too.'

'We can perhaps . . . publicise this? Put our case forward?' Nellie was thinking of the reporter she'd met. He would be keen to write a story on this, she was sure. And she wanted everyone to know the truth. It had helped her to start to understand and the community deserved that same chance to come to terms with what had happened.

Mrs Bolton shook her head. 'I'm informed by the Home Office that we must keep this quiet. They do not want this report in enemy hands, neither do they want it widely circulated in case it damages morale. Our hands are tied. There is nothing to be done.'

'It doesn't seem right.' Nellie sighed. 'They've used us, made us a . . .' She frowned, trying to remember the right term.

'Scapegoat. Yes, that's exactly what they've done, Nellie. But you and I and the other councillors know the truth. We know we did everything we could, to improve safety. None of what happened is our fault.' The Mayor spoke with passion, and Nellie realised she was saying this for her own benefit as much as for Nellie's. She'd been blaming herself too, Nellie guessed. As the person ultimately responsible for the borough, the Mayor must believe the buck stopped with her.

'You're right, Mrs Bolton. It isn't our fault.' All Nellie could do was repeat the words, and direct her anger towards the Home Office, not the Mayor. She'd thought that when the report was out, that would be an end to it, and they could get on with the process of grieving. But it seemed that it was all far from over yet. It was like a never-ending nightmare from which she could not wake.

Chapter 38

'Miss Morris, it's good to see you again. I hope you are keeping well and beginning to come to terms with your losses, now that a month has passed.' Stan Collins called after her as she walked down the steps of the town hall later that day, eager to get home.

'Hello, Mr Collins. I'm . . . managing. I hope you are too.'

'Yes. I miss my father very much, as I'm sure you miss yours too. And your sister. Terrible times.'

Terrible times indeed. He didn't know the half of what she'd been going through and how low she felt. 'What brings you here, Mr Collins?' He walked next to her as she moved briskly down the sidewalk.

'Well now, I hear . . . that there was a Home Office inquiry into what happened that night, and that the report has now been produced. But I'm unable to get a copy of it. I've been told it's not to be made available to the public. And I believe the inquiry was conducted in secret.' He caught hold of her arm and whirled her to a stop. 'Miss Morris, does this not seem wrong to you? Do you not think the public have a right to know? So many people are grieving still, do they not deserve to know exactly what happened? Don't I deserve to know how my father died?'

'Mr Collins, I—' Nellie began.

'I wrote a story, the day after, you know. Called it in to my paper. Didn't mention your name of course – I would never disclose a source. But my report was suppressed. The paper printed some old rubbish about it being a bomb. Strikes me the editor was leaned on by someone high up. He told me they didn't want people too frightened to use the tube station shelters.' He glanced around them, then pointed over the road at a Lyons Corner House. 'If you have a few minutes, let me buy you a cup of tea.'

She hesitated for a moment, unsure of whether she should be talking to him right now. 'All right, but I can't—'

'Don't worry, I'm not going to ask you to tell me anything if you've been told you must keep quiet,' Mr Collins said, with a comforting smile. He led her to the café and ushered her to a table by the window, ordering them each a tea. 'We're just two people bereaved by the accident.'

Nellie looked up at Stan. She knew she wasn't supposed to be doing this but she felt compelled to help him so she made her decision. Regardless of what the Mayor and the Home Office aides said, people did deserve more. She'd have to tread carefully. 'I do think the public have a right to know the truth, Mr Collins.'

'Stan, please.'

'All right. Stan. And please call me Nellie. But I really can't say too much. Been told not to.'

'Who by?'

'The Mayor. She says the government want it kept quiet, for morale and whatnot. It was the Home Office that ran the inquiry. And I think they . . . had decided the conclusions they wanted to reach, in advance.'

Stan stared at her. 'You think they manipulated the inquiry? Or the report?'

She took a sip of her tea before answering. 'I feel like the Council's been made a scapegoat. I think the Home Office wanted someone to blame and decided to blame us. The safety and upkeep of air raid shelters does fall to the Council, it's true, but—'

'That's so, and if the report suggests the Council was negligent in its duties, even if it wasn't actually, then that means victims' families could seek compensation.' Stan looked thoughtful, as though he was formulating a plan.

'Compensation?' She frowned, trying to understand what he was getting at.

'Yes. Your mother, for example. Losing her husband, the bread-winner, means she's – excuse me, for speaking bluntly – she's in danger of slipping into poverty, being unable to pay rent. Do you have any other brothers or sisters at home?'

'One brother, still at school.'

'Without your father's wages, how is your mother going to make ends meet and care for your brother?'

'I earn—' Nellie began. But he was right. Em had already been talking about taking in laundry to try to get by.

'I know you do, and I know you'll be doing everything you can to help your mother out, but it shouldn't be up to you to give up your wages. You should be saving for your own future. If the Council was found to be negligent then they need to pay out, to compensate your mother.'

'The Council wasn't negligent. We'd applied for funding to improve the shelter,' Nellie said.

'But the report says the Council didn't do enough, right? Look, I'm not saying it's your fault or the Mayor's or anyone's, but if the Home Office say the shelter wasn't adequate then there's a case for compensation. Your mother should seek it.'

'B-but how does that work?'

'She'd need to instruct a lawyer to take on her case and sue the Council.' Stan leaned back in his chair, regarding her. 'Nellie, it's worth a try.'

'Why don't you?' she asked. 'You lost your father . . .'

'But I'm not directly financially affected by my loss, the way your mother is, losing her husband. And her losing two family members, your little sister – forgive me but that's going to have much more of an impact if it goes to court.'

Nellie knew he was right. She felt the impact and burden of it every minute of every day. 'Mum wouldn't want a court case . . .' Nellie said, hesitantly. She was pretty sure Em would say no to all of this.

'May I meet her?' Stan drained the last of his tea as though he wanted to go right then.

'Well . . . I don't see why not. All right.' Let Em be

the one to decide whether to take this idea forward or not. Nellie finished her tea and pushed her chair back, ready to go.

'Thank you, Nellie,' Stan said as he pressed his trilby firmly onto his head. 'I feel strongly that justice must be done, here. Through no fault of her own, your mother and many others like her have been left without any means of support. Someone needs to pay up.'

Nellie agreed with that, though privately thought it should be London Civil Defence who were sued. They'd refused the funds to improve the entrance, after all. But rightly or wrongly, they weren't the ones the report had pointed the finger of blame at.

She led the reporter through the streets to her home, hoping she was doing the right thing in taking Stan Collins to meet Em. And if Em did decide to go ahead and sue the Council, what would that mean for her, Nellie's role in the town hall? It would certainly make things difficult between herself and the Mayor. Impossible even. Should she just let it be, avoid the risk of losing her job, and allow the whole thing to drop? Or . . . could this be a way of getting the truth told, in the end? They reached her home and she called out to Em as they entered. 'Mum? You here? I've brought a visitor!'

Em came out of the kitchen wiping floury hands on her apron. 'Oh! I was just making pastry . . .'

'Mum, this is Stan Collins. He's a reporter, but he's here about something else . . . Shall we sit in the front room?'

'Yes, of course, and let me . . .' Em turned back to the kitchen.

A couple of minutes later she came into the front room, hands clean, apron off and carrying a tray. 'Last of the shortbread I made last week there,' she said proudly, indicating a plate of biscuits. Oscar had followed her in, and after sniffing and wagging his tail at Stan, he slumped down at Nellie's feet, eyeing the biscuits hopefully.

'What can I do for you, Mr Collins?'

Stan explained again his idea about seeking compensation.

'I got to sue someone, you mean?' Em asked, as she handed round cups of tea.

'Yes. You have a strong case, I would think.'

'I might well do, but I ain't got no money to pay a solicitor to make my case,' Em replied. 'So there's an end to it, really.'

'I thought you might say that,' Stan went on. 'There's a way round it. Yours would be a test case. If you won, then lots of others might follow, knowing they too would win, and there'd be payouts for everybody. And I'm sure you would win.'

'Still, can't afford to do it.' Em folded her arms. 'We're struggling as it is, and I just don't see where we'd come up with even a small portion of what it'd cost.'

'And as everybody benefits in the end,' Stan went on as though Em hadn't spoken, 'then everyone ought to chip in to pay for the first case. If I set up a petition, and everyone in the neighbourhood who wants to, puts a bit in the pot, then I'm sure we'd raise enough.'

'I don't take no charity from no one.' Em pressed her lips together.

Nellie wasn't surprised. Her mother had always been a proud woman and had instilled in her family the need to stand on their own two feet and not expect nor accept handouts from anyone.

'It's not charity,' Stan said patiently. 'It's more like an investment. They pay for your case, which is sure to succeed, and they're repaid when the precedent is set and they can bring their own cases and get their own payout. Do you see?'

Nellie looked from Em to Stan and back again. Em was wavering. Her initial reluctance to sue was dissipating. 'So, I'm doing this for everyone else, like? Not for me. But to benefit all them others who lost people that night?'

'That's exactly it, Mum,' Nellie put in.

'Why me? Loads of us lost people then.'

'Because we lost two family members, Mum,' Nellie said. She bit her lip. While she wanted Em to go ahead, to get the truth told and win some compensation money, at the back of her mind was a worry about how it might jeopardise her position at the town hall.

'Losing your little girl as well as your husband makes your case more likely to touch a chord with the judge,' Stan said, keeping his tone carefully devoid of emotion.

Em swallowed and glanced away, then looked back at the reporter. 'In that case, it's my duty, innit? You set up that petition, Mr Collins, and find me a solicitor, and I'll do whatever I can to get them people their money. It's what my Charlie would want me to do.'

Em's expression was one of determination. She'd do this, and she might win, Nellie thought, and in the process it would give her a purpose, a reason for going on. It would be good for her. Nellie was proud of her, but horribly anxious at what would happen. Goodness, it was going to be difficult at work, knowing Em was suing Nellie's employer. Part of her wanted to tell Em, *No, don't do it, don't make my life any harder than it already is,* but she stopped herself. This could make a real difference for so many friends and neighbours in their community who were suffering. And there was no need to tell the Mayor about it immediately. If the petition didn't raise enough money it'd all come to nothing anyway, and if not . . . well, she'd cross that bridge when she came to it.

'Well done, Mum,' she said, reaching out to squeeze Em's hand.

'Right then, that's settled,' Stan said. 'I'll help you all I can, Mrs Morris.'

That was a good thing. They would need all the help they could get. Her family had never been involved with the courts, and now they were putting everything on the line, in Nellie's place of work no less. God, what a situation to be in. She didn't know which way to look – either direction made her skin prickle.

Chapter 39

Billy was glad there was no likelihood of an air raid that night, and that he hadn't been sent to the tube station. Lately the newspapers had been full of the 'dambuster' raids, in which so-called bouncing bombs had been deployed to destroy dams in Germany. There'd been fewer air raids over London lately. He dreaded going down the tube now. Every time he set foot on that stairway, he was haunted by that night. He felt the little red shoe that might have been Flo's in his hand, felt his grip loosen and his lungs constrict and the asthma attack take over. And then he'd be gasping for breath once again, needing to visit the first-aid post and use the nebuliser.

Thank goodness then, that tonight he was on blackout duty – patrolling the streets, making sure that the blackout regulations were being adhered to. Blitz or no Blitz, air raid or not, the people of Bethnal Green still needed to ensure their windows were covered after dark so that no light shone onto the streets that might guide an enemy bomber. Anyone walking out after dark could use a torch but it had to be shaded so that the minimum light possible shone onto the pavement. The streetlights were also shaded or removed. Anything to hide the presence of the city from enemy planes.

A man was walking towards him, probably on the way home from the pub. He was limping, and as he drew nearer Billy recognised him as a fellow who'd been a few years above him in school. He'd gone off to fight and come home minus a leg. He nodded as he passed him but the man seemed lost in his own thoughts, as Billy was too.

Billy worked his way up and down the network of Victorian terraced streets that made up this part of town. He'd done this so many times he swore he'd be able to tell which street he was on, which house numbers he was passing, blindfolded. The feel of the pavement underfoot, the smells coming from drains, open windows or plants in window boxes, the sounds of children at play or domestic arguments – all these would provide enough clues.

Now he was passing a gap in the houses where once Nellie's aunt and uncle had lived. The remains of their house had long since been bulldozed to make it safe, but there was still a pile of rubble, which local children would climb up to shout, 'I'm the King of the castle!' There were no children playing now, after dark, but the thought brought a smile to his face, remembering how he, Nellie and Babs had been inseparable when they were young. They'd played out in the street or in the parks together at every opportunity. Nellie would be the leader; Babs, a year younger, looked up to her and would follow her anywhere. He, Billy, despite being the eldest of the group, also worshipped Nellie – a childhood infatuation that had gradually blossomed into intense adult love. On his side at least.

They were growing closer again, both he and Babs had been rallying around Nellie since the American had been killed in action. She'd taken it so badly and he'd done what he could to support her. He always would, surely she knew that? He'd taken her and Babs to the pictures once or twice. Bought Nellie a bag of chips and sat with her on a park bench to eat them, just being there in case she wanted to talk.

And she'd smiled at him, told him she was grateful for his support. She'd reached out a hand once or twice, and touched his with her soft, warm fingertips. Tiny steps but certainly there was a new closeness forming between them that he hadn't felt since she'd met the American.

'If you were more of a man, Billy Waters, like that American airman was, you'd just take her in your arms and tell her how you really feel about her,' he muttered, as he turned a corner into the next street along. A cat darted out of the way and onto a doorstep a little way ahead, watching him pass.

If he was more of a man, Nellie would have fallen for him instead of still seeing him as just a friend. He knew it, but could not bring himself to even say the words to himself.

Damn his asthma. If not for that, he'd have been a soldier too, or perhaps he'd have joined the RAF and flown Spitfires and come home a hero, and Nellie would have loved him for it.

Or he'd have been shot down like Ray Fleming was, leaving Nellie alone. Or if he'd been in the army, he might have been killed like Amelia's fiancé had been. So perhaps it was better this way, better that he was stuck here in Bethnal Green doing the comparatively safe job of an air raid warden, able to stay near Nellie, to look after her, to be there for her whether or not they had a future together.

But who knew what would happen in the long term? Perhaps, in time, when she'd had a chance to fully grieve Ray, to get over her other losses as best she could. Perhaps later, when the war was over, she'd realise he, Billy, was still there and still loved her. And maybe then there'd be hope for him.

PART THREE

Spring–Summer 1945

Chapter 40

Over the past two years, Nellie, Em and George had done all they could to find ways to move on. It helped that there were moments to celebrate as the Allied troops made progress the previous year, after D-day, slowly pushing back German troops through the French countryside until Paris itself was liberated. But even while Bethnal Green applauded the advancement, there were new horrors to contend with, as flying bombs – first 'Doodlebugs' and later V2 rockets – rained down on the city. They flew so fast that no air raid warning was possible. People either slept in the shelters every night, or took their chances at home. In many ways it was just as hard as the early part of the war, hitting East London badly once again. But everyone was confident that victory was inching closer.

Money was tight and Em had been taking in laundry, but somehow they managed. Now fifteen, George had left school and was doing an apprenticeship to become an electrician, but it was still Nellie's wages that kept the family afloat.

For months, it didn't seem like Em's lawsuit would

ever go anywhere. Nellie had no idea how long it would take to raise the money, find a solicitor and bring the case to court. Thankfully Stan knew what he was doing. 'Everyone wanted to chip in with the costs,' Stan had told them, 'whether or not they'd lost someone in the accident. Like I said, if or when you win, it'll benefit everyone.'

Except me, Nellie thought. She still hadn't told Mrs Bolton about the lawsuit, anxious that if she did, she might lose her job. Even when the solicitor Stan found, a Mr Badcock, called on them to discuss it with Em, Nellie kept quiet when she was in the office. She and the Mayor didn't have as good a relationship as they used to. Not since Nellie's outburst after the Home Office report into the crush was published. It wasn't easy being at work with the Mayor, knowing about the forthcoming court case, and Nellie often wished she could just start over somewhere else, some place where she could be free of the burden she carried. She really felt she had no choice but to keep on at the town hall. There weren't many job opportunities, what with the war still over-shadowing everything they did, and it went without saying that the wages she received would not easily be matched elsewhere.

She arrived at work one Friday in February and greeted Mrs Bolton as usual. But the Mayor looked up and scowled.

'Is something wrong?' Nellie asked, as she took off her coat and hung it up.

The Mayor stabbed a finger at a pile of papers on her desk. 'Yes. This. I've had a letter from a solicitor named

Badcock who, it seems, is representing your mother. She's suing the Council, Nellie, for negligence over the tube accident! Did you know about this?'

It was the moment that she'd been dreading for many months. There was no point trying to deny it or downplay it now Mrs Bolton had got wind of the case. 'Erm, yes, Mrs Bolton. I did know. I was . . .'

'Why didn't you tell me? Why is she doing this?' The Mayor ran a hand through her hair. 'Nellie, you of all people, know the truth. You *know* we tried to improve the shelter entrance but were denied the funding. You know the Council is not to blame for the tragedy! And yet . . .' She poked at the solicitor's letter once more. 'And yet your mother is taking us to court. This is not a rich borough as you well know. What services are we going to cut, in order to pay her compensation if she wins, hmm? Who's going to suffer?'

Nellie was taken aback by the venom in the Mayor's tone, but her family came before her job. She needed to speak out. 'Mum's already suffering, Mrs Bolton. Without Dad to bring in a wage, money's tight, and here's a chance for her to get something back. It won't replace Dad and Flo, of course, but it might ease the pain of poverty a little. She deserves that at least.' She jutted out her chin as she spoke.

The Mayor blinked, looking shocked at Nellie's defensive words. 'I know it's hard, and your mother – and you – lost a lot that night. But this . . . I never expected this.'

Nellie stared at her. 'Just because I work for you, doesn't

mean my mother can't do whatever she can to get some compensation, Mrs Bolton. And I will support her, no matter what you say.' Nellie felt her temper rising, but with effort managed to keep it under control.

'It feels like a betrayal,' the Mayor went on. 'If it had been someone else, I'd . . . I'd have been cross, because it makes us – me – look bad, but I'd have understood. But *you*, your family . . .' She shook her head, looking sad now rather than angry. For a moment Nellie didn't know how to respond. This was exactly why she hadn't said anything about it before. She feared that everything she'd been worried about all these months would now come true. Mrs Bolton would fire her and she wouldn't be able to find a new job that offered enough compensation to provide for her family. She had to find a way to get the Mayor on her side. She thought back to the inquiry, remembered how the Council was so wrongly held accountable. And then she had an idea. 'Mrs Bolton, I wonder if this might work in the Council's favour, while still giving my mum some compensation?'

'Oh yes? How's that, then?' the Mayor asked, sounding sceptical.

'I mean, there'll be a hearing. Another chance for the truth to be told at last. Won't that mean it'll become public knowledge that we tried so hard to get funding to improve the shelter, and that it wasn't the Council that was neg-ligent, but that Civil Defence refused us funding? Then the government would have to admit liability and pay the compensation, and the Council would be vindicated. Isn't that how it would work out?'

The Mayor shook her head. 'It sounds so simple, put like that, but . . .'

'All you need to do is go public with it, tell the world you tried, you did all you could, but you were denied funding. I know a reporter for *The Daily Mail* – he'd write a story about it and get it published.'

'I can't.'

Nellie threw up her hands, exasperated as to why people couldn't be told the truth. She wanted to scream. It was maddening. 'Why not? Sorry, Mrs Bolton, but I don't see why not.'

'I can't, and that's all there is to it.' The Mayor sighed. 'This is a very tricky situation, Nellie, and I'm afraid you don't know quite everything about it.'

'Then tell me,' Nellie pleaded, desperate to know what Mrs Bolton was hiding.

'I can't, Nellie. I am bound not to say. I will, however, write to the Home Office and ask that they shoulder the cost of litigation and any compensation, should your mother win her case. Now, just accept that, please, and get on with your work for the day.'

Nellie stared at her, but Mrs Bolton gathered up her papers without catching Nellie's eye again, stuffed them in her briefcase and left the office.

'Bound not to say? What does she mean?' Nellie muttered, as she picked up a pile of typing from her in-tray and fed a sheet of paper into her typewriter to make a start. How could she concentrate with all of this going on? She did understand why Mrs Bolton had felt betrayed but hoped the Mayor also understood that firstly it was right for Em to take this opportunity to get a payout, and secondly that anything that helped tell the truth to the public was surely a good thing, no matter what the Home Office had said. She could only hope that Mrs Bolton would calm down and not decide to fire her.

Chapter 41

In March, a few days before the trial was scheduled, Stan Collins paid them an evening visit. Em ushered him into the front room and served him tea, insisting that Nellie stay too. 'You'll understand what he says better, and you'll remember it too.'

'You know, Mrs Morris, that you'll have to make a statement in court,' Stan said. 'I've reported on loads of these civil cases in the past, so I have a good idea of what happens. You might want to write something you can read out, that's often easier. And there may be a few follow-up questions from lawyers, from both sides.'

'I ain't on trial though, am I?' Em asked, wide-eyed in panic.

'No, it's not a criminal trial, merely a civil case. But they'll want to hear from you directly – how you lost your husband and daughter, that you still have a minor at home, that your daughter brings in the main income and without that, you wouldn't be able to afford the rent.'

George stuck his head through the door. 'Just off to sell eggs, Mum.'

'Be back for tea,' Em called to him.

'You can play that up, too,' Stan said after the door shut. 'That your son is selling eggs from his chickens to help make ends meet. You want the judge to feel sympathy for you. That way you'll win and achieve the maximum damages.'

'I dunno. Like airing me dirty laundry in public, it is.'

'Mr Badcock tells me it's to be a closed session. No one other than the judge, lawyers and other officials in the courtroom need ever hear what you say. They still want to keep the whole thing secret for some reason.' Stan sat forward in his chair and gazed at Em. 'Besides, you're doing it for the community, remember? Yours is the test case, and if – no, *when* – you win, they'll all benefit.'

Em sighed. 'Right. I'll do it. Nellie, you'll help me write a statement I can read out, will you?'

'Of course, Mum. We'll do it this evening.' Nellie squeezed Em's shoulder in support.

'And you'll be there with me, on the day?'

'I don't think I'll be allowed, Mum. Stan said it's to be a closed session. I'll ask, but . . .'

'I got to do it on me own, then,' Em said with determination.

Nellie needed fresh air. The approaching trial was weighing on her. She said goodbye to Stan and went out to the backyard to sit on the bench in the spring sunshine for a few minutes.

'Your mum ready for her court case?' Billy asked, coming out into the yard.

'Nearly. I've got to help her write a statement this evening.'

'If there's anything I can do, to help, like . . .'

Nellie shielded her eyes from the sun as she looked up at him. 'Thank you, Billy. For being there for us. Means a lot, you know.' He had been good to them. Taking her out with Babs now and again, buying her little treats. Being a friend, quietly supportive, helping them move on from their losses. Nobody could make her laugh like Billy. He always knew how to cheer her up. Bit by bit, he'd helped her feel more like her old self. Or perhaps, a *new* self. She was twenty-one now. More grown-up, quieter. Less prone to flashes of temper, she thought, with a pang of shame at some of the outbursts she'd had in the past.

'Any time. You know that, don't you, Nellie?' His eyes were filled with regard for her as he sat down beside her.

She smiled at him. 'I do, Billy.' She leaned in towards him, her head against his shoulder. He was such a comfort, he had been throughout these difficult times. He turned his head towards her, and she held her breath as she felt the brush of his lips against her hair.

'Any time,' he whispered again, and she knew he was referring to more than simply helping her with the court case.

*

On the day of the trial, Nellie took the day off work. The Mayor had to be in court anyway, and Nellie wanted to go with Em to the courthouse and wait for her there. They walked arm in arm through the streets, nervous and jittery as Em practised her statement for the umpteenth time.

'You'll do fine, Mum,' Nellie said, yet again, trying to reassure Em despite her own nerves.

'You think so? I ain't never spoken in front of so many people before.'

'Stan said there wouldn't be that many in court. A dozen, maybe. Before the war, we had that many round for Christmas dinner sometimes! If you can cook for that many you can surely speak to them. You have the written statement, don't you? So if you forget your words you can just read it.'

Em patted her coat pocket. 'Got it right here. Thanks, love, for supporting me.'

Nellie squeezed her arm. 'No problem, Mum. Wish I could come in with you, though.' She was worried about the consequences if this didn't go their way, but if they were awarded compensation then their future would be more secure and there'd be one less thing for them all to worry about.

'I'll be all right, knowing you're just outside,' Em said, putting on a brave smile.

*

Mr Badcock met them at the court, instructed Em, and led her toward the courtroom. 'It shouldn't be too long,' he said to Nellie. 'You can both go home as soon as Mrs Morris has made her statement, and rest assured I shall come to tell you the outcome as soon as the judge delivers a verdict.'

Nellie sat in a wood-panelled corridor outside the courtroom fidgeting with her hands as she tried to guess what was happening inside. There were oil paintings of prominent lawyers from days gone by lining the walls, all glaring down at her as though questioning her right to be there. Nellie glared defiantly back at them. She was proud of her mother for standing up for their neighbourhood and felt a sudden wave of confidence it would all work out. Didn't they deserve some good news? Ever since she'd lost Ruth and John, it felt like she couldn't avoid bad things happening. She shook her head, not wanting to get into that way of thinking. It's true life had not been easy since Flo and Charlie had died, but she knew she had things to be thankful for – her tight relationships with Em and George, the support of Babs and the steady presence of Billy. She smiled as she recalled a recent story he'd told her while they'd been out for a walk.

And then, suddenly, the courtroom door opened and Em was led out by a court official. She looked relieved that her part was over.

'How did it go, then?' Nellie asked Em, as soon as they were a safe distance away from the building.

'I said me piece, they asked a few questions – checking stuff I'd said, like, and that was it. Mr Badcock nodded at me. I think he thought I done all right.' Em was smiling, looking pleased with herself.

'Well done, Mum. Proud of you.' Nellie squeezed her arm.

'Thanks, love. Blinking glad it's all over though, I can tell you. Whether or not we win.'

Nellie nodded. She knew the feeling and was mightily relieved this part was over.

*

Mr Badcock came to Morpeth Street late the following day, looking delighted. 'Well, Mrs Morris, you won your case. As I was always sure you would. You are to be paid damages amounting to £1,550 for the loss of your husband and daughter. It's a substantial sum, one that will give you financial security so that you never have to worry about money again but no less than you deserve. There will be a letter sent confirming this.'

'Ooh, we won!' Em squealed. 'Listen to that, Nellie!'

George let out a whoop and Nellie gasped, then hugged her brother and then Em.

'What a relief,' said Em. 'But where on earth am I going to put all that cash?'

Mr Badcock smiled. 'I shall make arrangements for the money to be paid into your bank account.'

Em frowned. 'I ain't got no bank account.'

'Then we shall open one for you,' the solicitor said kindly.

'Hark at me, with me own bank account and all!' Em squealed, and Nellie laughed, hugging her mother. What a weight off her shoulders! Now the family would no longer need to rely on her salary.

The solicitor shook hands with each of them – Em, Nellie and George. 'A most satisfactory outcome, I would say, that should give you some security. And I suspect it won't be the only compensation the borough will need to pay. It's been a pleasure working with you. I'll send through my final bill in due course, and if you have any further need of my services, please don't hesitate to contact me. I shall leave you to celebrate. Good evening to you all.'

Nellie showed him out, then came back into the front room where Em and George were sitting, staring at each other. 'I can't believe we won. That's a lot of money. Mum, you could buy a house with it, and never again need worry about paying rent.'

'Won't bring our Flo and Charlie back though, will it?' Em said, looking up at Nellie with tears in her eyes. 'Don't matter how much money they pay me, or how many houses I can buy, or bank accounts I got. I'd rather have my Charlie and Flo here with me.'

'Of course, Mum. We all would. But the money will help.'

George nodded. 'It'll help, Mum.'

'Don't feel right, taking money when all I want is my Charlie and Flo.'

'Oh, Mum.' Nellie knelt at Em's feet and wrapped her

arms around her. George, after a hesitant look at Nellie, came over to sit on the arm of Em's chair – Charlie's chair, as they still thought of it – and he too wrapped his arms around her.

'The money'll make life a bit easier for you, and maybe help set George up in a business of his own when he's finished his apprenticeship. Dad would have wanted that, eh? The three of us got to stick together and make the best of our lives.'

Em sniffed back a tear. 'I know, love. I know. Hard though, innit?'

'Yes, Mum. It always will be hard.' And she thought of Ray, whose loss was just as hard for her to bear, and always would be. But with the case now over and money worries gone, perhaps she'd be able to move on at last.

Chapter 42

The compensation hearing may have been held behind closed doors, but the judge, Mr Justice Singleton, had other ideas about the verdict he reached, or so Nellie learnt the following day as she approached the town hall ready for her working day. There was a throng of people at the entrance – reporters, photographers and general public – and their mood was angry. Staff entering the town hall were being accosted and shouted at, though from where she was, Nellie couldn't make out what they were saying.

'Nellie! Can I have a quick word?' It was Stan Collins. 'Congratulations to your mother on winning the case. It's a good outcome and I'm not surprised. I was looking out for you, hoping to catch you before they all did.' He nodded in the direction of the crowd.

'What's it all about?' Nellie asked, feeling worried, as he drew her away into a side street that was quieter.

'The judge has published his verdict. Think he wants his moment in the spotlight.' Stan pulled a cigarette out of his pocket and lit it.

Nellie gasped. 'Can he do that? I thought it was all supposed to be secret?'

'It's up to the judge if he wants to publicise his findings. And it seems he does. The story's in all the papers this morning.'

'What did he say? I mean, of course I know my mother won compensation but . . .' Nellie was confused. She hadn't seen the morning papers.

'He said the shelter steps were a trap. He laid the blame firmly at the feet of the Borough Council,' Stan said. 'As the body responsible for the shelter and the safety of those using it, he judged that they are liable for compensation payouts. It's as we expected, and there will be a lot more lawsuits to come. I'll be making my own claim, for the loss of my father.' He took a puff of his cigarette and stared at the crowds across the road. 'So they,' he jabbed a finger in their direction, 'are now also blaming the Council.'

'You were right then. To persuade Mum to bring the case.' Nellie couldn't understand why Stan wasn't more excited by the verdict. They'd won. Stan could now seek compensation himself.

'Yes. But what I don't get is why the Council didn't defend itself. You told me they'd applied for funding and been denied it. Why didn't the Mayor say that, at the hearing? She gave evidence but she didn't say any of that. The judge said there was no attempt before the accident to improve the entrance and yet, we know there was.' He frowned and shook his head. 'Nellie, I thought this was our chance to get the truth told at last. The public deserves to know. If the Council had defended itself, then it'd all have come out. I don't get it. Is there anything . . . you can say? I don't want to push you, but we deserve to know.'

Nellie stared at him. It was just like at the initial inquiry. The Mayor had not taken the opportunity to tell the truth. 'I-I don't know. I don't understand either. I'll . . . see if I can find out anything . . . that I'm allowed to say.' She took a deep breath. 'I do agree, Mr Collins, that the public ought to know. We . . . I mean, the Council couldn't have tried harder to make the shelter safe. It ain't our fault.'

'I know. There's a cover-up. The government is using the Council as a scapegoat, like you said before. I suppose Home Secretary Morrison doesn't want to lose his job. Bloody politicians, eh? Always want what's best for their own careers.' He dropped his cigarette butt and ground it beneath his heel. 'Well, I won't keep you any longer. Hope to catch up with you again later.'

Nellie took a deep breath and left Stan, heading into the town hall and bracing herself for a difficult day ahead.

'Excuse me, miss, do you agree that the Council are negligent? How is the Council going to afford all the other lawsuits that will no doubt follow this one?' a man shouted at her as she began climbing the entrance steps.

She just shook her head and went on up. Behind her the noise of the crowd grew louder and there were angry shouts. 'Murderer! You killed my mum! You killed them all!

'How can you live with yourself, you cow!'

'Murderer! Murderer!'

Shocked, Nellie turned to see Mrs Bolton pushing her way through, looking small and frightened. She was being jostled by the crowd, photographers were shoving cameras in her face, reporters were waving notebooks. All were shouting questions at her, while others in the crowd were hurling abuse.

Nellie rushed to the Mayor's side and took her arm. 'Let's get inside, Mrs Bolton.' She elbowed a reporter out of the way as they climbed the remaining steps and pushed open the town hall doors.

Thankfully no one followed them and they went straight up to the mayor's office, where Mrs Bolton slumped down heavily onto her chair, her head in her hands. 'That was ugly. Thank you, Nellie, for coming to my aid.' She sounded utterly defeated.

'Are you all right, Mrs Bolton?' Nellie asked.

The Mayor looked up and regarded Nellie with a strained expression. 'No, not really. The judge didn't hold back in saying that the shelter and the safety of people using it are ultimately the responsibility of the borough. And it seems those people out there now think I *personally* killed their loved ones.' The Mayor's voice cracked then she seemed to remember who she was talking to. She glanced up at Nellie. 'I do understand why your mother brought this case and on a personal level I am glad she will get compensation. But, my God. That was horrible. I have given my all to this borough, to these people, I've done my best for them at all times, and now they call me a m-murderer.'

Nellie was astounded to see that the Mayor, normally so poised and calm and capable, was on the verge of tears. She felt awful that Mrs Bolton was now being blamed. She'd hoped the hearing would have cleared her of any wrongdoing or negligence, and there was something Nellie still couldn't understand.

'Mrs Bolton, why didn't you . . . the Council . . . defend yourself? Couldn't you have talked about all those times you tried to get funding? It was a closed session so it's not like it would affect morale and all that.' Nellie spoke gently, not at all sure whether she would get an answer.

'Ah, politics, politics,' said the Mayor. 'I am not at liberty to say.'

She left the office then, muttering about needing to fortify herself before she could face the day's business. Nellie watched her leave, the Mayor's shoulders slumped as though the weight of the world was upon them. At least, the weight of 173 needless deaths, according to the mob outside. And still Nellie was none the wiser as to why the Mayor hadn't defended the Council's actions.

*

Nellie kept out of the Mayor's way as much as possible that day, only working in the office when Mrs Bolton was in a meeting. Em's compensation claim had changed everything. All she could do was hope things would improve and that they would return to the mutual respect and friendship they'd had before.

Before.

That's how Nellie saw life now – before the tragedy, in which she included the news of Ray's death – and after. There was no going back, except for in her dreams, when she'd imagine Flo was still there in the other bed, clutching her Dollie, snuffling in her sleep, and that tomorrow Nellie would be breakfasting with all the family before going out for the day with Ray. And then she'd wake up and remember. Even now, two years on, it hurt so much. Every day was a struggle.

Only her friends, Babs, Amelia and of course Billy, helped her through. They took her out to the cinema or for a drink. They came round with little treats for her – a packet of biscuits, a few fresh oranges. They spent time sitting with her in the backyard, just being there so she could talk if she wanted to.

Billy's quiet, gentle presence had always been a constant in her life. Now that she was older, wiser, and had been through so much, she appreciated it more than ever.

In the late afternoon that day, she was heading back into the mayor's office after a tea break when she heard the Mayor talking to someone on the telephone, and she sounded irritated. Nellie turned to go but then something the Mayor said made her stop, and listen.

'So the government will foot the bill, if I am understanding you correctly?'

There was a pause as the Mayor listened to the person on the other end of the line. 'Uh huh, but you and I know the Council is not to blame—' She broke off as though she'd been interrupted and listened again.

'And any future compensation claims?' The Mayor's tone was hostile.

'I expect there could be dozens, Mr Macdonald Ross. An awful lot of families were affected. I'm not comfortable with this underhand arrangement, you must understand that, but you leave me no choice. The Council's insurance is limited to £5,000. That would only cover about three payouts the size of the Morrises'.'

Another pause.

'Please stop. There's no need to explain the Official Secrets Act to me yet again. It's not easy. My own people here are accusing me of effectively murdering their loved ones. But if the only way I can help them now is to allow myself to be scapegoated, then . . . so be it. *I* know the truth. I shall have to be content with that. Good afternoon.'

There was a clatter as the telephone receiver was put down violently. Nellie turned away from the door and headed back to the typing pool. She needed a few minutes to think about what she'd just heard. So the Mayor had agreed to accept responsibility in return for the government paying the compensation claims? That explained a lot. Nellie's heart went out to the Mayor, who was seemingly in an impossible situation.

*

When she left the town hall that day, Stan was waiting for her on the steps once more.

'Did you find anything out?'

She shook her head. Despite Stan becoming a friend of the family, she knew there was no possibility of her telling him what she'd overheard the Mayor say. If he wrote a story on it, even if he named no names, the government might withdraw their offer to pay the compensation. The losers would be the Bethnal Green people who'd already suffered so much. 'Sorry. The Mayor won't tell me anything more.'

Stan sighed. 'At least people will win compensation. There are already another fifteen writs served, including mine, and there will be more to come. I can't imagine how the borough is going to pay them all.' He rubbed his chin, looking thoughtful. 'Unless perhaps the government is quietly footing the bill.' He glanced at Nellie with a question in his eye.

She held his gaze and shrugged. 'Maybe. Who knows?'

'Hmm. Well, I imagine things will calm down around here soon. The anger will dissipate as the money is paid. Keep in touch, eh? Let me know if you do hear anything more. I would still dearly love to cover the truth of this in my paper.'

He left then, and Nellie heaved a sigh of relief as she headed homewards. She realised she was in pretty much the same situation as the Mayor. Bound to hide the truth, for the good of the community. She was exhausted by it all. Every time she thought there'd be a path forward, she reached a new roadblock. Would there ever be a future in which she'd find peace and closure?

Chapter 43

'How long, do you think, before Germany surrenders?' Nellie asked Billy as they walked in the park one fine spring morning. It had become a ritual for them lately. A bag of chips, a walk through the park and a chat about the state of the world.

'It's only a matter of time, I reckon,' Billy replied. 'Few weeks, month or two perhaps.' He took her hand to steady her as they negotiated a rough section of path and somehow she left her hand in his. It felt comfortable. It felt right.

Lately, she was happiest when in his company, and there was no denying he, more than anyone, knew what to do or what to say to make her feel better.

He was a good man, she thought, as they walked on, hand in hand, commenting on how Amelia's son, little William, had grown up so fast. 'Running everywhere now, trying to kick a football even, can you believe it!' Nellie said.

Billy smiled. 'He's talking too. He chatted to me non-stop when I last visited Amelia. Calls me Beeyeey.'

Nellie laughed at Billy's impersonation of the little boy. He'd make a good father, some day. A doting, caring, wonderful father. And husband.

'Nell?' Billy had stopped walking and pulled her to face him, a nervous yet serious expression on his face. 'Do you think, one day . . . we might . . .'

Her stomach gave a flutter. What was he going to say? She was excited but also nervous that he'd say something that would change things, pushing her in a direction she wasn't quite ready for. Not yet.

'. . . you and I . . . go to the pictures together? Without Babs, I mean. Just . . . the two of us?'

She turned and grinned at him. 'I would love that, Billy. *Brewster's Millions* is showing, and I haven't seen it yet, so why don't we go tomorrow?'

The delighted look on his face was infectious, and she laughed and caught his arm, pulling him close to her side. 'It'll be fun! Looking forward to it!'

This was the way to do it. Gradually, bit by bit, step by step, they could allow their friendship to turn into something deeper. She'd always been fond of him, and now that they were older, it felt right for their relationship to develop. There was an inevitability about it, Nellie thought. There always had been. It would take time, but that was all right, wasn't it? Her romance with Ray had been a whirlwind, the uncertainty of his job had forced that. This, with Billy, if it was indeed to be a romance, could and should progress so much slower, if it was to have any chance of succeeding. And she hoped, she realised, that it would.

Billy went home that day jubilant. He and Nellie had held hands as they strolled and made plans to go to the cinema, just the two of them – on a date. At least, he hoped that was how she saw it. He'd been so careful not to push her, not to rush her into anything, but now . . . now he dared to think they might have a future together. Just as Allied troops were winning battle after battle in Europe, liberating towns and cities one by one, so he might win her heart, bit by bit. He knew he'd never take Ray's place in her heart, but maybe there'd be space in it somewhere for him.

He hoped that soon he and Nellie would be going steady as their relationship had at last headed in that direction. His dreams, for so long buried, once more had a chance to surface. The future was looking bright.

Chapter 44

In May at long last came the news that everyone had hoped for. Hitler was dead, and the war in Europe was finally over. Every church's bells had been ringing non-stop, people were going about with grins on their faces, the pubs were running out of beer and the atmosphere of joy and relief was so tangible Nellie felt that if only she could bottle it and sell it, she'd make a fortune.

So many families had been torn apart by the war, and perhaps none more so than Nellie's. But today was V-E Day, and Morpeth Street was having a hastily arranged party to celebrate the news, broadcast on the wireless the day before, that Germany had unconditionally surrendered.

'Flo would have loved it, wouldn't she?' Em said to Nellie, as she popped a batch of shortbread biscuits into the oven. 'She'd have been in the kitchen helping us, loving every minute.'

Nellie smiled wistfully. 'Yes, and Dad would have been busy shifting the table and chairs out into the street, organising the other blokes.'

'Breaks my heart that they're not here with us,' Em said, and Nellie crossed the kitchen to give her a hug.

'I know. But they wouldn't want us to be sad. Not today, eh Mum?' She gazed around the kitchen where every surface was covered with plates crammed with all manner of good things to eat. Every house on the street would be the same – all using every bit of their ration to provide sandwiches, pies, cakes and biscuits for everyone to enjoy. After all it wasn't every day that your country and her allies were victorious in a war that had lasted nearly six years. 'Do you think there's enough food?'

''Course there is! We'll be eating the leftovers for days. Just as well, 'cos we ain't got no more ration coupons.' Em smiled as she wiped the table clear of flour. 'If you can find your brother, you can carry this table out with him. Or get Billy to do it with George.'

'Did I hear my name, Em?' Billy came in the back door. 'Want me to bring the table out? Quite a few people are out there already.'

'Yes please, Billy, love.'

'I'll help too, Mum,' Nellie said. 'Come on then, Billy.'

It wasn't easy – the large kitchen table had to be upended and fed through the doors two legs at a time, all the while Em was yelling at them to mind the paintwork. As they tried to get it through the front door, somehow Billy ended up stuck between its legs and the door frame. 'Ha! I got you trapped now! Mine forever!' Nellie said with a laugh.

'I'll always be yours, Nell, you know that,' he replied

with a grin and a wink, but the wistful expression in his eyes told her he was serious despite his joking tone. She knew it, and some day soon she'd have to let him know she knew it. And tell that if he wanted to take things further, well . . . she was probably ready for that now. They'd been stepping out for a while now. It wasn't the passionate fireworks she'd felt with Ray, but a comforting, warm love that made her feel safe and secure. And that was best for her now.

'Gonna be quite a party!' Babs said, as she arranged her family's chairs at the next table along.

'It is! What're you gonna wear?' Nellie said.

'I got a new dress!' Babs said, proudly. 'Saved up all me clothing coupons for weeks, just for this event. Red, white and blue, it is. What about you?'

'My old blue thing.'

'You always look lovely in that. Coming, Mum!' Babs ran off to answer a yell from Mrs Waters.

Nellie felt a sudden pang of sadness. Ray had always liked her blue dress the best. She'd been wearing it the day she'd met him. He was another person not here to join in the celebrations. If things had turned out differently, perhaps they'd be arranging a wedding by now. That had been the plan, once the war was over. She sighed and pulled herself together. Over two years on and she still missed him. But she owed it to his memory to be as cheerful as she could, he'd have hated to think of her moping. *Have a happy life*, he'd said on that wonderful day when they'd ridden a bicycle all around the borough.

She couldn't see a bicycle in the park without thinking of that day. So often there'd be some little thing to remind her of him – an American accent overheard, a knitted scarf like the one she'd made him, a discordant jazz band on the wireless. She was grateful for the memories but life was moving forward and she was okay with that. She had Billy, and she'd build herself a happy life as Ray had told her she must.

*

The party, when it got going, was riotous. The entire street turned out, with every household contributing twice as much food as they could eat themselves. They'd arranged the tables down the centre of the street and children chased each other up and down either side. Someone had set up a gramophone and was playing dance records at full volume. George came back with Oscar just as they'd finished setting up and were about to start eating. 'Typical boy, just in time for the food!' Em said, ruffling his hair fondly.

Mrs Waters had made bunting and strung it from house to house, but halfway through eating it fell down, right across the many trifles that adorned the tables. She blushed but everyone laughed, and then a small boy caught hold of one end and ran off pulling it and whooping gleefully, with all the other children following.

'Who needs paper chains when you've got a chain of kids?' Nellie shouted over the noise.

'Come on, let's join in. It's not just for the children!' Billy pulled her to her feet.

'We can be big kids!' Nellie chuckled, and soon they too had joined the chain, with Billy behind Nellie and Babs behind him, all laughing hard as they gripped the bunting and followed the line of children, dancing their way along the street.

'One day we'll look back and wonder if we ever really grew up,' Nellie yelled back at Billy.

'One day I'll marry you, Nellie Morris!' he called out, in the way he always used to.

Something shifted inside her at this, a warmth rose up in her. This was as good a time as any. A better time than any other, if you thought about it. Suddenly she knew that was what she wanted – the safe, contented life that Billy could offer her. The security of staying in Bethnal Green near her family. The quiet, easy life that once she would have sneered at but now . . . things were different. *She* was different. She let go of the bunting, and stepped aside out of the chain of children, Billy did the same.

'Had enough already?' Babs said, closing the gap to carry on with the dance, which moved on up the street leaving Nellie and Billy at the side.

Nellie looked directly at Billy. 'All right, then. Why not?'

'You mean, you will . . .'

'Marry you. Yes.' She cocked her head on one side and smiled. 'But only if you propose to me properly, Billy Waters!'

He gaped for a moment, and then, with the broadest grin she'd ever seen on anyone, he dropped to his knees in front of her, took her hand and kissed it. 'Nellie Morris, the love of my life. Would you do me the honour of marrying me, making me the happiest man in a very happy city on a very happy day?'

She laughed and he blushed, a flicker of worry crossing his face as though he wondered if he'd got it all wrong, if she was teasing him. She pulled him to his feet and into her arms. 'Yes, Billy Waters. I'll marry you, and I'll be very pleased to do so.'

Around them, everyone had stopped talking and dancing when Billy dropped to his knees. When they heard Nellie's reply, an enormous cheer went up and everyone clapped.

'War's over, it's a new beginning for everyone, and I'll be very happy to spend the future with you,' she whispered to him. He turned to gaze at her, his eyes filled with love and also astonishment. She'd made all his dreams come true, she knew it, and it was a good feeling.

'Congratulations, lad!' Mr Waters said, clapping his son on the shoulder. 'And Nellie, you will be so welcome in our family.'

'Nellie!' Em came bustling over, her eyes brimming with tears. 'I am so pleased for you, love. After all that happened, this is the best thing. Billy, love, let me give you a kiss.'

'Propose to one Morris woman, get two!' Babs

quipped. 'My best friend marrying my brother. At long last!' She kissed each of them in turn.

'George, come here. Give your old sister a kiss,' Nellie said, seeing her brother standing back a little, behind the crowd that was gathered around them. It'd be strange for him – a new man joining the family.

'Well done, Nellie,' he said, as she planted a big wet kiss on his cheek. He rubbed it off immediately. 'I'll miss you, if you move out.' He looked thoughtful for a moment. 'You'll be Mrs Waters, I s'pose.'

'I'll always be Nellie to you, Georgie-boy.'

He grinned at the old nickname and gave her a play-punch on the arm. Maybe they weren't growing up, not just yet.

The whole street, her friends and family, all dancing and laughing, celebrating the end of the war and the start of her new life with Billy at her side.

He'd be a good husband. He'd be steady and kind and thoughtful, and he'd worship her. They'd have a calm, quiet life here in Bethnal Green, surrounded by their friends and family. Right now that was all she wanted.

Chapter 45

The celebrations went on late into the evening. Some of the men were still in the street drinking beer and singing raucous songs, but Em, Nellie and George finally called it a day. Billy hugged Nellie goodnight. 'You have made me so happy, Nellie. I can't believe my luck.'

She smiled and stroked his face. 'You've work tomorrow. Better get to bed now, eh?' He kissed her cheek and went inside.

Nellie joined Em in their kitchen to help wash up and set things straight.

'You'll soon have your own kitchen, when you're married,' Em said. 'You'll get your own little place and it'll be just me and George here.'

'Wherever we live, it won't be far away, Mum,' Nellie said. 'We'll stay in Bethnal Green.' She pictured a little house nearby for her and Billy, his slippers by the fire, her apron hanging on a peg in the kitchen. Like her parents before her and her grandparents before that. It wasn't what she used to dream of, but it was a good future that awaited her. A safe, comfortable one. She felt her stomach twist a little at the idea of being a wife. With excitement, yes, but also nerves. How could this be happening to her? It was a world away from how she'd felt when she was promised to Ray. More grown up. More serious. But the right thing to do now.

'I can help you out with the rent. Or buy you a house outright. With my compensation money.' Em took a tea towel from a drawer and began drying the dishes Nellie had washed. There were tears in her eyes, Nellie noticed. It was a big moment, her getting engaged, and Em must be feeling the pain of not having Charlie there to share it with.

'Oh, Mum, that's for you and George. Billy and I will have enough money with two wages.'

'Well, then, I shall pay for your wedding. And I won't hear no arguments about it.'

'You don't need—' Nellie started, but Em interrupted her, wagging her finger.

'What did I just say? No arguments. My girl's going to have the best and biggest wedding Bethnal Green has ever seen. I got the money. I know your reporter friend Stan said I could buy me own house but I don't want to. I want to stay in this house. I got more than enough to pay the rent and help George out and buy some new curtains for the front room, so I'm going to spend some of it on your wedding. We'll hire the Angel and Crown for the reception. We'll invite everyone in the street. You'll have the most beautiful dress, the best we can get. We'll go up west to buy it. And there'll be so much food! A three-tier wedding cake. No, five tiers! Why not!'

Nellie laughed. 'Mum, you are getting carried away. We don't need all that, Billy and me. We'll just want our family and friends there.'

'You ain't gonna stop me paying for a big party for you.' Em stopped drying up for a moment and looked thoughtful. 'I can't help but think how much Flo would have liked seeing you as a bride. She'd have loved to wear a bridesmaid dress. And how proud your dad would have been, Nellie, walking you up the aisle.'

'I wish he were still here to walk me up the aisle too,' Nellie said quietly. 'And I'd have had Flo as a brides-maid, of course. Imagine her in a pretty frilly frock with a ribbon in her hair and a bouquet in her hand – she'd have loved it.'

'She would've.' Em sniffed, and rubbed her eye with the back of her hand. 'Who'll walk you up the aisle now, I wonder? George?'

'He's a bit young. Also, he's my brother. He can't "give me away", can he?'

'Frank Waters?'

'He's Billy's dad. That doesn't seem right either.' Nellie had an idea. She looked at Em questioningly. 'What about you, Mum? There's nothing that says it has to be a man, is there? I don't see why it can't be you.'

'Me? But . . .' Em blinked, as though not sure how to respond, but Nellie saw pride in her eyes that she'd been asked.

'I would love you to do it, Mum. Imagine, the two of us walking up the aisle together, to meet Billy at the altar . . .' She tailed off, for briefly in her mind it had been Ray she'd seen, waiting for her at the end of the aisle. Ray, looking handsome in his smart uniform, with his broad smile and love shining from his face. She felt tears prick at her eyes and she pinched the bridge of her nose.

Em rubbed her arm. 'There now, love. I know it's all a bit overwhelming for you, ain't it? You'll be all right. And yes, I'll walk you up the aisle. It'll be quite something, won't it? No one round here would ever forget your wedding, would they? When's it going to be, then?'

Nellie rubbed away her tears. 'Mum, he only proposed to me a few hours ago. Give us chance to get it all arranged, eh?'

'Well, don't leave it too long. Gawd knows, if the war taught us anything, it's that if you've a chance of happiness, take it straight away, as you don't know what's round the corner.'

'That's true enough,' Nellie said, kissing her mum on the cheek.

Chapter 46

They decided on a June date for their wedding. It was just a few weeks away and there was hardly any time for Nellie to catch her breath. 'No point waiting too long,' Billy said, and Nellie agreed, remembering what Em had said about taking your chances while you could. Now that they were engaged they spent all their free time together, going to the pictures, spending nights out at the Angel and Crown, or walking in parks making plans for their future. Billy had more time since he didn't have to work shifts or nights at his new job as a clerk for a construction company. Nellie had a different job too. She still worked for the Council but in a more general administrative role. Mrs Bolton had stood down as mayor and retired a few months earlier.

A week after V-E Day, on their way home from the Angel and Crown one night, Billy suggested to Nellie that they walk the long way round, through Bethnal Green Gardens.

'Let's sit here a minute,' he said, pulling her towards a bench.

'So do you think we should have wine at the reception?' Nellie said, continuing the conversation about their wedding they'd been having. 'I mean most people drink beer, or gin and tonic . . .' She broke off, noticing that Billy was regarding her with an intensity she hadn't seen before.

'What is it, Billy? What's on your—' On your mind, she'd been going to say, but he interrupted her by reaching for her, tugging her close, and then his lips were on hers, his hands around her back. She responded, wrapping her arms around his neck and pulling him in close. It wasn't like kissing Ray, which had made her melt inside every time. But it was warm and pleasant, and she knew Billy loved her with all his soul.

He let out a low moan, and when the kiss ended he blushed. 'S-sorry, Nellie, I couldn't help myself, and we are . . . engaged now.'

She smiled. 'It's all right. Really. In fact . . . it was very nice.' And she meant it, it was.

Perhaps you could only truly love one person in your lifetime, in the all-consuming way she'd loved Ray. She was lucky to have Billy and grateful to him, but she knew she'd never feel for him the intense passion she'd had for Ray. Maybe friendship was more important in the long run for a long, happy marriage. She wasn't sure. Rather than dwell on it any more, she leaned in and kissed Billy again.

'I love you, Nellie Morris,' Billy said, when at last they broke apart.

'And . . . I, you,' she replied, and he kissed her once more.

*

They debated which church to marry in. St John's held so many painful memories for Nellie – seeing Flo and Charlie's bodies there, watching Ray carve their initials in the stone. But it was the community's church and in the end Em insisted. 'It's where I married your dad, and where I always imagined you marrying, Nellie. We have to bury the bad memories under new, good ones.'

Throughout the rest of May, their wedding plans came together quickly. As she'd expected, Billy refused to take any money from Em for a honeymoon but did agree to let her pay for a reception at the Angel and Crown. Amelia was excited to help them organise that part of the day. With a dress bought, Babs roped in as bridesmaid and George agreeing to be best man, everything was arranged. They'd found a flat to rent, two streets away from Morpeth Street. Her future was mapped out, and it wasn't a bad one at all, not when she considered how dark things had been two and a half years earlier. Not for the first time, Nellie thanked her lucky stars for Billy, good, strong, dependable Billy to whom she'd so soon be married.

*

Two days before the wedding, Nellie and Billy spent the evening in the Angel and Crown. Babs was there too, with the new man she'd started seeing. Her factory had reverted to making silky underwear and nightwear, to her enormous joy, and she had a new supervisor – an ex-army captain named Peter, whom Babs had immediately taken a shine to and asked out. Nellie was glad that it looked like Babs was forging a good new life for herself.

'He's nice,' she said to Babs, when Peter was at the bar fetching another round of drinks for the four of them.

'He is, yes. We both got ourselves decent men,' Babs said. 'You'll soon be married. Then you'll have kids, and I'll be an aunty!'

'Oh! I don't know if we'll have children straight away,' Nellie said, glancing at Billy. Truth be told, she hadn't much thought about that aspect of marriage. Her, a mum? Was that what Billy expected, that they'd start a family immediately? Em had been twenty-one when she'd had Nellie, but Nellie felt too young, still. She wanted to enjoy life with just Billy, first.

'Not straight away,' Billy said, looking embarrassed. Peter returned then with the drinks and began a conversation with Babs. 'Actually, Nellie,' Billy went on, talking quietly in her ear, 'I, erm, went to the chemist today. To . . . you know. Get myself equipped. For . . . our wedding night. So we don't have to have babies straight away, if you don't want to.'

'Oh!' She vaguely understood what he was referring to.

'They . . . come in packs of three,' Billy said, 'and you

can only buy three at a time. Even love is on the ration, it seems.'

At this, Nellie threw back her head and laughed aloud. 'Love on the ration! Oh dear!'

Billy seemed pleased he'd made her laugh, but less so when Babs turned to him demanding to know what was so funny. 'Sorry, there are some things a man can't talk about to his sister.'

'Tell you later,' Nellie whispered to her, which for some reason made both girls dissolve into fits of giggles. Now it was Billy's turn to ask what they were laughing about.

It was a fun evening. Billy and Nellie left first, walking home slowly on the fine summer's night. 'Won't be long, Nellie, until you and I are walking back to our own little home, together,' Billy said, as she took his arm. 'But we'll have a honeymoon first. I have it all booked.'

'Ooh! Where to?'

He grinned. 'You'll have to wait and see.'

'Oh, go on. Tell me! I'm longing to know!' She squeezed his arm close to her and stretched up to kiss his cheek.

'Not saying. I want it to be a surprise.'

'Oh please!' She stopped him and turned him to face her, kissing him soundly.

'Ahem. Not even that will make me tell you,' he said, when they broke apart. 'Go on, inside. You need your beauty sleep before the big day.'

And with one last kiss he'd gone into his own home, waving at her from the doorstep as he closed the door.

Nellie stayed outside for a moment longer, enjoying

the balmy night air as she gazed up at the stars. Once, so long ago, she'd done exactly this with Ray. It was harder to see them now the blackout had ended and streetlights were no longer shaded. But they were the same stars as on that other night, long past.

There was a figure standing at the end of the street. Something about him looked familiar, achingly familiar – his height and build, the way he held himself. She began walking back up the street towards the man, then broke into a run, not believing what she was seeing until she was just a few feet from him. He was thinner and older-looking; there were lines on his face that hadn't been there before. He was wearing an ill-fitting set of civilian clothes, not the handsome blue uniform she remembered. But it was him. Definitely, unmistakably and remarkably *him*.

'R-Ray? But . . . how . . .' she gasped. Her legs felt like jelly as she stared at him, unable to trust what she could see with her own eyes.

'Nellie. Oh, my Nellie,' he said, holding out his arms to her. Her instinct was to fall into them, but she couldn't, not right here, with neighbours' curtains twitching. And Billy was inside, just a few feet away . . .

'How . . . how are you here?' She had so many questions, but no idea how to start. And so much she needed him to know, but where could she even begin? She thought she'd lost him, she'd been told he was dead, and yet . . . here he was, right in front of her. It was a miracle, and yet . . . the timing could hardly have been worse.

'I was shot down,' he said. 'I crash-landed over German

territory and was taken prisoner.' He shrugged, as though dismissing his experiences as unimportant. He didn't want to talk about it, at least not now, Nellie guessed. The idea of him being a prisoner horrified her, but he'd survived, he was right here. 'I've been in a POW camp, and I was only released after the war was over.' Ray kept his eyes on Nellie's the whole time he was talking, and she kept hers on his, drinking him in, unable to believe that he was here, her own, dear Ray standing right here in front of her. 'Nellie, I'm sorry I couldn't come sooner. It took a while to make arrangements, and then . . . I didn't write first because I wasn't sure . . . I thought I'd just come and see . . .'

It seemed such a cruel twist of fate, that so close to her wedding Ray had returned. The man she'd always wanted, within reach, yet out of her grasp. Her mind was in turmoil. She loved Billy, she was marrying him in two days yet how could she turn her back on Ray? It was Ray, for goodness sake! Ray, the man she'd loved so very much!

They needed to talk. That much was clear. Somewhere quiet, private. Not here, where even now Billy, her fiancé, might be watching from his bedroom window. 'Come on,' she said. 'I know where we can go to talk.'

Chapter 47

She led him through the familiar streets towards the tube station entrance, and from there across the road to the church. St John's church, Ray recalled, where once he'd carved their initials into the stonework. That seemed so long ago, in a different life. The gates to its grounds were open, although the church was locked. Down the side, past their initials, was a bench and here she motioned to him to sit beside her.

'God, Ray. I can't believe it. I just can't,' she said, staring at him as though drinking in every inch of him. 'Why didn't you write?'

'I did, in the camp, but we found out afterwards that none of our letters were sent. The guards destroyed them all. When we were released, I was torn whether to write first or just come straight here. In France there was no opportunity, we were shuffled from place to place. Repatriation takes ages. Then when I arrived at Dover, I figured it'd be quicker to take a train directly here rather than write a letter first. I saw Clayton at Dover, briefly. He was part of the team meeting released prisoners and getting them kitted out with a set of clothes and train tickets. He told me he'd been to see you back in '43 and shared the bad news.'

He smiled at her, longing for her to fall into his arms so he could kiss her, so it could be like it had been. But she was gazing at him with something like regret in her eyes, biting her lip nervously. Did she still hate him for what had happened on that terrible night?

He glanced away from her, across the street to the tube station entrance. It was quiet, deserted and calm. So unlike the last time he'd seen it, the last time he'd been here. The view, in his mind, was overlaid by what he'd witnessed that night – his borrowed car parked there, ambulances all around, bodies covered with blankets and coats, bewildered and traumatised rescue workers doing their best. And Nellie, with her mother and brother, wondering where the rest of their family was. That agonising time he spent comforting George while Nellie and Mrs Morris checked the bodies in the church. That wail of anguish he'd heard coming from the church when they found Flo.

And all of it had been his fault. His fault, for driving a backfiring car so near a crowd of people who were only trying to reach safety during an air raid.

Night after night in the POW camp he'd lain awake, replaying the events of that night over and over, wishing he'd parked farther away, wishing he'd shouted that no, it wasn't the Nazis firing on them, it was only a car. Wishing he could have pulled people out sooner. Imagining himself seeing the top of Flo's head, grabbing her and saving her.

Clearing a path for Mr Morris. Anything, to make it *not his fault* that they died. How many died, he didn't know, but Clayton had told him, when they met in Dover, that it was thought to be dozens. All of them on his conscience.

'I'm sorry, Nellie,' he said again. 'I destroyed your family. If you don't want me any more, I'll go.'

'What do you mean, destroyed my family?' She was looking at him quizzically.

'The . . . accident. My car, backfiring, starting the panic.' He hated that she'd made him say it aloud.

'Your car didn't start the panic,' Nellie said carefully. 'The survivors said there was no panic. People were hurrying but that was all. And if there was more rush than usual, it was because of the new anti-aircraft rockets they'd fired from Vicky Park. Nothing to do with your car.'

'But . . .'

'I wrote to tell you this, as soon as I knew.' She'd turned to him again, and was holding his hands on her lap, squeezing them. 'Oh Ray. I prayed you'd received that letter before . . . I hated thinking you might have d-died without knowing it wasn't your fault.'

He frowned. 'I never had any letter . . .'

'It must have arrived too late,' she said, crying now, but still not leaning into him for comfort. 'There was an inquiry, I was there taking notes as part of my job, and I heard it all. I heard all the witnesses. None of them mentioned shots, or anything that could have been your motorcar. None of them! They all said people were calm as they went down the steps.'

'Not a panic?'

'No.'

'Then how . . .'

'A woman fell, at the bottom. She was holding a child. Someone else fell right by her, and then those behind fell forward on top of them, and then more came. The whole thing happened so quickly, they say. In seconds. There was no chance of stopping it.'

'How many?' Ray had to know.

'One hundred and seventy-three.' Nellie's answer came in a whisper, so quiet he thought he'd misheard.

'One hundred . . .' he began, repeating her.

' . . . and seventy-three. Yes.'

He pulled his hands away from her then, burying his face in them to silently mourn those poor souls, dear little Flo and decent, hard-working Mr Morris among them. But it wasn't his fault. *It wasn't his fault.* 'All this time I've thought . . .'

'We've all blamed ourselves,' Nellie said, a sympathetic tone now in her voice. 'For taking Flo off the bus. For delaying getting to the tube that night. Even Billy, for not doing more down below to pull people out. But he was a hero that night. He did save a few people, just like you did.' A note of pride had crept in as she said this last part, and Ray was glad that it sounded as though she'd come to terms, as far as possible, with those terrible losses of 1943.

But there was something else in her voice when she'd mentioned Billy. An intimacy. He remembered the skinny boy, Babs's brother, the air raid warden, who'd been besotted by her. He waited for her to carry on speaking, half knowing what she was about to say, dreading it but knowing he had to hear it.

'Ray, this is so hard for me . . . but I'm engaged to Billy,' she said. Her voice broke on the words and his heart went out to her. 'We marry in just two days. In there.' She nodded towards the church.

He'd known, of course, there was a possibility she'd have found someone else. If she'd been married already, there'd be no chance for them. If she'd been free, they could pick up where they left off. But this – this no-man's-land between her being simultaneously out of reach and accessible – this was the most painful of all the possibilities.

'Do you love him?' he asked quietly. It was the key question, the one that had to be answered, even though he dreaded hearing her reply.

She nodded, slowly, biting her lip. 'I do. I-I always have, in some ways. I've known him all my life. We've always been the best of friends. And he's been kind to me. I think, if it hadn't been for Billy, I wouldn't have got through the last two years.' She pushed away a tear. 'After the . . . accident at the tube station, and then you going, and then Clayton telling me you were dead . . . I was at rock bottom, Ray. Billy helped me through that. It brought us closer together.'

He felt grateful to the other man for that, at least. 'He always loved you. That was obvious.'

'Yes. He always has,' she said with resignation.

'And you agreed to marry him?'

She gazed up at him for a moment before answering. 'I thought you were dead. I had to keep living. Billy is a good man, and it felt like the right thing to do. He makes me happy, and I know he will be a good husband to me.'

'And now?' He whispered the words. He held his breath, waiting for the answer. A minute passed, an hour, a day, a lifetime, while he waited.

'And now,' she whispered back, looking down at her hands that were clasped together in her lap, 'now . . . the wedding is in two days. It's all been arranged.'

'But . . .'

'I'm still going to marry him, Ray.' She let out an enormous sigh, the weight of the world exhaled through her mouth. 'I can't let him down. It would end him. And . . . I do love him, and it'll be a good marriage. I was told you were dead.' She grabbed his hand then and held it to her heart. 'Please believe me – I'd have waited forever if I'd believed there was the slightest chance! I love you, Ray, I will always love you, but I can't leave Billy. I can't. I love him too.'

And then she was sobbing, and he was holding her and she was clutching at him like a drowning man clutches at a lifebelt and he was forcing himself to see her point of view, to understand, to accept it.

He said nothing for a minute, letting her sobs subside. He gently unwrapped his arms from around her and passed her a handkerchief. She sat upright again, smiled weakly at him and mopped her tears.

'I understand,' he said, and they were the hardest two words he had ever spoken. 'I won't stand in your way. You deserve a happy marriage and I'm only sorry it can't be me who gives you that.'

She gasped and the tears began to fall again. It broke his heart seeing her like this, and it was *his* fault. She should be happy, excited about her upcoming wedding, longing to be joined to the man she loved. And he'd spoiled all that for her. 'Nellie, I'd never have come back if I'd known about you and Billy. I'd have kept away. I am sorry, so sorry, I put you through this.'

They sat in silence for another few minutes, each lost in their own thoughts. Ray had made a decision. He lifted his head to gaze at her one last time, and found she was staring at him, love and longing and loss reflected in her eyes.

'I wish you . . . all the best, for your wedding day. And I hope you and Billy have a long and happy life together.' As he said this, he meant it. He only wanted her to be happy. 'I'll leave here tonight, and I won't come back. I have to go to my old airbase and be formally discharged anyway. And they will make arrangements to get me back home to the US.'

'Ray, I—' she began, but he held up a hand.

'There's no more to be said, Nellie. Just . . . let me hold you, one last time.'

As though she'd been waiting for him to say that, she fell into his arms again and he held her tight, stroking her back, her hair, longing to kiss her but knowing that would be their undoing. She nuzzled her face against his cheek as though she too was battling the same desires, and then, as one, they pushed each other away.

'Goodbye then, Nellie.'

'Goodbye, Ray. I hope you find . . . someone . . . I hope you'll be happy too.'

They stood. He watched as she walked away, gratified when she stopped and glanced back, just once more. He lifted a hand to wave at her, and she did the same, and then she was gone, into the night, and he was alone.

***

Nellie let herself into her house quietly, praying that Em would be already in bed and wouldn't wake. She tiptoed up the stairs and into her room, collapsing onto her bed, staring at the ceiling.

She'd lost Ray before, she'd spent the last two years coming to terms with that and now . . . now she had to do it all over again. It was a miracle he was alive and her heart surged with joy to think of it, but he couldn't be hers. She couldn't and wouldn't let Billy down. It would destroy him. She had to be strong, and not think of Ray again, and think only of the quiet, settled life she'd been planning with Billy.

And put Ray, her darling Ray whom she loved with all her heart, out of her mind for ever.

Chapter 48

The day of Nellie's wedding, the morning was filled with last-minute jitters and passed in a whirl of getting ready, people calling at the house, packing a case ready for the honeymoon. Babs arrived at Nellie's at nine o'clock to do her hair and make-up and get dressed. Em insisted on both girls having a large breakfast of scrambled eggs courtesy of George's chickens, and bacon for which she'd saved ration coupons. 'Can't have you fainting at the altar,' she said, wagging her finger. 'I knew a girl who did that once. Ate nothing on her wedding morning, keeled over saying her vows and banged her head, got blood all over her wedding dress. Whole wedding had to be postponed.'

But Nellie could hardly eat. For two days she had carried her big secret inside her – the knowledge that Ray was alive, that she'd seen him. She couldn't help but wonder if the wedding hadn't been so close, if she'd had longer to consider her choice, might she have made a different decision? Would she have somehow found a way to gently let Billy down, even knowing it'd devastate him? She couldn't answer this, not now, not while everything was happening so fast and she had no time to think. She'd made her decision, she reminded herself for the hundredth time. She was sticking with Billy. She'd promised Babs she wouldn't break his heart. It was the right thing to do.

She tried hard to be as a girl should be on her wedding day – excited, fluttery, giggly. Like Em and Babs, who were skipping around, unable to wipe the grins off their faces. Nellie did her best to join in, but it was all an act. She knew it, she felt it, but she just had to hope that no one, not Em or Babs or God forbid, Billy, ever realised. She would never tell him about Ray, she'd decided. This was her cross to bear. Hers and no one else's. She'd made her decision and she knew it was the right one.

* * *

Nellie and Babs washed their hair and went upstairs to set it in curlers. 'You nervous?' Babs asked. ''Cos I am, and I ain't the bride!'

Nellie smiled. 'Yes, a bit. Looking forward to it but also I'll be glad when all the fuss is over.' It would have been so different if Ray hadn't come back. She'd have been nervous but excited. Right now she just wanted the day to go to plan, a ring to be on her finger, and she and Billy setting off for wherever their honeymoon was to be. She couldn't take any more surprises. She needed to start her new life with Billy. A life that she was confident would be loving and stable. Although she still hadn't got used to the idea that very soon she would be a married woman.

'It's your day. Of course there's lots of fuss!' Babs laughed. 'Billy's as jittery too, if it's any consolation. I couldn't wait to get out of there this morning. He was charging around the house looking for his Brylcreem he'd bought specially. As though the wedding couldn't go ahead without it! I said to him, if that's the worst thing that goes wrong today then the day will have gone well. Men, eh? They're more vain than we are, I reckon.'

Nellie forced a little laugh, wondering if she should tell Billy about Ray. Was it wrong to start married life keeping such an enormous secret from your husband? Even if it was for his own benefit, to save him from anguish. 'You could be right, there. Did he find it?'

'What?'

'The Brylcreem?'

'Oh, yeah, in his bedroom under the shirt Mum had ironed and laid out for him to wear.' Babs chuckled. 'You know what Mum said? She said that'll be the last shirt she ever irons for Billy, and from today on it's your responsibility. Hope you're looking forward to ironing my brother's shirts!'

'Hmm. He can iron his own. I'll teach him,' Nellie said. A couple of days ago, the image of her ironing Billy's shirts while he toiled in the garden or painted walls or simply sat with the newspaper was one she'd have relished – a quiet, comfortable domestic scene. The future she'd thought was ahead of her, that she'd thought she'd be happy with. But now, she knew that whenever she was doing something for Billy she'd be imagining doing it for Ray, now she knew he was alive, and she'd forever wonder how different her life could have been. He would always be her first love, but she knew without a doubt she was doing the right thing in staying with Billy.

'There's an idea. Men ironing! Ha!' Babs looked at Nellie quizzically. 'What's up, Nell? You all right?'

Nellie smiled at her friend, forcing herself to look happy. 'Just nervous, I suppose. Come on, let me do your hair now. You got to look gorgeous for Peter too, you know!'

'I will, in that dress your mum bought me.' Babs cocked her head towards the pale lemon, full-length lace dress that hung on the back of Nellie's bedroom door. 'It's gorgeous. And yours is even more lovely.'

Nellie glanced over at her own dress – white lace, full length, with a sweetheart neckline and a short train. It was the kind of wedding gown she'd always dreamed of wearing. Em had insisted on her and Babs having the very best. The three of them had gone up west together to shop round all the department stores before finding ones they loved in John Lewis. 'It is, yeah,' she said, smiling brightly at her sister-in-law-to-be, and trying to inject as much enthusiasm as possible into her voice. It was going to be a difficult day but she owed it to everyone – Mum, Babs and not least Billy – to play the part and at least try to enjoy her wedding day.

*

The wedding ceremony was at twelve. At half past eleven George stuck his head into Nellie's room. 'Nell, I'm going round – oh wow, look at you two!' He gaped at Nellie and Babs.

'You never seen us looking this gorgeous before, have you?' Babs said, fluttering her eyelashes at George. He blushed and backed out, calling through the door that he was going next door to be on hand for his best man duties.

'You embarrassed him, the poor little sod,' Nellie said with a laugh. 'Right, with him out the house we can go downstairs. Think Mum's got a little something to fortify us.' And Nellie definitely felt as though she needed a little fortification.

Downstairs, Em was waiting for them in the front room. A tray held three mismatched glasses, each containing a tot of brandy. 'Present from Amelia's landlord,' she said, passing them each a glass. 'Here's to Nellie and Billy. A long and happy marriage to you both.'

Nellie laughed, sounding nervous even to herself. 'Toasts ought to wait till after we've said the vows, Mum. You'll jinx it.'

'No, I won't. Not this close.' Em set down her glass and put her hands on Nellie's shoulders. 'And can I just say, you look stunning.' Her eyes were suspiciously bright. 'How proud your dad would have been, at this moment.'

Nellie brushed away a tear and lifted her glass. 'To Dad. And Flo. And Auntie Ruth and Uncle John. Love you always.'

'Charlie and Flo, Ruth and John,' Em and Babs echoed.

Em gave Nellie a sad little twisted smile, as she dabbed at her eyes. 'We'll always miss them, won't we? All those we've lost.'

'We will,' Nellie agreed. Up until two days ago that would have included Ray. She pressed her lips together. She wasn't going to cry, not now, with her make-up done and the ceremony just minutes away.

Em glanced at the mantelpiece clock. 'Righty-ho, it's time. Come on, girls. We need to get a shift on. Don't want to be late, do we?'

They set off, Nellie clutching Em's arm. Babs, holding both her own posy and Nellie's bouquet, followed behind. A few neighbours at the top of the street who weren't coming to the wedding were on their doorsteps, clapping and wolf-whistling as they walked past. There were a few people milling about outside the church, smoking and chatting, but when they saw the bridal party approaching they all went inside the church to take their seats.

All except one. Nellie held her breath, unable to see his face from this distance but knowing without a doubt who it was. They walked on, the three of them silent now they were so close.

And then it was Em who recognised him first. ''Ere, ain't that . . . I thought he was . . . bloody hell, Nellie, that's your Ray! Look, large as life, waiting there!'

'What? Can't be, Mrs Morris,' Babs said, skipping onto the street to pass Nellie and Em so she could take a look for herself. 'Bloody hell, it is! Ray! Ray!'

He was already looking, already watching, and lifted

a hand in acknowledgement of Babs's shout. He'd known, of course, the place and time of the wedding, and here he was, and somehow it felt inevitable that he'd be here. If their places were reversed Nellie knew she'd have had to come to see him get married, to know for sure he was out of her reach. She held her mother's arm still tighter as butterflies fluttered in her stomach at seeing Ray again.

'We thought you was . . .' Babs said. 'You survived! I'm so glad.' She gave him a spontaneous hug and a kiss on his cheek, but his eyes never left Nellie's.

'How did you know . . . Nellie, did you know he was . . .' Em stuttered.

'I bumped into her two days ago, Mrs Morris,' Ray said. 'I'd been in a POW camp. I'm not here to . . . disrupt anything. I just wanted to pay my respects and . . . see Nellie one last time. In her wedding dress. I couldn't help myself.' He gazed at her, anguish in his eyes. 'You look incredible, Nellie. Billy's . . . a lucky man. As long as he knows it.'

'Oh my God,' Babs muttered. Nellie glanced at her bridesmaid. Babs had a hand across her mouth, her eyes wide. She'd seen the love that Ray still held for Nellie.

'Ray. Oh, Ray.' All she could do was whisper his name. She couldn't think straight. Here he was again, and she loved him so much. She couldn't deny it, not with him standing there in front of her, looking at her with such longing. She couldn't take her eyes off him.

Beside her, Em looked from Nellie to Ray and back again.

'Well, this is a pretty pickle, ain't it? What we gonna do now?'

Nellie swallowed hard. 'We're going to go in that church, Mum, and I'm going to marry Billy Waters.'

'Come here, love. Let me talk to you.' Em drew her to one side, away from the others. 'You sure you're doing the right thing, Nellie? 'Cos there's one thing the war taught us and that's to grab your chances while you can. You never know what's around the corner. Things change in an instant, don't they? Like the bomb that took Ruth and John, the crush that took my Charlie and Flo. There's no predicting what might happen, and you only get one chance at it. One chance at life, at happiness.' She tipped her head to one side and smiled. 'Though it looks to me like you've been given a second chance.'

Nellie tried to reply but no words came out. If she could go back, replay V-E Day, not say yes so spontaneously to Billy . . . if she'd had any inkling Ray hadn't been killed . . . if the wedding date hadn't been so close . . . So many ifs. But here she was, and Billy was in there, in the church waiting for her, and she couldn't let him down. She couldn't lose him, lose Babs's friendship, too, no doubt . . . That safe, secure life in Bethnal Green she'd begun to look forward to, the little house she and Billy were going to live in, the children they'd have in time – it was all still there for her. It was what she'd thought she wanted . . . until two days ago.

Em hadn't finished. She wagged a finger at Nellie. 'So if you're going to go ahead and marry Billy, you'd better be totally sure, my girl. You've been through so much, we all have, and I just want you to be happy, with no regrets.'

'I'm sure,' Nellie said, though her voice held no conviction, even to herself. Grab her chances, Em had said. Grab her chance to have that quiet, comfortable life with a steady man who adored her. Yes, that was the decision she'd made, and she was sticking with it.

Chapter 49

Billy stood proudly at the top of the aisle, in his new suit bought especially for the occasion. A yellow rose was tucked into his buttonhole, and beside him, George, who wore a borrowed suit, had a similar rose.

It was nearly time, by his reckoning. He'd checked his watch a few minutes ago and it had been five to twelve, so any moment now Nellie would arrive, walking down the aisle towards him on her mother's arm. She would be here, and within the hour she would be his wife. He'd love and cherish her until the day he died.

He turned to look back down the aisle, longing for the moment he'd see her for the first time in her wedding dress.

He spotted Amelia, a few rows back, with little William on her lap. She was in a navy dress trimmed with white that suited her very well. She gave him a smile of encouragement that warmed his heart. Behind her were Mr and Mrs Bolton, the former chief air raid warden and former mayor, both now retired. They looked proud to be attending the wedding of their protégés. There were other friends present from his new job and Nellie's. All there, gathered to witness the great occasion.

The doors to the church stood open, and through them he could see her, Em and Babs. His heart swelled with pride – she looked as beautiful as he'd known she would.

There was someone else there, someone they were talking to, out of sight from him but as he watched them and saw Nellie's expression he could guess who it was. She looked starry-eyed yet almost pained with feeling. There was only one person she'd ever look at like that. But he was dead, shot down over France . . . As he watched they moved and he caught a glimpse of the man. His stomach lurched. No, it couldn't be. It couldn't! And why had he come back, today of all days? The one person in the world who could smash his dreams to pieces. Nellie loved him, he knew, but she loved that other man more. She always had done, and now he was here, not dead at all, and Nellie was out there staring at him, deciding what choice she should make.

Billy thought of being in her shoes and imagined himself having to turn his back on the person he loved most in all the world, to marry someone else. No. There was no way he could do it. And now, his only chance for happiness was if Nellie was stronger than him and could bring herself to leave Ray and come inside to him.

'I'm just . . . going to check on her,' he muttered to George, who apparently hadn't noticed what was going on outside. Neither had the congregation – they were all chatting quietly to those around them, unaware. He hurried back down the aisle to the entrance followed by George, who pulled the inner church doors shut behind him, gasping when he saw Ray.

'Nellie, I'm here,' Billy said. Em was staring at Ray, Babs was staring at Nellie, and those two were gazing at each other. None of them turned to look at him, Billy.

He looked from one to the other. From Nellie to Ray, and back again.

She looked broken. He knew, he'd always known, that her first love was Ray, her greatest love was Ray. But he also knew that she loved him, Billy, too. Perhaps with less passion, but it was still a deep love, born of all the years they'd spent growing up together. They would make a fine couple. They would have a happy, equal marriage, sharing their lives, bringing up children.

But now Ray was here, back from the dead, and Billy could see the love he had for Nellie. And the love she had for him.

He knew it was greater than what she'd ever feel for him. He could see that, as clearly as if it was printed on her face. She never looked at him like that, with that passion, that intensity. And she never would.

Why had Ray come back? Why couldn't he have stayed dead? Or stayed away. He must have guessed she'd have found someone else in the last two years. It was so unfair. Just as he'd finally and so nearly achieved his longheld wish, here was the one person who could snatch it all away from him. He let out a groan of despair. He wanted to shout at the injustice of the world that had done this to him. He wished Ray could simply disappear so that Nellie was left with only one choice. For he knew there was only one choice. There could only be one.

Everyone was silent. Waiting, he realised, for him to say or do something. 'Nellie,' he said again, his voice emerging as a croak, and this time she turned to look at him with anguish written on her face.

'Billy, I'm just coming in . . . Ray wanted to . . . pay his respects and say goodbye.'

'How long have you known he was . . . alive?'

'I found out only two days ago.' Her voice was flat.

'You didn't tell me.'

'I was . . . protecting you. I thought you'd think I wouldn't marry you.' She took a step towards him, away from Ray. 'Don't worry, though. It changes nothing, Billy.'

Oh, but it did. It changed everything. If she was protecting him, it was because she didn't want to hurt him with her true feelings. It was as though he could see into the future. Or rather, two possible futures, simultaneously. One in which he married Nellie today, and one in which he let her go, free to be with Ray. The love she had for him, Billy, would turn bitter in time, if she married him, knowing she could have had Ray. He knew it, and he could not let it happen. He couldn't watch her feelings for him turn to resentment. He knew what he must do, now that he'd seen the love between her and Ray, the love that would never fade, that he could never compete with. It was the only thing he could do. He loved her with every fibre of his being.

'He's come to win you back.' And as he said the words he felt his anger, his despair dissipate and turn to acceptance.

'No, Billy, it's nothing like that,' Nellie said, and Ray shook his head also. 'She's yours. I'm not—'

Billy held up a hand, silencing their protests. 'I can see how it is.'

'It's not—'

'We're not—'

'You are. You love each other.' No one tried to deny it. It was plain to see.

'Billy, I'm marrying you today.' Nellie's voice cracked but she sounded determined, that much was clear, and for that he loved her more than ever.

But still, he had to do this. The hardest thing he'd ever have to do. He shook his head. 'No, Nellie, you're not. You can't do this. *We* can't do this.' Behind him, Em and Babs both gasped, but he ignored them.

He took a step forward and pulled Nellie towards him, into his arms. He leaned into her and spoke softly, so only she could hear. 'Nellie, my love, my darling. I couldn't save Flo. But I can save you, from a lifetime of regret. You've lost so much. I can't, I *won't* take this second chance from you. We won't get married. I know how you feel for Ray, and all I want is for you to be happy. As happy as it's possible to be. So I'm . . . setting you free. Go . . . with him. Marry him, one day.'

She pulled back slightly so she could look into his eyes, and he held her gaze, willing her to believe that he meant it. It broke his heart but it was the right thing, the honourable thing, to do. For all of them.

'Billy, I—' Tears began rolling down her cheeks. Tears that he wanted to wipe away, to kiss away. He put a finger to her lips.

'Ssh. It's all right. Really, it's all right.' He smiled at her, and she smiled back, and he realised that yes, it would be all right in time. This way she'd still love him. She'd never grow to hate him, to resent him for blocking her path to her true love. He wouldn't have been able to stand that. This way her love for him would stay pure and untainted, and that was all he wanted, now.

'George,' he called. 'Give me the . . .'

George came over, put his hand in his pocket and pulled out the ring. Billy reached into his own inside pocket and took out an envelope. He handed it to Ray. 'Here. You might want these. Train tickets to Brighton, and confirmation of a hotel room I booked.'

The ring he handed to Nellie.

She held out her hand and he dropped it onto her palm. Not the way he'd imagined giving her this ring, he thought wryly, but maybe there'd be some comfort in knowing it'd be on her finger anyway.

She hugged him and spoke quietly into his ear, her voice cracking 'You're a wonderful man, Billy Waters.'

'Thank you.' He squeezed her, relishing the feel of her pressed against him for what might be the last time, then let her go, holding her gaze another moment, seeing the love there, the lasting love of childhood friends now grown up. The love that would never die, if he gave her up now to Ray.

Behind her, a few people were coming out of the church, wondering what was going on.

'Oh God, the explaining we'll have to do,' Em said, but she was smiling through her tears. Babs, at her side, put an arm around her.

'Thank you, sir,' Ray said, holding out his hand for Billy to shake.

He stared at it for a moment, and then took it. 'Look after her and give her the lifetime of love she deserves.'

Ray nodded. 'I will. I promise.'

And that was all Billy could wish for.

Chapter 50

Nellie watched as the two men she loved best in the world shook hands. It was hard to believe what was happening and her heart was racing with joy, with excitement, with love.

'Just go!' Billy urged them, again. 'Be happy!' His expression was a mix of determination and anguish. She could see how much it was costing him, emotionally, to release her from her promise to him, and her heart ached for him. Yet deep down she knew that he was right to do this, for all their sakes. Behind him, people were coming out of the church, wondering what was going on. George, bless him, was trying to make excuses, to usher them back inside.

She glanced down at her dress, her beautiful wedding dress. 'I can't face those people.'

'Best be quick then, before all those people come out. I'll think of some explanation.' Billy darted back towards the church. 'We'll meet again, Nellie Morris!' he shouted over his shoulder.

She saw him telling everyone to go back inside, that there was to be a change of plan and he'd explain, and then he went inside and closed the church doors.

Nellie turned to Em, who was smiling and crying at the same time. 'Mum? I don't know what to say.'

'Say nothing, lovey. Go, as Billy said. You have my blessing, and I reckon your dad and your sister would want you to do this too.'

'I'll be leaving you all alone,' Nellie said.

'Not alone. Got my George and my friends. And I'll be happy knowing you're happy, living life to the full.' Em smiled once more at her. 'I think this is what your dad would have wanted for you. A life of excitement and adventure, with the fellow you love the best. It was what you always dreamed of, remember?'

Nellie hugged her mother tightly, then turned to Babs who looked stunned by the whole thing. 'Babs, I'm sorry.'

Babs stepped forward and hugged her too. 'It's all right. And Billy will be okay, I promise. You should go now, like he said. He won't be able to keep all those people inside for long. They'll want to know what's going on.'

Ray held out a hand to Nellie.

She took it, but turned back to Em and Babs.

'Thank you. I'll . . .'

'Go!' Both Em and Babs shooed them away, crying and laughing at the same time.

And then, with Ray's hand in hers, she hurried back along the street she'd so recently walked with her mother and bridesmaid. Not Mrs Waters, but Mrs Fleming-to-be, and the hand in hers belonged to the man she would love forever and spend the rest of her life with.

'Nellie! Wait!' It was George, pounding after them along the street.

She stopped and turned. 'George!'

He skidded to a halt in front of them, and held out his hand, palm open. In it was Flo's little china dog ornament. 'I found this. Day after the accident. Flo had dropped it on the stairs at home. Kept it on me ever since, as a reminder of her. You should have it now.'

She took it from him, tears pouring down her face. 'Thank you. And George?'

'Yeah, I know. Look after Mum for you. 'Course I will, Nellie. You don't need to worry.' He gave them both a military-style salute, and ran to the church, to Em and Babs and Billy.

She watched him go back to them. The life she'd thought she would have seemed to be fading already, and a new one was within her grasp. A new start.

'They'll be all right,' Ray said. 'And so will we. God, I love you, Nellie Morris. Don't know where life's going to take us but we have each other, and we'll have a lifetime of love and adventure, I promise.' He pulled her into his arms and kissed her, and it was as though the last years crumbled to dust. Here they were, together, the war over, the danger passed, and the blessing of everyone that mattered was with them.

'Come on, Mrs Fleming-to-be! Before they all realise there's not going to be a wedding and come piling out of the church.' Ray grinned at her, that familiar smile she'd loved so much. 'Let's go to Brighton!'

'To Brighton!' It would be the first of many adventures they would have together, the first step on their travels, and Nellie couldn't wait. She hoisted up her dress with one hand, kept hold of Ray with the other, and together they ran up the street, laughing, unable to believe what had just happened, suddenly seeing a future that was bright and joyful and full of love. A future that Billy, out of his love for her, had given them.

Epilogue

March 1993

'You won't fall. I've got you.' Strong hands gripped Nellie's upper arms and held her steady while the students charged past on the tube station steps. 'Come on, let's get you out of here.'

Nellie allowed herself to be led up the rest of the nineteen steps, out into the bright spring sunlight and fresh air. Her heart was still pounding, her breath coming in gasps, but she was safe, she was not in the crush that had killed Flo and her father and all those others. It was only as she emerged out of the tube entrance and into Bethnal Green Gardens that she realised she'd recognised the voice of her saviour and turned to look at him properly.

'Billy! Oh, it's you!'

'Babs told me you were expected around this time, so I was there waiting for you, in the ticket hall. Walked right past me, you did, like you were in a world of your own. It's good to see you, Nellie.'

She smiled at him. Those same kind eyes, the same dimple in his cheek, the same old Billy. Just seeing him calmed her down. 'Good to see you too. Been too long.'

'Come on, let's sit while you get your breath back. We've got a lot of catching up to do, and Babs'll no doubt hog your time later. I want you all to myself for a few minutes, now.' Billy led her to a bench in the corner of the park.

She looked around her. The park was better kept, more luxuriantly planted than it had been in the war years. The street had a mix of old and new buildings – the newer ones, she realised, had taken the place of the bombed-out gaps she remembered. 'It's all so different.'

'Yes. Of course it is. Forty-eight years since you left, if I've done me sums right,' Billy said.

'Almost forty-eight. Not quite. Summer of '45, I left. Billy . . . I've never forgotten what you did back then. You gave us, me and Ray, a wonderful life together.'

Billy smiled at her, a smile of long-standing friendship. 'I knew we'd have regretted it in time, if we'd gone ahead and married. You'd have resented me for keeping you apart from Ray. I'd have grown bitter towards you, for not loving me the way you loved him.' He took her hand. 'I pushed you away that day, because I suddenly had a clear vision of the future, as it would be, if we married. And I didn't like what I saw.'

'Thank you. We had many very happy years.'

'It all worked out for me too, didn't it?'

She did know – there'd been constant letters back and

forth across the Atlantic, between herself and Babs, who'd passed on all Billy's news. Babs had even visited, with her husband, Peter. As had George twice, and her mother, once. Em had been delighted to have the chance to visit a new country, to see the place where her daughter had made her home. And Nellie and Ray had made many trips to England, staying with George and his family in west London, meeting Em there too. 'How is Amelia? And the kids?'

'She's very well, and so excited to see you. William's visiting at the weekend with his brood, and our twins both still live locally anyway.' Billy looked away from her then, staring across the gardens. 'I adore her, you know. I thought back then that you were the only girl for me, that I could never love anyone else. But I was wrong. I've had a wonderful marriage too. Amelia's been so good for me. I was so lucky, getting to know her through you.'

'I'm so glad.' Funny, she thought, how things had worked out for them both. The only thing she would have changed, if she could, was for Ray not to have had cancer, that horrible, awful disease that had ended his life far too soon. She twisted the ring on her right finger – the ring Billy had bought for her, that she'd worn throughout her forty-five-year marriage to Ray, to remind her of the selfless, wonderful man who'd made it all possible.

'You still have it?' Billy said, noticing her hand.

'Worn it always,' she replied, with a smile.

'I can't believe the memorial service is tomorrow.'

'Yes, I know.' Fifty years on from the tragedy that had taken so many lives, it would be the first service commemorating those people. A chance for the community to get together to remember them, to talk about what had happened.

'The Council was absolved of all blame, you know. I read a long piece in the paper about it. You always said it wasn't Mrs Bolton's fault, that she'd done all she could, and now she's been vindicated.'

'Just, she's not here to see it happen,' Nellie said, and there was a moment's quiet while she remembered her kind, hard-working old boss.

She turned to look at the church across the road, St John's, where the service was to be held. The same church where so many victims of the tragedy had been taken, where she and Em had found Flo and Charlie.

'Shall we go to Babs's house now?' he said.

Nellie looked back at the church. 'Do you mind if I do something first? On my own. Flo's grave.'

He gazed at her with compassion. 'Of course. I'll take your case, and I'll see you at Babs's a bit later. She won't mind. You know the way? Her house is near the old cemetery anyway.'

'I know it.' Even after all these years, the streets of Bethnal Green were imprinted on her memory.

They walked together out of the park. 'I'll see you later, then.' Billy kissed her cheek and took her suitcase from her, waving as he headed down the street.

She took a deep breath and crossed the road to the church. She went inside and sat quietly for a few minutes, gathering her thoughts, letting the air of the East End seep into her soul. And then she went outside, along the side of the church, and peered at the stonework.

It was still there. *NM and RF, February 1943*. Their initials, after all this time. Ray's carving, lasting longer than his life had, but not longer than their love. She traced the letters with her finger. 'Oh Ray, my love. I wish you were here with me today. I'll never forget you.' A gentle breeze blew about her face, lifting a strand of hair, as though Ray was listening, as though he were there beside her, as he had been for forty-five wonderful years. She smiled. 'Thanks, love. For all of it.' For all the years together, for all the travelling they'd done, exploring the world as she'd always dreamed. The places they'd been to, the fun they'd had. The family they'd raised together. Their three beautiful daughters.

All three of them, separately, had suggested coming on the trip with her, but Nellie had said no. They had busy lives, children, husbands and jobs, so much to keep them in Michigan. She'd wanted to do this on her own. A companion would have meant less chance for her to lose herself in her memories. It would have been harder to feel the ghosts of the past around her, if any of them had come along.

With a last look back at the initials she headed away from the church, through the familiar yet changed streets that teemed with people as they always had.

To think that the last time she'd gone this way she'd been running, decked out in her wedding dress, hand in hand with Ray.

She walked up Morpeth Street. The old terraced houses where she, Babs and Billy had lived were no longer there, bulldozed to make way for characterless blocks of flats. But the school where she'd been taught still stood at the end of the road, and there were one or two older houses on the opposite side. It didn't feel like home any more. Home was people, not places. Home was Michigan, on the shores of the great lake, where her daughters and their families lived. As soon as her passport came through, Ray had taken her there and they had married with Ray's parents in attendance. They'd been so happy, with no regrets.

She headed south, towards Bow Cemetery. It had been renamed, along with the rest of the borough, to Tower Hamlets Cemetery now, but it was still where it had always been, and in it were Charlie's and Flo's graves. Nellie wanted to spend some time there, alone, before the service tomorrow, before her time was taken up seeing old friends. Em was buried elsewhere, as Bow Cemetery had closed for new burials in 1966. Nellie planned to visit her mother's grave later in the week, to pay her respects to the wonderful woman who'd urged her to take her chances while she could – a mantra she'd used throughout her life.

Her route took her through a park that she didn't remember at all. Back during the war that area had been streets of Victorian terraced housing, along the Regent's Canal. It had been badly bombed, she recalled, and clearly after the war the authorities must have bulldozed it all and created a park in its place. A pleasant, green oasis that linked up with Victoria Park in the north and the cemetery to the south. She wandered through the cemetery and found what she'd been looking for.

Charles Francis Morris, 1896–1943, beloved husband and father. Rest in peace. She read it aloud, her hand on the headstone, remembering her larger-than-life father who'd sometimes been angry or hard to please but who'd been loving and caring, wanting the best for his family at all times.

And beside him, the smaller grave of Flo. *Flora Emily Morris, 1935–1943, beloved sister and daughter. May heaven be a place of play, always and forever.*

She remembered how she and Em had struggled to find the right words for Flo's headstone. 'Nothing trite. Nothing too religious. She was only a nipper, the poor lamb.'

Nellie knelt beside Flo's grave and put her hands on the earth, roughly where Flo's heart would have been. 'Miss you, little sis,' she said. 'I always have and always will.' All these years later, and it was still true.

A single tear escaped and ran down her cheek. 'The service tomorrow is for you, Flo. And Dad. And the other 171 people who died that night. But this moment's just for you.'

She sang, then. Softly, quietly, so that only Flo, deep

beneath the earth, would hear. The last verse of the lullaby she'd so often used to sing Flo to sleep.

> 'Hark, a solemn bell is ringing, clear through the night
> Thou, my love, art heavenward winging, home through the night
> Earthly dust from off thee shaken, soul immortal shalt thou awaken
> With thy last dim journey taken, home through the night.'

Acknowledgements

To my family: Mom, Dad, Charlie Rachel, Paige, Sam and Ava. I love you all more than anything in this world. Thank you for your consistent love, support and guidance.

To Jake, my partner in life, thank you for holding my hand and being a guiding light for me. Nanny Ruth would've loved you, no doubt.

To my incredible agents at WME thank you for nurturing this idea and carving out a space for me to create such a story. Andrew, TJ, Steve, Huy, James, Matilda and Alyssa you all are the wind in the sails that pushed this story from being a seed of an idea to publication. To Jenny and Cara, thank you for always having my back and protecting me in this crazy world.

Thank you to the publication team at HarperCollins who believed in this story and never took no for an answer, especially my editors Katie and Liz. And to the brilliant Kathleen McGurl for working with me to bring it to life .

Thank you to my wonderful dogs Winnie, Max, Barbie

and Marley who faithfully stayed by my feet during the restless nights of trying to craft the next chapter.

Lastly, to my Nanny Ruth. Without you no one would be holding this book in their hands. Without you there would be no me. This is your story, a testimony to your hardships and inner-strength that I draw from every day. This is for you. I love you and present *Nineteen Steps* in your honour.

ONE PLACE. MANY STORIES

Bold, innovative and
empowering publishing.

FOLLOW US ON:

@HQStories